WHY?

PJ DODGE

PAGE PUBLISHING, INC.
New York, NY

First originally published by Page Publishing, Inc. 2017

ISBN 978-1-64027-407-5 (Paperback)
ISBN 978-1-64027-408-2 (Digital)

Printed in the United States of America

IT BEGINS

When Raoul showed up at the VA for his appointment to try to fast-track his benefits request, he knew deep down in his heart it was a lost cause. Having been homeless for more years than he cared to count, this was his opportunity to start life anew, and while hoping for the best, he was not sure this would be the answer. The security guard, Randy, nodded hello and waved him through.

Half an hour later he passed back through, looking as if he had lost his last friend, and Randy stopped him, seeing the look of despair once too often and, in a moment of kindness, asked if he was okay.

Raoul responded with a head shake, and mumbled something unintelligible. For some reason, Randy felt the need to reach out. This was a fellow Vet, obviously in pain, and he invited him to his house on Sunday for a barbeque.

"Can't, no car" was the response.

"Five-minute walk from here, man. Does that work better? Looks like it would do you good to talk to someone."

After a bit of back and forth and info exchanged, the dinner was a go. Randy did not need to know Raoul was homeless because the shelter he could shower at was also very close.

Sunday rolled around. It was one of those gorgeous spring days. Raoul actually felt good about his decision, only having a brief moment of panic as he walked up to the apartment building. Randy had assured him no one else would be there, he lived alone, and the balcony was his, which was where they would be to cook and hang.

However, Raoul was a bit nervous about his social skills. They definitely suffer when on the streets and in shelters.

He rang the bell for entrance, was buzzed in, and proceeded to Randy's apartment, being greeted by a seventy-pound yellow lab and Randy, who handed him a beer immediately.

"Meet Fred. He's my stabilizer. Best friend a guy could ever want! Took me a while to realize that he could be my bestie, but now, wouldn't trade him for anything. And how do you like your steak?"

"Medium well, please" was the response as he rubbed Fred's ears.

The discussion did move on. Raoul became a bit more comfortable, sharing his history.

Born in '46, he was raised in Yuma, Arizona, joined the Army at twenty, ended up in Vietnam in '69–'70, lost his hearing 80 percent in one ear, but did manage to complete his tour stateside as a desk jockey, and got out in '76, disgruntled because he couldn't keep his chosen rate and desk jobs didn't fly. He did hold down odd jobs, construction mostly, but nothing to give a good retirement, so in '98 when he was diagnosed with diabetes, he tried to take care of himself, but the cost was overwhelming. He was told the VA could assist, based on the Agent Orange correlation, and they did assist. His meds were taken care of, but they couldn't help him get a job. By the time he went to the VA in '98, he couldn't work and was moving from shelter to shelter. He was receiving his meds, and while that did help, no income meant no stability.

Randy sympathized, seeing many others who were fighting for the benefits they were entitled to, and a friendship was formed. "Dinner is served, Fred. You do get the bones, and we need to shift to a lighter conversation. However, let me state this: the VA needs to get back on track and support those who served without the delays. I think they take way too much advantage of situations and are not serving us!"

As the evening wound down and the beers disappeared (Raoul only having two), Raoul figured it was time to go. At 9:00 p.m., he stood up, stretched, and stated, "This has been a great evening, but I think I need to hit the road now. Thank you is not enough, but it is all I can offer. Fred, great dad you got here. Keep him well."

Randy considered options, either a ride or his couch, but knew that might come off as condescending, so after the good-byes, he walked Raoul out and decided this was a friendship that needed to continue. In the back of his mind, however, a seed was germinating, and he was seriously trying to figure out how the entire VA issue had gotten so out of hand. It was so obvious that the Vets were not receiving the medical care nor financial support they earned and deserved. He had read somewhere that in January 2014, almost fifty thousand Vets were homeless and wondered how many of those were partly or fully caused because of the VA's lack of assistance. And also, was that a true figure? We all were aware that those figures were never 100 percent accurate. Too many variables came into play.

So was there any solution? He was going to mull this over and perhaps come up with something that might assist those in need. He also felt lucky. Joining the National Guard in 2001, his unit was called to serve in Iraq in 2001, and he ended up doing two tours there. Most of 2002 and 2003 were spent in that hell, and when '05 rolled around, he decided enough of that life, got out, spent a little time with his family in Vermont, then when the offer came in for the VA security job, he moved to DC and settled in. But seeing the people pass by day after day leaving with sad faces and/or pissed-off expressions made you wonder. Was the VA actually trying to help those in need, or had they perfected the art of making it look like they were helping but, in actuality, blowing off everyone they could and giving no assistance? Or was it a case of being overcautious because of known fraud issues (look at Social Security) and trying not to have that happen within their system? When he contemplated the options, it seemed overwhelming, but sometimes answers came in mysterious ways.

Perhaps synchronicity comes into play more often than we realize. People band together and bond, at times with no known reason, until something brings it all to light.

VA HOSPITAL, DC

MARY HINES HAD WORKED AT the VA hospital since 2010. She had served in Iraq as a triage nurse in '06–'07, and when her tour ended, she knew military life was not for her. Four years was enough, but she also knew that she could somehow help those who passed through the VA because she understood their mind-set better than those who had no experience in conflict situations. So after separating from the military, she found a position at the hospital in DC, moving from Grand Rapids, Michigan, to do so.

As her background was so varied, she became a floater, working many departments, depending on where needed, and quite often did intake exams prior to the Vet seeing the doctor. She would do the vital checks then forward the patient on for the exam or recheck as needed.

On this day, when Raoul walked in, she was surprised to see him in an upbeat mood. She was aware of his issues. With the diabetes and minimal benefits from the VA, it made his life on the streets seem endless.

"Raoul, what's up? You seem really happy today. Win the lotto?" Mary asked.

While she took his blood pressure and got ready to check his blood sugar levels, he replied, "Don't I wish. That would solve all my problems, wouldn't it? But nope... I had dinner last weekend with a guy I met at the VA, and it was an enjoyable evening, kinda gave me a break, and well... it was just nice."

"Great to hear. And your BP looks good. Let's get the blood work done, and the doc can check you out the rest of the way."

As he went back out to the waiting area to be called, Mary mulled over his words for a few minutes then had to go back to work. The VA was always busy, and time for reflection wasn't in her schedule. However, later that evening, she found herself with some time to reflect. Mulling over what Raoul had said, she realized that a lot of the burden that rested on these Vets' shoulders would be lessened if they had someone to talk to. And not necessarily a psychiatrist or someone in the system, but a friend. Maybe she was not that person for them, but maybe she could help them find one another. In her mind, if she could help anyone, it was worth the effort. She well knew how careful she needed to be, but as her thoughts progressed, she realized that it might not be completely impossible—perhaps as easy as introducing them in the waiting area. She knew enough about their history to make that potentially work. Now just to wait for the opportunity.

A week or so later, as Mary was checking a Vet in, she glanced up to see a familiar face. While in Iraq, she had met Ben Goodman, who was from Alexandria, Virginia, and had lost his leg in a firefight that took place near Arbil in the region of Kurdistan.

"Sergeant Goodman?" she exclaimed.

"Mary, Mary Hines? Wow, I have never forgotten the talks we had before I was flown out of Iraq. Your concern and compassion were a great comfort to me and kept me going quite often once I came home! Are you due lunch soon? Would love to continue talking."

She advised him her lunch was at twelve thirty and she would be happy to meet him in the cafeteria, to which he replied, "I will be there!"

As Mary entered the cafeteria at twelve thirty, Ben immediately spotted her, smiled a happy smile, and stood up to hug her. After the usual you-look-good conversation, they discussed how she ended up in the VA in DC and his experiences in getting his prosthetic leg, as well as the therapy and acclimating himself to having the limb.

While Mary (and Ben) could have gone on for hours, Mary realized her lunch was over. "I really have to get back to work, and with so much more to discuss and catch up on, we need to keep in touch."

She handed him her card and told him to call when he had time, and he provided his card with a resounding "Oh, I will."

VFW, DOWNTOWN DC

MIKE JACKSON, A MARINE STATIONED in Vietnam, was sitting having a beer at the VFW. A young man, Durham Murdit, walked up to his table and asked if he minded if he joined him. Mike said, "Hey, fine, sit, take a load off."

As they sat there, they started discussing their involvements in the different wars they participated in. Durham asked Mike what he was involved in. Mike responded, "I was a Marine in Vietnam."

Durham responded, "Wow, that was worse than what I went through. I was a Ranger in Iraq."

Mike said, "You think I had it worse? Weren't you shot at and had rockets coming at you and IEDs?" Durham responded with a yes. Mike asked if he was sniped at and got another yes. Mike looked at him and stated, "It wasn't any worse in Vietnam than Iraq. There is only one thing different, and that is as in any war, the one you were in, I was in, and any other war ever fought, and that was the real estate we fought over! One isn't any worse or better than the other."

After a moments reflection, Durham stated, "You know, you are right. What type of involvement did you have in Vietnam?"

Mike responded, "I was at Khe Sanh, one of the worst battles that was fought there in the Vietnam conflict, or war, whatever they want to call it! It lasted seventy-seven days, with heavy artillery, constant bombardment, and hand-to-hand combat. These battles lasted all night long, and we had major casualties and injuries. I lost a lot of my Marine buddies. It was pure hell, something you can't *ever* forget.

We were on a hill in northwest South Vietnam, an outpost of Khe Sanh. So you were in Iraq... How did that go?"

Durham looked at him and said, "Well, I was involved in urban warfare. We had to go through cities and towns, driving the bad guys out, al-Qaeda specifically. We had a lot of firefights, like you mentioned, IEDs to try to avoid, not always successfully grenades, and snipers as well, and yeah, we had a lot of casualties too. I lost quite a few of my Ranger buddies also."

"Wow, not a good time, was it?" from Mike.

"No, not a good thing at all," responded Durham.

"So how were things when you came home?" asked Mike.

"Not too good. Had some problems with the VA, and I am not too sure that's not a bigger problem than the ones we dealt with in the field! Those people don't listen! What about you?"

"Well, pretty much the same thing. And in your case, you didn't get a very nice reception when you returned home from Vietnam, did you?

Mike replied, "Not at all! I can't tell you how often civilian guys would attack us. We had to wear civilian clothes so we couldn't be recognized. Like the military haircuts and bearing didn't give us away! But I will tell you one thing, those boys weren't as well trained as I and my buddies were. They usually ended up in the hospital for at least a day or two, some even longer. And on that note, think I need to get my butt home. Is this a normal hangout for you? I get in here at least once a week, and maybe next time we can discuss a more pleasant topic."

Durham advised Mike he was somewhat of a regular as well and would enjoy further conversation, and they exchanged phone numbers.

As Raoul went back to one of the shelters he frequented (and that allowed him to keep his insulin refrigerated at), he saw a familiar face as he entered. "Hawk? Long time no see, bud. Where ya hiding?"

He and Hawk (Jason Hawk) had crossed paths periodically at homeless shelters and occasionally on the street. Hawk explained that at the beginning of the past winter, he knew he couldn't take the DC weather and managed to get to Florida, where he did find some buddies to stay with and day labor to keep his head afloat. But as he was also trying to get his benefits for the PTSD, he knew he needed to be back in DC.

"Ya know, Raoul, sometimes I wonder if it is even worth it to continue fighting these people. Their shrink gives me this four-question test, tells me I don't have PTSD, and yet I still have nightmares that I *will not* try to remember and jump forty feet when a car backfires or fireworks go off! When anyone speaks any language other than Spanish or English, that throws me into panic mode as well. I cannot hold a job, and yet they say I am fine!"

Raoul thought a moment and responded, "I get it and agree. Wish the VA would provide us with the things promised without making us feel like we are trying to take advantage of them. Or at least that is how I feel. We Vets gave up a lot to help our country, and now how many of us are homeless and jobless? Are you due to go back to the VA anytime soon?"

"Not really due, but am going by to ask why this is all taking so long. I filed over a year ago, and not even one letter to acknowledge my request for a review. But I will tell you this, I am grateful to the shelters here that will take our mail and let us use their address. At least I have some point of contact."

"I do agree. Some of them are great! And, man, I need to get rolling, shower, and insulin time! But when you go into the VA office, if Randy Lopez is at the guard station, tell him hi for me please."

After Hawk left for the VA, Raoul got thinking about the conversations he and Jason had in the past. Hawk had been a Navy SEAL in Vietnam and also worked as an operative for the CIA, which meant his involvement was top secret and classified, making it something he still could not talk about. Raoul knew that that was a very heavy load to carry without being able to share with anyone. At least Raoul could discuss things with people, like the battle that took over Hill 881 and other gory battles he took part in when serving with the Army Infantry in the sixties. It didn't lessen the pain of the memories, but it did help sometimes, which was more than Jason could do.

VIETNAM VETS' GATHERING IN SEATTLE

Sergeant Lewis (Sarge) walked into the convention he attended annually that was being held in Seattle this year. As he walked around looking for Tony Rice, and anyone else he might know, there was a tap on his shoulder. Swiveling around, he faced Tony. "Hey, Sarge," said Tony, "good to see you. Ya know, you never were that good-looking, but, man, that gray hair, well, it doesn't help you at all!"

Sarge replied, with a big grin on his face, "Look who's talking! A man who looks like he got into a fight with twenty Marines with ugly sticks, and you were empty-handed!" Sarge then chuckled and followed up with, "Please, no bar fights like the one in Orlando. I didn't bring bail money."

"Who, me? Nuh-uh, I behave always... well, almost always," responded Tony.

At that moment, Tim Morris, who had been a Radioman in Vietnam, and Raoul Martinez walked up. Hellos and handshakes were given, and Sarge then turned to Tony and asked if he brought the D cell batteries. As Tony handed them over, they shared a smile, and Tony's response was a quick, "Yes, sir!" It seemed that during a firefight west of Da Nang, the battery in the radio died as Tony had forgotten spares. In the Vietnam era, it was the only communication method available; cell phones and/or satellite radios were not even invented yet. Therefore, Tony had to bring Sarge two batteries as a reminder of the importance of being prepared always. It also strengthened the bond, with the two being aware of always having each other's backs.

Raoul at that point looked at Sarge, stating, "I want you to know how much I appreciate you and anyone else who chipped in to pay my way to come here. You know you don't have to do it, but I really enjoy the chance to see some of the guys I served with. Thank you again."

"Raoul, they say when someone saves your life, you are indebted forever. When we were pinned down by Charlie [the Viet Cong], you are the one who saved us. I feel the least I can do is keep us in touch. You were the one shot, and you deserve to be here with us!"

As they separated to see everyone else, Raoul did thank Sarge one last time.

As gatherings of this type go, great food and camaraderie were shared. There were updates on family and moves, and two who had passed were honored with a short service in their honor. Lieutenant Nelson and Private Wilson had both passed from cancer, and the chaplain offered a prayer for them as well as an invocation for all to be well. Then Sarge closed with thanks to all and a reminder that next year was a big year, when the gathering was in Washington, DC.

"Looking forward to seeing everyone there, and get the word out to everyone you can. We need to be sure we support all our brothers and they are aware we are here and care."

As this was an informal group of Veterans who gathered each year, there were no dues paid or official communications. It had started many years ago as a word-of-mouth group and continued that way, but it gave those that came an opportunity to find out what was new with other Vets, learn potential sources for help as needed and/or jobs that may be out there, and just enjoy fellowship with others. It was always a three-day affair (kind of like a class reunion), with one night of dinner and dancing for spouses to attend (usually a small turnout), one day to see the city they were having the gathering in, and the final day for the Veterans to gather, share, and of course, tell some tall tales.

NEW FRIENDS, NEW HOME, CHARLOTTE, NORTH CAROLINA

GERALD WASHINGTON, FORMER GREEN BERET in the Vietnam era, was just settling in his new home in Charlotte, North Carolina. Three days into the move and working on unpacking, he was taking a breakfast break at 9:30 a.m, Bud being his breakfast of choice.

"Welcome to the neighborhood," he heard as the neighbor strolled over, holding out his hand for a shake. "James Becker here. Jim will do. Noticed the Vietnam Vet sticker on the back of the truck when you pulled in. What branch?"

Gerald gave his name, shook hands, and said, "Army, Green Beret. Would you like a beer?"

"Nah, I'm good! Small world, though. I was a Green Beret too but spent my time from '68 to the end in a concentration camp," responded Jim. "Ya know what, that beer sounds good, thanks."

Gerald opened the garage door, pulled one out of the fridge there, and pulled out two lawn chairs and told Jim, "It's break time. Sit and join me." Then he asked Jim where in Nam he was, adding, "If it's okay to discuss."

Jim replied, "I was Special Forces Operational Detachment, Alpha Team. There was a firefight with Charlie the first week we were there. Ten didn't survive. Two of us were wounded and brought to a concentration camp west of Da Nang, until '71, when we were moved to Hanoi."

"You were in there a long time," Gerald responded. "I was with Special Forces Group, B Team, at Nha Trang that originated out of Saigon but didn't join them 'til after you guys were wiped out. However, we knew about you guys. Your insignia was the Trojan horse—*de oppresso liber* [to liberate from oppression], right?"

"That was us! However, look at how long it took us to get out of the concentration camp. Seemed like a lifetime."

"Man, do I agree! And I think I need to go help the old lady unpack some more boxes. Great meeting you."

"Next time I will have the brew on ice whenever you are ready. Let me know if you need anything," responded Jim as he walked away.

LAKE CASCADE, IDAHO

WHEN TONY LEFT THE CONVENTION in Seattle, he headed back to his cabin on Lake Cascade in Idaho. He had settled there with his wife, who died in a car wreck after only seven years of marriage and no children. She slid on an icy road head-on into a tree. They said she didn't suffer; it was all so quick. Tony had been Marine Infantry in Vietnam, served on the Cascade Police Department for twenty-five years, then sold his house in Cascade and bought the cabin on the lake, where he enjoyed his quiet life, never remarrying, keeping Susan's memory close to his heart.

However, it was not a totally lonely existence. His best friend, Robert Ellis, with whom he grew up, spent a lot of time with him hunting, camping, and fishing. They had grown up together, living two houses apart, playing football together (and, of course, getting into things as do all teens), and deciding to join the Marines upon graduation. Robert ended up in a tank division, and when he returned home, he became a fireman in Cascade.

They both served in Vietnam in the late sixties, early seventies, taking part in the Tet Offensive that began in January 1968. The North Vietnamese decided to start that attack at that time knowing that that was usually a time of peace and hoping it would turn the tide and help end this "conflict" and in their favor. Mass attacks by the VC began, hitting major cities, military bases, and airports throughout Southern Vietnam. They brought massive troops, weapons, and ammo through Laos on the Ho Chi Minh trail, as well as by sea on motor junks. Robert and Tony were there through the entire time (which was basically all of 1968), and when they did return to Cascade, both had multiple ribbons, including Purple Hearts and Bronze Stars. They then settled in and finished their respective careers, now enjoying the lake and trying to let all the past go.

Robert did still technically live in town, but he and Jill were married in name only.

They had a daughter, who became a lawyer, moved to Boise to work for a law firm there in 2002, and within two years, died of cancer. Neither he nor Jill handled this well, and it drove a deeper wedge between them, giving him another reason to hide out at the cabin with Tony.

BEN'S GYM, DC AREA

AFTER BEN GOODMAN FINISHED HIS therapy, to adjust to life with his prosthetic leg, he took his lump sum back pay received from the VA and bought a thirty-two-thousand-square-foot warehouse just outside DC. The building was in great shape and ready to move in gym equipment. Plus the price was right. In time, he was able to add and upgrade his gym equipment, as well as add a ten-foot-by-fifty-foot lap pool, as well as a nutrition bar that served healthy drinks and snacks.

He had also decided two years ago that all Vets would qualify for discounted rates.

His manager at the gym was Tyrell Dyer. Tyrell had been in the National Guard out of Jacksonville, Florida, where he had grown up. Eight years and multiple tours in Afghanistan was enough. It took him a total of three years to receive his VA benefits for PTSD. The VA originally turned down his request for those benefits based on a test they ran for Alzheimer's and dementia rather than a test for PTSD. Tyrell had a certified psychological exam from an independent psychologist, who diagnosed PTSD, and they refused that also. But once he retained a lawyer and appealed his case (which was denied), he finally received a hearing, and after a year and four months for that process, he was approved the claim for PTSD.

Tyrell had done jobs as a laborer in construction, but as the summers were so hot and humid in Jacksonville, it became more than he could stand.

The gym he belonged to, because of his build, knowledge, and dedication, as well as his willingness to always help others, offered him a job as assistant manager. He gladly accepted the position. However, three years later, while visiting his cousin in DC, he visited his cousin's gym, met Ben Goodman, and yes, he now was the manager of Ben's Gym.

CHARLOTTE, NORTH CAROLINA

GERALD WASHINGTON HAD SPENT A week unpacking and organizing his house. Yesterday was computer hookup day, so today he could log in to the Vets' chat room, where he and a group of like-minded Vets kept one another up to date on one another's lives, as well as issues that affected them, and could perhaps help others. The Vets knew they could share everything, feelings, troubles, benefits and issues with benefits, and successes they had achieved.

Right after he logged in and opened the chat, he saw Mike Jackson on. "Hi, Mike!"

Mike replied, "Hi, Gerald. Are you all moved in up there in Charlotte?"

"Yes, all moved in, and this place really is the city of my dreams. People are really friendly! My neighbor noticed the Vietnam sticker on my truck and came over to welcome me to the neighborhood. We had a beer and talked a little about Nam. He was actually in a concentration camp for a number of years."

"I know a couple guys who were caught," responded Mike. "I can't even imagine the torture they went through. If you wouldn't give them the information they wanted or sign the documents of war crimes, Charlie would shove a bamboo stick a little bigger than a toothpick under your fingernail until you cooperated."

"Yep, and the food wasn't that great either!" typed Gerald. "A bird could have starved to death on the amount of food they got every day."

Mike typed back, "Well, Gerald, thanks for the update. I am so glad everything is good and you are settling into your new home and finding new friends. And especially a fellow Marine... hurrah... hurrah. And on that note, I need to sign off."

BACK AT THE VFW

MIKE JACKSON AND DURHAM MURDIT were drinking a beer at the VFW when Ben walked in. Mike looked up when he walked in, noticed him, and yelled, "Ben, over here, join us!"

Ben walked over, sat down, and ordered his beer, and Mike introduced him to Durham, stating, "Durham was a Ranger in Iraq. Durham, Ben was in the National Guard there also."

Ben replied, "I came in here to relax, enjoy a cold one. Can we find something better to talk about?"

"Matter of fact, think I can," stated Durham. "What do you think about the Vet who walked into a VA clinic and shot his doctor?"

"I think that may be a good start. Maybe it will put some attention on the crappy ways the VA treats Vets!" Mike stated.

Thinking about Mary and how hard she worked to help the Vets, Ben responded, "I think a lot of the doctors and medical staff are trying to do a good job, but their hands are tied by what the regional offices allow. I sometimes think about going in there and getting locked and loaded and killing those bastards to make a point. That may be a start to resolving the issues!"

Durham said, "Can't say that hasn't crossed my mind!"

Mike said, "Haven't we all?"

From there, the conversation went on to more pleasant topics and tales with a lot of beer being consumed until 2:00 a.m., when everyone decided to call it a night and head for their respective homes.

BEN AND MARY PLAN A DATE

BEN DECIDED IT WAS TIME to give Mary a call on a Tuesday and asked her if she would like to have dinner on Friday evening. She explained that Friday was not good as she was working another nurse's shift but Saturday would be great. Asking if that worked for him, she also said, "I can meet you somewhere, if that is easier."

"No, you won't meet me somewhere. I will pick you up. Does seven work for you?"

"Looking forward to it, Ben. See you then."

Saturday came quickly, both anticipating time spent together as they enjoyed each other's company. Ben pulled into her drive promptly at seven and rang the bell, and within minutes, Mary opened the door, commenting, "Hi, Ben, you must know I am starving. Between laundry cleaning and shopping, I didn't stop to grab lunch, so thank you for being so on time." She closed the door and proceeded down the walk ahead of him.

"Well, then, let us get going. Can't have you collapsing on me, can we?" asked Ben as he opened the car door for Mary. "Italian sound good?"

"Italian sounds great, Ben, and promise... no collapsing for me!"

On the way to the restaurant, they discussed their work weeks, Ben sharing the story about the girl who came in to check out his gym, knowing by watching her, she knew a lot of military guys worked out there (acting like she was looking for a hookup!), then proceeding to try out some equipment and splitting her drawers right there in front of God and country! Mary tried to hold back her laugh, and they both had mental pictures that kept them going 'til they arrived at the restaurant.

As they pulled into the restaurant parking lot, Mary advised Ben she had been here before and their food was excellent. He agreed wholeheartedly.

Entering the restaurant, they were seated immediately and handed menus, then the waiter discreetly left them to decide what was for dinner.

"So tell me, Ben, you made the reservation here, but what if I said I don't eat Italian? Then would we have had hot dogs at the corner stand?"

"Mary, ye of little faith. You know the steak house two blocks over, right?" As she nodded, he continued, "That was reservation number two, and bear with me one sec, let me go call and cancel that one!"

She broke out in laughter. "No, you did not, did you?"

Ben said, "Yes, I did, and we still could make it if you prefer that big juicy steak."

"Nope, next time maybe. Pasta tonight!"

Dinner progressed with conversation covering their pasts and how they ended up where they both were now. Over dessert, Mary mentioned that she had been thinking about getting some of the Vets together to discuss and vent about the issues with the VA that so many of them encountered. Or if not, to discuss issues, to relax, enjoy others' company, and eat!

She explained, "When Raoul told me about Randy, who works security at the VA office, had invited him for a barbecue and made him feel like a real human, it really made me think. I have this huge house, monstrous backyard, and pool, and it begs for people to come visit. I don't entertain much, but feel this is worthwhile. What's your thought, Ben?" "Absolutely a great idea! And I can help set up or do whatever you need me too!" said Ben with enthusiasm.

The drive home was quiet, but a companionable quiet, both thinking about what needed to be done to plan the gathering. As they got to Mary's, they both had big smiles, and big hugs were given as well as promises for many future times together. During the next few weeks, they did talk periodically about the barbecue and met for lunch a couple of times.

A few weeks later, Raoul came in for his labs, and Mary mentioned the barbecue, asking him if he knew anyone who might want to join in.

"I can talk to Hawk. I've known him a while, and I think he would enjoy that. And Randy, definitely Randy. I can check with some others too! You really want us, a bunch of misfits, at your place?"

Mary responded quickly, "Raoul, I consider no one a misfit. We all served our country in one capacity or another, and it is important that we have each other to support, even if no one else does. Now take my number and talk to those people and let me know who is interested."

PLOTTING A BARBECUE

MEANWHILE, BACK AT THE BEN'S GYM, Ben and Tyrell were hard at work. Coaching and helping people stay on their fitness regimes was hard work, especially for those who were not sure if this was what they wanted to do (and they needed extra attention) and also for those who were dedicated and loyal to the routine (the potential overdoers that could harm themselves if not careful). Neither Ben nor Tyrell wanted either to fall off their scheduled workouts and goals, and they worked relentlessly to keep everyone on track.

"Break time, Tyrell!" stated Ben at about one thirty. "Let's go to the bar, get a drink, and compare notes to be sure everyone is on track."

One power bar and smoothie later, they had made sure the day was progressing as it should for all, and Ben mentioned the barbecue Mary was thinking about.

Tyrell looked at Ben, nudged him with his elbow, winked, and said, "You and Mary got something goin' besides a cookout?"

"No, no. Get serious, Tyrell. We are just good friends with a shared history! But seriously, what do you think? And do you know anyone who may want to come?"

"Actually, I do think it is a great idea. I have a couple of guys in mind and will ask them and see if I can think of anyone else. Let's get back to getting these people to work!"

HOMELESS SHELTER IN DC

RAOUL WAS SITTING AT THE shelter one morning having breakfast. He noticed Hawk walking in and flagged him over to sit with him. "Where have you been hiding, Hawk? Haven't seen you in a while."

"Well, as we talked about, I did apply to stay here, and it looks like a bed will open in the next couple of days. So I have been bouncing around some, spent some time at that camping spot we used to hide out at. Nobody has ever discovered that place, luckily."

The guy next to Hawk overheard that comment and, as homeless are always trying to find safe places, asked where this place was.

Hawk, realizing the guy was trying to potentially take over this spot, responded tersely, "None of your damn business! Quit eavesdropping and eat your breakfast!" He looked back at Raoul. "What's new with you, Raoul?"

"Not much, same old street stuff. The cops and others are about as friendly as snakes in a mouse cage."

"I know what you mean. Never changes. People don't realize how hard it is to be placed in a position like this, when you don't know for sure where your head hits a pillow at night, if you are lucky enough to have the pillow, and where the next meal comes from! Luckily we have some of those places here we can use, and perhaps one day, if and when the VA gives us our due, we can actually have a place that we call home! But I guess we can say for now we are in good shape for the shape we are in!"

"Couldn't have said it better, Hawk! And on a happier note, how does barbecue sound to you? A friend has invited me and asked if I knew anyone else who may want to go. You in?"

"Nah."

"Seriously? Man there will be ribs, hot dogs, burgers, potato salad, desserts, God knows what else, oh yeah, and beer!"

"Okay, the food sounds good, but when you said beer, you got the Hawk's attention! Got a date for this?"

"Not yet. But I will be sure to let you know as soon I know."

They finished breakfast and went their separate ways, Raoul heading over to the VA to see if Randy was working, and he was. When he saw him, he offered a wave and a hello, thanking him again for the dinner and chance to meet Fred. "You know, if you ever need a dog sitter… I think I am Fred approved!"

"Hmmm, I will keep that in mind. How are you at fetch? Are you here for an appointment today?" responded Randy.

"Nope, not today. Social visit. I just wanted to let you know about a barbecue coming up. I would really like you there."

"Raoul, this isn't a back-alley barbecue with alley cats being cooked over a fifty-five-gallon drum and dumpster sides, is it?" asked Randy with a wry smile.

"And if I said yes, would you supply the beer? I know you've heard of beer-can chicken, but how about beer-can kitty? But no, this is a real barbecue. A nurse, Mary Hines, over at the VA hospital, is putting it together."

After a bit more discussion, Randy said he would go if not working on the day of the cookout, and Raoul assured him he would let him know the date ASAP. Raoul then left, and Randy went back to work.

MORE TIME AT VFW, MORE GUESTS FOR THE BARBECUE

On a Friday, Ben called his buddy Mike Jackson, stating, "I am ready for a VFW night. Saturday around six to six thirty work for you?"

Mike responded, "See you then."

Ben said, "And invite that guy Durham that was with you before. I enjoyed talking with him, and he could probably use a night out too."

"He enjoyed your conversation too, Ben. I will ask him, but either way, will see you then!"

Saturday rolled around. Mike and Durham arrived at the VFW about 6:15 p.m., chugged one beer by 7:00 p.m., when Ben came in and apologized for being late.

Mike, smiling, said, "You're only one beer late!"

After the good to see-yous went around, the evening progressed to military stories (some all true, some like fish stories, getting bigger and better with time), telling one another about life since the military. It was a great bonding experience, allowing a camaraderie to form between all three men.

At about 10:00 p.m., they were all ready to wrap things up and go home. Ben asked if the barbecue that was being planned sounded good to all. "There would be lots of good food and beer, and as soon as a date is confirmed, will let you know." They agreed that it sounded great and would love to come as soon as they knew when.

Then Durham asked, "Any chance Jim Beam may make an appearance?"

Ben grinned and winked, replying, "Well, if Bud and Mich are there, why not Jim too!" And on that note, they all headed home.

Upon arriving home, Ben noticed a message on his phone (he had not turned it on at all while having guys' night). Mary was calling to advise him lunch was at her house tomorrow. "See you then." He smiled as he headed for the bedroom, kicked off his shoes, and fell onto the bed and was asleep before the smile was off his face.

BEN VISITS MARY

He woke up around 8:00 a.m. on Sunday, put on a pot of coffee, and managed to find his paper in the bushes next to the front porch. With winters being so miserable lately, as soon as warmer weather hit, Ben was on that porch with coffee and paper every morning possible. Every few moments this morning, he caught himself putting down the paper and just staring at the yard. Green grass and cherry blossoms in bloom, who could ask for more?

He did call Mary at about 10:00 a.m. to confirm lunch. Voice mail kicked in, so he left a message and then proceeded to shave, shower, and dress.

Today, he arrived right on time. As he had picked Mary up for dinner, he knew his way but had never been in the house. The few lunches they had before, Ben either went to the VA or they met somewhere due to work schedules.

He commented upon stepping into the entry, "What a gorgeous place! Big too. And from what I see, you like comfortable too. I like the decor, Mary."

Mary replied, "Thanks, 3,600 square feet, 5 beds, 3 baths, eat in kitchen, formal dining, rec room in basement. Want the whole tour?"

"Sure, but a question first. Was a wedding and 5 or 6 kids in your future when you bought this? 'Cause it sure could support that lifestyle."

Laughing, Mary responded, "Nope. I was apparently in the right place at the right time. This house belonged to a doctor at the hospital. He had major parties here. I attended some of them and always commented on how much I liked his house. When he was retiring, I told him I would love to own this. Rather than listing with a realtor, we haggled, he moved to Florida, and here I am! I even got to keep a lot of the furnishings, 'cause condos in Florida don't need this much stuff. Hungry?"

As they stepped out onto the back patio, Ben gasped, "Oh my." The patio had a full outside kitchen with a large grill, fridge, sink, counter space galore, and even a pizza oven. The yard sloped gently down to a large flat expanse where the pool was, along with a Jacuzzi.

Mary had a spread of sandwiches, salads, and drinks, and they both filled their plates. Ben asked if Mary had figured out a date for the cookout, and she explained that a week from the next Saturday, the twenty-second, would work nicely. They discussed details, deciding that fifteen to twenty people would be attending, and Ben expressed concern that that may be a lot for her to handle, with her response being, "Ben, I've had forty-plus here. I love entertaining. This house screams to have parties. Let's get this one rolling!"

"OK," said Ben, "but promise me, if you need help, you will ask. And I provide the beer and help pay for the food. Plus, anyone who can, we ask to bring either a side or dessert?"

She agreed with his plan. They discussed the cookout a little more to be sure they were on the same page then moved on to discuss other things until Ben realized the time, having to stop by the gym before his day ended.

With thirteen days left to finish planning and setting this up, Mary and Ben both swung into high gear. Calls back and forth were made to assure one another they had the proper amounts of meats, booze, etc., and also notifying everyone of the date and time.

Mary notified Raoul at his next hospital check, who in turn told Hawk and Randy. At that point, he did give Randy Mary's phone number, and Randy did call, offering to bring a dish, booze, whatever needed, and telling Mary she was doing a great thing. She asked if he would mind bringing coleslaw, to which he was more than happy to do.

Ben told Mike, who of course told Durham and Tyrell. Tyrell did ask if it was okay to bring his girl, Sue, and was told yes as Mary would probably like a little female company. That prompted a call-back to Mike, who said that he and Durham's wife would be happy to join them. Matter of fact, that may extend their lives not going partying without them.

Raoul called Mary from the shelter one evening to let her know two other guys he knew would be there and asked if that was okay. She of course said yes, and Tom Harris and Ron Woods were in.

AN INFAMOUS BARBECUE

FINALLY, ALL WAS IN PLACE for the Barbecue. Ben had taken over the last of the ribs last night and helped Mary check to be sure the propane tanks were full for the grill and that everything they could set up in advance was done. He knew he had enough time to enjoy his coffee and paper before picking up the ice (you always need more ice), grabbing the last two suitcases of beer, and heading over to pick up Raoul and the other three. Thinking to himself as he drained the last of his coffee, *It just doesn't get any better than this.*

Ben finished his coffee, loaded the beer in the trunk, and stopped at the shelter for his prearranged pickup of Raoul, Hawk, Tom, and Ron. They were eagerly awaiting his arrival, all clean-shaven (except for Hawk—the beard would never go!) had on clean clothes, freshly showered, but a little heavy-handed on that Old Spice.

On the way to Mary's, they compared military history. Tom and Ron commented they had been Army National Guard Infantry in Afghanistan, with Ben responding, that he had been with the Guard in Iraq and that future talks would follow.

They stopped, grabbed the ice, and arrived at Mary's a bit later than they should have. People had already started arriving. Ben recognized two of the women who were helping Mary cart the last of the food out to the patio kitchen area. He said hi to Sue (Tyrell's girl) and Jean (Mike's wife) and was introduced to Durham's wife, Shawna. He then introduced the ladies to Raoul and the others, then with their help, carried the rest of the beer and the ice out to the patio area.

Mary had made all the guys go out back and headed back into the house for one last food run. As she came out the back door, she yelled, "The last of the meat is coming out... Who's gonna be the chef?"

Raoul volunteered Randy's services, advising he was a pro, and Randy responded with, "Raoul, you just became my assistant. Now light that gorgeous grill. It makes my little hibachi look really pathetic!"

From down in the yard, there was a voice heard, "Vets, let the party begin!" followed by yells loud enough to be heard all the way down the street, followed by the sound of pop-tops opening. While this was going on outside, the ladies were inside smiling. Mary led them into the living room, where there was wine (chilled, if needed) and finger foods for them to enjoy and get acquainted over before joining the guys for the main meal.

Outside, Hawk was telling Raoul about a situation in Miami that happened last winter. Apparently another homeless man thought he could take Hawk's blanket from him and got a surprise when Hawk beat him up instead of giving up the blanket. Unfortunately, the cops were close by, heard the commotion, and because the other guy was injured, Hawk ended up in jail for a week.

Raoul stated, "Man, that sucks. Shouldn't the other guy have gone to jail too?"

Hawk replied, "Hell, Raoul, think about it, seven days of hots and a cot! As well as rec time, hot showers, and air... Miami is warm during the day, even in winter! That was my vacation."

Ben, Tyrell, Ron, and Tom were sharing their experiences in Iraq and Afghanistan, comparing engagements in urban warfare as well as al-Qaeda attacks that occurred in mountain outposts. They touched on people they had known, trying to see if any common bonds surfaced, but no one was familiar to all, so they moved on.

Mike and Durham found seats out on the lawn and were sitting quietly, absorbing the movement around them, realizing new friendships were being formed and old ones strengthened. At one point, Mike did comment on what a great thing Mary and Ben were doing to set up this and allow everyone to overtake her home. Durham agreed, then heard Randy yell out, "Hey, y'all, grab your mess gear. Chow's on!"

The spread laid out was phenomenal. Potato and macaroni salad, coleslaw, baked beans, all the condiments necessary for hot dogs and burgers, and those ribs! If anyone went hungry here today, they had only themselves to blame. For about an hour, food was the main focus. Not a lot of conversation, but movement back to the patio was consistent. As Mary noticed the interest in the main course dying down, she and the others came out, Jean asking if anyone had room for dessert. When the guys saw the two apple pies and two peach pies hit the table, as well as a big platter of brownies, a line formed. Someone stated, "My eyes may be bigger than my stomach, but I sure am gonna give it my all!" After assuring herself that the guys were all good, Mary herded the ladies back inside. She figured the guys needed bonding time without feeling the need to entertain the ladies, and they could get better acquainted as well.

Hawk, Raoul, and Tyrell were off to the side, and Hawk stated, "Gentlemen, we can leave the pie and brownies for others. I have our dessert here! Can you say Beam? Jim Beam?"

Raoul said, "Now you're talking! One and only one for me, though. Can really spike my sugar level, but this is a party!"

A while later, Hawk, Durham, Mike, Raoul, Tyrell, and Randy were sitting discussing the military and VA. Mike shared that he had undergone seed implant and radiation treatment for prostate cancer and had been put at 100 percent permanent and total disability with no future medical eval necessary. Even though it appeared the cancer was not completely gone (his PSA had kept rising), they lowered his benefit to 30 percent. His PSA had dropped from 55 to .5 after treatment, so he thought maybe they felt that was grounds to go back on their word, meaning their word was no good as they could retract at will when it benefited them.

Randy stated, "Well, in some ways, you are lucky, Mike. If you had retired and were in that position where the VA drops compensation, they can take from your retirement."

Hawk emphatically stated, "They can't do that!"

Randy replied, "Oh yeah! As an example, if you had 100 percent dropped to 30 percent, which, to pick a figure, is 550 per month, they can take that from your retirement. I know guys who actually are in the boat now, and when all is said and done, they are actually getting between 100 and 200 from the VA. And they were getting 2K or more a month before!"

Tyrell confirmed that, advising them that for retirees, anything under 40 percent was subject to the corresponding loss from your retirement pay.

Mike chimed in, stating, "And you don't dare question their decisions or they will retaliate. During an exam, I was told my nuts were two-thirds their normal size, and that entitled me to a 10 percent rating. I asked if that was per nut, and they said they would get back to me. Well, getting back to me meant another exam, and all of a sudden, my nuts were normal. Guess they grew and I missed it!"

Durham mentioned the Vet who went into a clinic and shot his doctor. Tyrell sympathized, asking if you could blame the poor guy. And expressed his surprise that that had only happened once. Mike explained that Ben felt most of the issues the Vets experience were from the regional offices and not the hospitals.

At that point, Ben heard his name and told Tim and Ron they needed to go see what the other three were up too. They walked over, Ben asking, "Now what did I do?"

Mike then recapped what he said to the others, adding what he had not previously stated, and that was that the VA regional office even controlled the doctors' final decisions.

"Wow," said Ben with a wry laugh, "I thought you might be using my name in vain, but nope, you were surmising wonderfully my thoughts. That poor Vet shouldn't have shot the doctor. It would have made more sense to go to his regional VA office and picked someone off there! Matter of fact, it wouldn't surprise me if a Vet or a group of Vets did just that! Can't say I haven't thought of it occasionally. Anyone here gonna deny they have thought the same or would applaud anyone who did that?"

"Okay, Ben, when do we go?" chimed in Raoul.

"I did not say that to recruit you guys to attack the VA. But it's the way things are. Everyone has a breaking point. When we were kids, remember what happened when the bullies kept picking on one kid 'til he retaliated? Remember the movie *Carrie*? Isn't the VA bullying a lot of Vets? And getting away with it…"

Everyone became silent. What Ben had said rang true, and they all needed a few moments to absorb and internalize the thoughts. Ron finally advised everyone that it was time for a subject change and drink.

Hawk chimed in, "I'll drink to that!" and took a drink of the Beam from the bottle he still held. Then he asked, "Who's ready for more booze?" And they moved on to safer topics.

Around 2:30 a.m., things had quieted down. Everyone had gathered out back by the patio, and Mary announced, "No one is driving home this morning. There will be no KIAs on my watch." The couples all were assigned bedrooms, Randy and Ben got a room, and Hawk got a couch and was given a blanket and pillow. Tom and Randy were sound asleep, or passed out, in lounge chairs on the patio, so Mary threw blankets over them as well, hoping if they woke up to pee, they headed for the house and not the bushes.

By about ten thirty on Sunday, everyone had woken up, and Mary had a big pot of coffee waiting. Ben offered to go get donuts. Everyone groaned, claiming they were still full from last night. Mary then offered leftovers to anyone who wanted some, advising them she had to-go boxes like restaurants so there would be no worries about returning containers. (That was also her way of being sensitive to the homeless. They could take one good meal to have later today with no guilt.) Plus she could only eat so much of what was left.

Everyone pitched in to clean the yard and patio, also to be sure no dirty dishes were left in the inside kitchen. The guys bagged and deposited the trash appropriately, and with warm hugs and thanks, everyone left.

PEOPLE START MULLING OVER OPTIONS

RAOUL SPENT THE NEXT FEW days mulling over what had been said about attacking the VA. When he and Hawk would speak, that subject was their main conversation, with Hawk saying, "If I had a gun, I would do it in a microsecond!"

After a few days of going back and forth on the subject, Raoul finally asked, "Hawk, what if we got together a group of guys and took on the office here in DC?"

They stared at each other for what seemed like forever in total silence, each thinking this over, then Hawk said, "Why not? It would really take some planning, and we have nothing but time to do that. Who would we get to join us that we trust completely though?"

"From the sound of things of the group at Mary's, most if not all have at least thought of it, thinking that would be a good start. The more I think about this, Hawk, the more I want to go through with it. You in?"

"Got nothin' to lose. Let's see who we can recruit and start planning, Raoul!" Hawk said with a bit of excitement in his voice. Having a mission was something he had missed.

RECRUITING

HAWK WAS HAVING LUNCH AT the shelter one day, and when he noticed Tom and Ron sitting at a table alone, he picked up his plate, grabbed his drink, and went over to join them. They discussed what a great time they had all had at the cookout at Mary's and having people who understand what life was like for the Vets to share and commiserate with. Then he said, "You know, there are some of us Vets who would get great satisfaction out of going into a VA regional office and just blowing away everyone we could! It may get the attention of politicians who seem to turn a blind eye to our situations and change some things! Ever had that thought cross your mind?"

Tom responded, "Hawk, I would be lying if I said it had never crossed my mind, but I really want to be able to go back to Georgia and work on getting my marriage back together and a life! I know that some of the issues are because of the VA not helping like they should, but..."

Ron chimed in, "At the party, I really got worked up when the VA discussion started. I get that. I have issues too! Yes, there are days I could cheerfully go annihilate some of those idiots! Then other days, I feel it would do no good. Would I? I don't know, honestly."

"Ron," stated Hawk, "maybe on one of the days you feel like doing a cleanse, we could go together to the VA and straighten them out!" he said that with a laugh and a grin, but Ron and Tom both noticed the hardness in his gaze.

WHY?

After Hawk said he was going to go over to the park and see if he could bum some money for cigs and a bottle, he left the table. Ron and Tom spent a couple of moments discussing the conversation, decided it was idle talk, and went their separate ways as well.

MIKE PREPS FOR AN NORTH CAROLINA VISIT

GERALD WAS ONLINE CHATTING ONE evening, and Mike popped in asking how things were going in North Carolina and if Gerald felt settled yet. Washington replied he was as settled as he could be and the bass boat he had purchased was awaiting Mike to visit.

Mike informed him he would love to come down to fish, and BTW he knew he could outfish Gerald, so if Mike had a convenient date that worked for Gerald, he would be happy to book a room. To which Gerald replied, "Motel? Uh-uh, buddy. I invited you. We have room. You stay here, meet Becker, and we all go out for at least one day!"

At that point, they both checked schedules and very happily decided that two weeks away, they both had clear schedules, and Mike could drive down for four days. After that was determined and all decided, they both disconnected with see-ya-soon and can't-waits.

RAOUL PAYS A VISIT TO BEN'S GYM

RAOUL STOPPED BY THE GYM to say hi and talk to Ben about those VA bullies. All that had transpired was really weighing heavy on his mind.

When Ben assured him he had time to talk, they stopped by the snack bar, grabbed smoothies, and headed for Ben's office. Raoul looked straight into Ben's eyes and asked if he had seen last night's 11:00 p.m. news. "No, why?" responded Ben.

"Well, Ben, the VA really screwed us over good this time. They got caught stealing our money, or *embezzlement* may be the better term! It appears to be billions. One person got over 2.4 mil alone!"

Ben realized Raoul was really upset over this situation and broke in, "Raoul, buddy, calm down. Seriously, how could that even happen?"

Raoul responded with, "They buy prepaid debit cards, load them with money that the Vets need and deserve, and give it to employees as bonus or incentive money! It has been going on for at least a year, God knows how much longer! Ben, I got ahold of a nine-millimeter pistol and twenty magazines! When I leave here, I plan to go to the VA and clean house. This is so out of hand and wrong!"

"Raoul… please, please wait and think this through. Without planning something like this, the odds aren't in your favor for a good outcome. Going in half-cocked would *not* achieve anything. But if there are others to join and a plan in place…"

Raoul said, "Hawk would join us in a heartbeat."

"So let's see who we know and trust completely to plan this," Ben responded, thinking what he should say next. "Remember My Lai? That would be the type of statement we want to make."

"I think anyone who was ever in Vietnam remembers My Lai, Ben. That is the way I would want this to go down! Let's start planning and putting this mission together."

After a moment of silence when you could tell both men were contemplating what had just been said, they nodded to each other and man-hugged with the back pats, Ben made sure Raoul had all his contact numbers, and they parted with the standard "Keep in touch. Keep me posted."

A PLAN COMES INTO BEING

RAOUL HEADED BACK TO THE shelter hoping Hawk would be there for lunch today. He got in line for the food looking for Hawk and spotted him at his usual corner table. As he joined Hawk, Hawk asked what was new, and Raoul informed him there was plenty new, and if Hawk had no plans after lunch, a walk in the park would be nice.

Hawk knew by the urgent tone in Raoul's voice something was definitely up, and he wasn't sure it was good. So he immediately responded and stated that that really sounded like a nice finish to the gourmet meal they were eating.

Raoul, trying not to spit out his bite of ham and cheese sandwich, actually managed a grin and followed up with, "Yeah right!"

Finishing lunch, they headed to a nearby park, where they knew it would be quiet enough and safe to talk openly. Raoul filled Hawk in on his earlier conversation with Ben. Without a second's hesitation, Hawk stated, "I'm in! Man, do you know how often that thought has crossed my mind? Even thought about turning it into my own one-man band. Kinda being like the Oklahoma bombing experience. Maybe I never told you this, but as a SEAL, ordnance was my specialty."

"Good to know, man, and now what we need to do is concentrate on finding Vets who are capable and willing to be part of this, as well as trustworthy! The easy part is over. We are done talking about doing this… Time to prepare for the attack!"

"Agreed, the time has come. We need to make this happen!" responded Hawk with conviction.

AT BEN'S, MORE DISCUSSION

AFTER RAOUL LEFT THE GYM, Ben sat in his office for a few moments, then called Tyrell, using his cell phone in case someone on staff picked up the work line and heard the conversation. He told Tyrell all Raoul had shared, concerning the attack on the VA, and waited for a response.

Tyrell replied, "Are you really serious about doing this, Ben?"

"Yes, yes I am."

"Wow, I am not gonna lie and tell you it has never crossed my mind, especially when I see people like Hawk and Raoul, who are homeless because of the VA's ineptitude, but to actually do this?"

"I understand how you feel, Tyrell. But there comes a point where they just push it too far, and for me this is that point! This is the proof that the VA does not care about us Vets. It is only what they can do to improve their lives, and I for one am not gonna tolerate it anymore!"

"Ben, I am not saying I won't get involved. I need time to absorb all this, do a little recon on my own to find out just what is going on, then decide. If this is as bad as it looks from what you have told me so far, the VA needs to be held accountable. No argument there."

"Tyrell, this is total disrespect for Veterans, those who died for this country of ours, not to mention those who have disabilities and health issues they have to deal with for the rest of their lives and, in some cases, their children's. The VA tells Congress there is not enough money to take care of the Vets, after they stuff their pockets with that kind of money! Then they ask for more money and want it to be 'discretionary money.' You realize that means they can also use those millions as they see fit, right? And of course that could mean more bonuses."

"I get it, Ben, torques me too. Let me mull things over, and we can talk later. Please go home and relax tonight, Ben. Don't obsess over this, okay?"

"Thanks, Ty. I will respect any decision you make, as well as assure you your job is safe! See you later."

RAOUL UPDATES SARGE

As evening settled in, Raoul realized he had one more thing to do. Sargent Bill Lewis provided Raoul with a calling card to allow him to check in with him and he was due his call. Raoul called, they exchanged the hellos and all good stuff, and Raoul asked if Sarge had heard about the VA and money issue. Sarge informed him that he had heard about it and inquired as to whether or not Raoul had heard about the Christmas party.

"Do I want to? No, but you can tell me," responded Raoul.

"Well, it seems those incentives and bonuses extended to holiday gift giving as well. Apparently across the various regionals, people got boats, cars, grills, RVS, and four-wheel drives. Now, gonna be honest, if those items were Tonka brand, I would still be pissed, on principle alone!"

"Agree," said Raoul, "Vets get a 1.7 percent raise, and some get their compensation dropped completely or lowered to an unacceptable level, and yet they get this crap!"

"And this on top of those hefty bonuses they already got. Oh yeah, they earned it for the great service they provide to our Vets. Nice…" stated Sarge.

Raoul then mentioned that he thought that there probably were some Vets who would attack the VA offices (like the regional in DC itself) and maybe that would help straighten things out! "What do you think, Sarge, do you really think that could happen?"

Sarge did not directly address that comment but responded by telling Raoul about his discussion with Rice and Ellis in Idaho, and they had commented when he mentioned the Christmas parties and gifts that this could be the straw that might have broken the camel's back. Then he asked, "Raoul, would you like to join us on a fishing expedition in Idaho soon? I have enough frequent flyer miles to get you out here at no cost!"

"Sarge, you are so good to me, and if it really is nothing out of pocket on your side, I would love it. I can clean and fry a mean fish to earn my keep while there. Let me know, and I will clear my calendar."

And with that, they closed the call.

BACK AT THE VFW

A COUPLE OF DAYS LATER, Ben had had some time to mull over the whole situation and decided it was time to talk to Mike Jackson and Durham Murdit. When he finally got to talk to them both, it was decided they would meet at the VFW the twenty-eighth around 4:00 p.m. Raoul dropped by the gym and told him about the fishing trip to Idaho and his discussion with Sarge that led up to that. Ben said he would be talking to two other guys in a couple of days and perhaps Tyrell would be in. They promised to keep in touch, and Raoul left.

The next day, Tyrell informed Ben that after careful consideration, he was in. "I cannot in good conscience stand by and do nothing. I was in Iraq and Afghanistan fighting for freedom for all Americans, thinking that the US had our backs, and to realize they don't care about the Vets who died for that freedom, as well as those who will suffer for the rest of their lives. Our enemy is now the VA!"

Ben thought over what Tyrell had just said and responded, "The VA will pay for their actions in the worst possible way! Thank you, Tyrell, for deciding to join us."

When Ben walked into the VFW around four fifteen, he declared, "Guess I am consistent. A beer late again, huh?"

Mike replied, "Nope, two beers! We got here early and started without ya."

After the usual guy talk, Ben asked if they had heard about the VA stealing Vets' money.

Durham replied, "They need an ass kicking. I know a few Rangers who would be more than happy to assist with that and smile the whole time."

Mike responded, "Kick butt, hell! My shotgun, nine-millimeter handgun, and Ka-Bar could walk in there, and there is no guesswork as to the outcome of that meeting. One big blood bath, not ending 'til I go down too!"

Ben, after glancing around the room to be sure no one was eavesdropping, asked, "Would a Marine consider taking someone like me on this suicide mission?"

Mike's response was, "Two can kill twice as many as one."

Ben replied, "Okay... seriously, when are we gonna do this?"

Mike replied, "Pick a date. Only don't wait too long or I will go it alone. I refuse to let the cancer take me first, so let's get serious if you mean it."

"I am," replied Ben.

Murdit had sat very quietly during this whole conversation. Now he looked back and forth at the two of them and stated, "Guys, you throw in a Ranger, me, and we could kill three times as many as one, so the big question now is, when?"

Ben paused for a moment then advised them that if they really were serious, this could happen. He explained that there were two others for sure and feelers out for more that would be willing to become a part of the group and fit in well. Things were in the planning stage now, but whoever else joined needed to be committed and capable and bring something necessary to the table.

Mike and Durham both confirmed their commitment to the mission, and then they decided they needed to toast one another, requesting a full pitcher. They then spent the rest of the evening just relaxing and drinking, each one catching the other's eyes and knowing they all would be thinking over this conversation.

MIKE APPROACHES GERALD

A FEW NIGHTS LATER, MIKE was in the Vets' chat on his computer when he noticed Gerald come in. He knew this was not the time nor place to discuss the mission but was going to ask Gerald later if he wanted in, thinking he would be a good fit. So he started with asking Gerald how things were going, and Gerald replied they were not good. It looked like his marriage was on the rocks, but his buddies Jim Beam and Bud were doing fine. Mike typed back with a LOL and that he could relate. "Those two will never let us down, huh?" They chatted back and forth awhile, then Mike asked for a phone number and a heads-up on a good time to call. "Got something rather interesting to discuss!"

Gerald provided his cell number and said, "Three days from today is totally yours. We can talk then."

Time flew by, and Mike called Gerald that day. "What's up, Mike? You sure have me curious," Gerald stated.

"What is your take on the VA spending Vets' money on themselves, Gerald?"

"Are you serious? Guess I have my head too far in the sand lately, try not to watch the news, but... what is going on?"

"Well, let me tell you, Gerald. It seems that for at least the last couple of years, the VA has been using their funds to support themselves rather than us. For incentives and bonuses, they place money on debit cards and give them to staff. We are not talking about fifty or one hundred dollars, buddy. I hear one higher-up got over two mil. It appears that it has added up to a minimum of one billion so far!"

"Are you kidding me? And how did this get out?"

"Apparently there was a whistle-blower in the VA who leaked it to the media. I'm guessing someone who didn't get any goodies was the one. And there's more. At the annual Christmas parties, people got cars, ATVs, and a bunch of other crap. And we get a 1.7 percent raise!"

Gerald was quiet for a moment, then he said, "You know, Mike, maybe it is time someone goes into the VA and blows away the guy in charge."

"The guy who was in charge is gone, about eight months ago. It appears the new guy can't or won't do anything, not sure which, and the government is either covering it up or really doesn't care about the Vets, 'cause no criminal charges have been filed against anyone!"

"Mike, this really sucks and is so unfair. Do you think there is anything Vets or anyone can do to stop this crap?"

"That depends, Gerald, on how far you would be willing to go to help stop this."

"What do you mean, Mike? Do you know something or have something in mind?"

"Something like a group of Veterans who are planning an attack on the VA? Something like that, Gerald? And would you join the group?"

"What are you saying, Mike, by attack? Something with picket signs and spray paint or guns and ammo?"

"If I told you that there are Vets who are planning to attack a VA office with weapons and the intent of killing VA employees, would you join the mission with no qualms or regrets?" asked Mike.

"Are you in this group, Mike?"

"I plead the fifth!"

There was a long pause here. Mike could hear Gerald tapping either a pen or his fingers on the table, mulling this over. Finally, Gerald spoke, "Well, Mike, we are both Marines. We always cover each other's back, and we never leave anyone behind. Are there other Marines involved in this?"

"Yes!"

"Then I am in. I will help cover their backs but need to know you are there to cover mine."

"You know it. We will talk soon. The mission is on, and will keep you posted. Arrah, arrah."

GERALD AND JAMES TAKE A WALK

By 9:00 A.M., GERALD HAD already downed one beer and was thinking about the VA and what they had got caught doing with funds that should have been used for Vets. The whole issue kept running through his mind in a vicious cycle. He knew that he and James were due a walk. It was both of their solutions when things weighed heavy on their minds. With the thought of a walk and talk, Gerald grabbed two beers and headed next door.

When James looked out and saw two beers, he immediately opened the door, smiled a wry smile, confiscated one beer, and said, "Let's walk."

They walked in silence for about a block, then Gerald shared all with James, from what the VA had done with the money to the conversations and plans that were in process.

After about another minute of complete silence on James's behalf, he said, "Are you asking me to go with you, Gerald?"

"No," replied Gerald, "but I really needed to talk to someone. I trust you not to turn me in, me nor the other guys, even if I share everything with you, James."

"Do you really feel this is going to go off as planned, Gerald? This is some heavy shit you got going here!"

"I do," responded Gerald, "regardless of the loss on our side as well."

"For the short time we have known each other, Gerald, we have shared a lot. What we did in Nam, how we have dealt with it since,

55

and even what we would like to see happen to the VA. I have often wondered if anyone had the cojones to go in and kill those SOBs, especially after the one that did blow away his doctor. Now you tell me you are part of a group that is thinking about doing just that! I have always felt the government did not work hard enough to get me out of that concentration camp sooner nor end the conflict sooner. I always thought that if there were a way to get payback, or at least get even, I would. Charlie broke me, and I am still not the fighting man I once was. Could I get involved in something like this? I really don't know. While I understand the many reasons you and others would pursue this, I really do not know if it is for me. But no way would I break the confidence and trust you have placed on me!"

"I know it is safe with you, James, and I feel really lucky to have a friend like you who I can talk to about anything and everything. Thanks, buddy!"

"You are welcome, my friend, and I am aware that works both ways! On a lighter note, though, I spoke to Dee to be sure all is set up at Lake Marion for our fishing trip. I am oh-so ready to go! She assured me we are set, same cabin as before, and free day with the pontoon again. That is, as long as we provide her with cleaned fish to take home for dinner that night. We will have to gas up the boat when we return it, but that sure works for me!"

"Yeah, well let's see how this trip plays out. Last time, Gerald, you kicked my butt, got the biggest cat and bass. This time, if I have to fish 24-7, I am gonna kick your butt!"

"Sure, James, that's gonna happen! Maybe when it snows in the far south… Now I gotta go get the lawn mower ready for summer, it won't do it itself, so we'll talk later," said Gerald as they landed back in front of the house.

"Yeah, guess I should accomplish something too. Later."

BEN AND RAOUL

BACK IN DC, RAOUL STOPPED by the VA to say hi to Randy and was informed Randy had been off sick for the past two days. He then called Randy to see if he was okay or needed anything, even taking Fred for a walk if required. Randy assured him they were both fine and should be back at work the next day, after profusely thanking him for checking on him.

Raoul then headed over to the gym to update Ben on everything he knew so far. Ben had given an open invite to everyone at the cookout, and Raoul had stopped in periodically. As usual, the gym was swamped, so he said to Ben, "Man, business is good, oh-so glad! I can catch up with you later." To which Ben extended a dinner invite, and it was agreed that Raoul would be at Ben's place Friday evening.

Friday rolled around, and when Raoul showed up, Ben had pizza on the counter and beer in the fridge. They grabbed the pizza and a beer and headed for the patio. Ben knew from the small grin on Raoul's face he had info to share and asked him what was up.

Raoul smiled a bit broader smile, took a deep breath, and said, "Well, Ben, got some good guys lined up. Ready? Sergeant Lewis and Tony Rice were with me in Nam. A Robert Ellis, who grew up with Tony in Idaho, also Nam. And of course, Jason Hawk, who you have already met. He was a Navy SEAL. You?"

"Let's see. Tyrell Dyer, Army, Durham Murdit, Ranger, Mike Jackson, Marine, and a friend of Mike's, Gerald Washington, who was a Green Beret in Vietnam who happens to be Mikes neighbor. Got no one else yet, but that could change. You? Anyone else you may want to approach?"

Raoul said he was thinking about talking to Ron Woods, who also was at the barbecue and also lived at the shelter. He would feel him out and let Ben know.

Ben then asked if Raoul remembered a Tom from the cookout, and Raoul did. He advised Ben, "You mean Tom Harris. He is definitely a no! He is working with some missionaries, trying to become a priest, I think Mormon, and hoping to reconnect with his wife."

"Sounds like he has a full plate. Anyone else?"

"You know, one more to consider. Do you remember Randy Lopez from Mary's? He is a security guard at the VA."

"Seriously, Raoul? Need to be extra careful talking to him. His ties could fall on the other side."

Raoul thought for a minute and responded, "I don't think that is an issue, Ben. He had me over for dinner one night, and it seems he is as upset as we are over treatment of Vets. As the only Vet in security there, he feels kinda left out of the group. The others are always making smart cracks about how screwed up the Vets are that come into the VA. He works, he goes home. No connection there."

"Just remember, loose lips sink ships… so be very careful!"

"Oh yeah, trust me, I will. And guess I should boogie on. Pizza was good. Thanks!"

"You are welcome. Same time, same place next week to see what else we have?"

"Ben, do you think Mary is willing to have another cookout? Be a great way to get together with everyone, and she did offer."

"I will check with her, but not tonight, too late and work tomorrow. Will let ya know."

DINNER AND BEN AND MARY

BEN REALIZED THE NEXT DAY while working that Mary had been on his mind since that conversation with Raoul. So he called to invite her to dinner.

Mary responded, "It's been over two weeks of late nights, cafeteria food, and you are offering me food? Yes, pick me up at six, and take me to that steak place!"

"I love a woman who is direct and to the point! You said six? See you then!"

"Okay, I will start getting ready now. The older I get, the longer it takes!" said Mary with a chuckle.

"Mary... don't talk like that. You don't need to put on war paint to look good. I have seen you without any, and you do look good! You are still young and good-looking to boot, regardless of what you think. Now let me go finish my day so we can enjoy this evening," Ben said in a more serious tone.

"Gee, you gonna stop there, handsome? Or is that just a taste of what is to be this evening?"

With a laugh, Ben stated, "Bye, love."

"Later, you!"

Ben arrived right at the stroke of six. Mary was sitting on the porch on the swing, and when she saw him, she got up and headed for the car. He got out of the car to greet her, and they exchanged a very warm embrace and a kiss. Ben released her to open the car door for her then rushed around to the driver's side with a laugh as he looked through the windshield.

When Mary advised him there was no need to run, he informed her she was the one that was starving and that he did not want to be the reason for a fainting woman then proceeded to start the car and punch the accelerator hard enough to lay a little rubber as they left the driveway.

"Well, thanks for being so considerate and rushing on my behalf, but let's not get a ticket on the way to the restaurant, okay? Then I just may pass out!" she said. At that point, they shared the laugh and went on to the restaurant.

At the restaurant, the greeter recognized them both (even though they had not been there together, they both were regular enough to be known). She said hello to them, seated them at a nice table overlooking the small courtyard, and advised them Linda would bring their water and take their orders. This was one of those places where you needed time to review the menu, so they both took their time, but strangely enough, both ordered the same cut of steak, requested medium rare, with baked potato and salad on the side. And Italian dressing! Linda looked at the two of them with a quizzical look on her face and asked, "You two been together long?"

Once they realized what she meant (and what they had done), they chuckled, and Ben responded, "No, but I think we can change that. Any woman who knows what kind of steak to order and what sides go with it deserves my full attention."

Mary replied, "Good point, but I will let you choose the wine."

As they waited for the food, Mary asked Ben about the gym. He informed her they kept busy improving things, setting the pool up with lines and ropes to allow four to do laps at the same time, as well as changing the filtration system to a saltwater system, which meant a savings on chlorine. He then asked how her work was going, and she said, "We are getting more and more new patients, but the staff doesn't increase accordingly. There have always been money issues, but since the information has come out about the higher-ups stealing money for their own benefit, everyone affiliated with the VA looks bad! But tonight is a night I am gonna pretend work, problems, nothing of that nature exists! I am going to enjoy the steak and the company. One question, though, if I end up in a food coma, will you get me home safely?"

Ben replied, "Of course I will, and look, here are the salads. Let's see how you do with that."

They both dug into their salads, and when the steaks came, they enjoyed those as well. Other than comments on how good the food was, it was a quiet meal, but not at all awkward, both feeling very comfortable with each other. Linda did ask if dessert was in order, got two major groans in response, complimented them on finishing the whole meal, then they paid and got up to leave. Mary commented that she had yet been invited to the gym, and after looking at his watch, Ben stated that if they stopped for a coffee, it would be after eleven before they got to the gym and he could show her around with no interruptions. He stated that they could go over to the gym, park there, walk a few blocks for coffee, and then go back for the tour, to which she responded, "Great idea. We can walk off some of the food, which, as always, was incredible. Thank you, Ben."

They drove over to Ben's, chitchatting, her telling about patients, mostly the cute, funny stories, him talking about people at the gym and also the cute, interesting stories, neither wanting to be serious and just enjoying each other's company. They parked at the gym, walked four blocks to a nearby coffee shop, enjoyed their coffees (and shared a piece of apple pie), then headed over to the gym. Ben had called Tyrell so that he would not see his car in the lot and be concerned, so lights were left on for them.

"This is the reception area," stated Ben.

"Got it. The sign gave it away," Mary said with a laugh.

"Guess you caught on to the Cafe and Bar too, huh? You are not only pretty, you are smart!"

"Ya got me, Ben," said Mary, and now they were both smiling and laughing.

As they walked through the different areas, Ben pointed out the different machines and what they did. As they entered the pool, Mary gasped. "Ben, I didn't expect a pool in a gym to be so pretty.

The water is so clear, and you even have plants around to give it a warm feeling."

"I firmly believe, Mary, that if you bust your butt working out then want a swim to relax, it should be nice!"

"Well, that it is! Is it heated too?"

"Yes, Mary."

Mary kicked off her shoes, walked over to the steps, stepped down to feel the water, sighed a sigh of contentment, then stepped back out of the water. "Ben, this has to be the best part of the whole gym! I bet you swim often."

"Yes."

"And I bet a lot of times it is after hours? And occasionally skinny-dip too, I bet!"

Ben said not one word but did smile at her.

Mary smiled a shy smile and removed her blouse. That was followed by her skirt, bra, and panties when Ben did not stop her nor move. All her clothes were placed on a nearby chair, and Mary then went to the edge of the pool and dove in. (Even though the pool was lap length, Ben had it designed with a shallow and deep end so down the road they could have meets or lessons.)

Mary swam the width of the pool then back and looked up at Ben, asking him to join her. He very quickly undressed, removed his prosthesis, and dove in. As he came up for air, Mary was there. They gazed into each other's eyes for a few moments, kissed, and made love for the first time in the warmth of the pool. Then they proceeded to shower together and learned each other's bodies even more fully in the shower.

When they were dressing, Mary asked Ben if he was a big breakfast eater or not. He knew that to mean only one thing and reached out to give her a big hug, stating, "Coffee... black, and I can take that as an invite?"

"I was hoping you'd catch on. But I don't think I can do a round three!" Mary said. "But sleep, oh yeah, that I can do!"

"Agree! Let's go."

They headed back to Mary's and settled in for the night, cuddling comfortably close. It was as if this was an old established ritual. No awkwardness for these two.

When Ben awoke, he was alone in the bed. There was a note on the nightstand telling him there was a toothbrush in the bathroom and she had coffee waiting for him. He smiled, headed for the bathroom, brushed his teeth, washed up, and threw on his pants. Mary was on the patio enjoying her coffee, with a carafe and cup sitting there waiting for him.

"Good morning, Ben! Have some coffee, and should you be hungry, I have croissants in the kitchen."

"Oh yeah, Mary, it is most definitely a great morning, but the coffee will do me fine for breakfast."

"Well, seeing as how it is almost lunch, I thought you may want something to eat."

Ben chuckled and said, "Mary, I had a great time last night. You swim wonderfully and are a great back washer. We need to spend more time together for sure."

"Thank you, Ben, I couldn't agree more. And you cuddle nicely too" was stated with a shy smile.

Ben reached over, took Mary's hand, and squeezed it lightly, then leaned over and gave her a kiss. They sat quietly and finished their coffee, and Ben realized he needed to get over to the gym. Tyrell would be wondering where he was, and it was his night to close.

"See you later?" he asked as he was ready to go with a soft kiss.

"I hope so. Call me," she responded.

When Ben got to the gym that day, Tyrell couldn't resist. Smiling, he asked, "How was your evening with Mary? Did you stay up all night... talking?"

With a small grin and big blush, Ben responded, "Time to get to work, isn't it?"

STATUS QUO

Everyone was having a quiet week. Raoul, Tom, and Hawk were spending a lot of time at the park, heading for the shelter at dinnertime and to get some rest. Sarge Lewis was hard at work on his farm, getting his garden in, doing some repairs, and enjoying the mild weather in Cañon City, Colorado. Gerald and James were doing the usual, hanging out and telling bigger and better fish stories as each day passed! And beer, let us not forget the beer, because they didn't! Gerald was so happy he chose the Charlotte area to move to; he would never would have met James.

Tony Rice and Robert Ellis were creating fish stories as they enjoyed some time on the river in Idaho, and they took some time to discuss the things they had learned and seen at the Militia meeting they had recently attended there. It seemed that what had started as a survivalist group had morphed into so much more, and now it appeared they not only had survival plans down pat but they could also get almost any and every weapon possible in the event of a war on US soil.

PLOTTING BEGINS IN EARNEST

THE TIME HAD COME FOR Ben and Raoul to meet for beer pizza and planning. Ben left a message at the shelter for Raoul, and their Friday-night pizza date was on.

Settling on the patio, Ben asked, "Raoul, have you any idea how this whole thing is going to play out?"

"Been thinking about it a lot," stated Raoul. "Pretty much all the time, if I am to be honest. I'm thinking those of us who know the VA layout should go with someone who may not be as familiar with the building. That would be you, Tom, Hawk, Tyrell, and me. And we will need to figure out who fits best with who from Sarge Lewis, Rice, Ellis, Jackson, Murdit, and Washington. Kinda thinking it is easier to plan and execute the mission if we are no bigger than a squad was in the military. That way we have a little leeway to add others if that ends up happening."

"Okay, I am impressed! Great start, or prebriefing, as we used to say. Now, how do we get everyone together to work out the logistics? Any ideas there, O wise man?"

"I think we need to get everyone here that we can. They need to be familiar with the city, and we need time to get to know who will work best with who and who can do what when it all goes into play. Seven of us are already here, so far two are in North Carolina, two in Idaho, and Sarge in Colorado. The two in NC are close enough to drive up but still go home when they want to, but the others would need to come out for a while and have a place to stay. Any ideas on your part, Ben?"

"Easy, Raoul. There is already one camper out back of the gym. That's where I keep mine. It's a big area, nice trees, and 24-7 access to all the gym has to offer. There is room too if anyone else brings in a camper, and should there be any questions, the guys we knew in service are visiting DC or family."

"Hmm, that sounds perfect. But now I am wondering, could those of us from the shelter stay here too?"

"Of course, once we get closer to go on this, I think you guys should be here. But you guys get to stay in the building in the back. We can clean that up for sleeping quarters and actually have real living space there. We will have to figure out just how that plays out and when and what the best way is to get you guys moved in. Don't want to bring you guys over too soon, though. Let's get the rest set up."

"So is there a timeline for this?" asked Raoul.

"I am thinking if we start prep work in August and if the ones outside DC are willing to come out by the end of September, that would be good. Of course, if we plan correctly, they can show up later, as long as everyone knows their part by the day!"

"Are you telling me we are putting this off 'til the end of the year?"

"Think about it, Raoul. Cold weather makes more sense. It will be easier to conceal weapons under big bulky coats. And another thing that just crossed my mind. It makes it easier to get you guys here and free up space at the shelter. I can play good guy! So I have been thinking January or February should work."

"Makes sense when you explain it like that. At first I thought you'd slipped a gear," said Raoul. "And it gives everyone time to get themselves lined up, personal stuff arranged, and still make all the necessary plans. I can talk to Sarge, Ellis, and of course, the guys at the shelter."

"Great! I've got the other three to talk to. Oh yeah, one more thing: cell phone, unlimited minutes. Remember, though, don't talk too much, 'cause for now I think we are okay, but if we say too much, we could hang ourselves. Later we may need to switch to throwaways, but for now… here. That way too when you travel, 'cause I do see at least a couple trips in your future."

"Ben…"

"No, no Ben. You are important to this whole mission, so let it be."

They then spent the next hour eating pizza and discussing other things. They tried to stay off the subject of the VA but couldn't help wondering what the VA's and public's response would be when the first round went off.

After their discussion that night, Ben knew he needed to get Jackson and Murdit together, so he called them the next day, planning a VFW night the following week.

A couple of days later, Raoul asked Hawk and Tom to join him at their favorite park. He proceeded to catch them up on plans, and both got really excited about the plans and the chance to spend part of winter in a place that wasn't the shelter. Hawk stated, "Man, this is really gonna happen, isn't it? And you guys know as bad as I do how stinky this place can be in the winter, so we get an added bonus there."

Later that afternoon, Raoul took advantage of that nice weather to find a spot where he knew no one would see him on the cell and called Sarge.

"Hi, Sarge. Know who this is?"

"Hmmm, sounds like my buddy Raoul, but the phone says Ben Goodman."

"You got me. Ben got me a phone to help plan things. We got some thoughts on the table, but I sure would like a face-to-face! Can we work something out?"

"Know what? I think you need a working vacation. Couple of things I could use help with here, and it would be worth the plane ticket to get help from someone I trust. Or I do have those miles we talked about earlier, and we can take that fishing trip too. Combine work with pleasure. Let me set that up and call you with dates. You will fly into Colorado Springs, then we will drive here."

"Sounds great, and you know anytime you need help, I am happy too. Let me know, and I will be there with bells on, or is that not a good idea 'cause the cows may get confused?"

"Smartass! Talk soon."

BACK AT THE VFW, MORE DISCUSSION

When Ben walked into the VFW, Murdit and Jackson both stood up and applauded him, confirming he was the usual one beer late. Murdit laughingly informed him the only way he could ever hope to keep up was if he showed up when the party was at least half over.

"Low blow," replied Ben. "I could start six hours ahead of you two and continue on after you give up."

"Uh-huh. Ben, we know good, and well after six hours, you would spend the night hugging that porcelain god and waking up with her the next morning!" exclaimed Jackson.

They harassed each other a while longer, then Jackson looked at Ben and asked what was up with the plan?

Ben explained the information they had so far, from getting the guys to DC to how they would be working together. At this point, it looked like a January or February completion date.

Jackson got a contemplative look on his face and, after a couple moments of silence, said, "How about this for a thought: you guys ever hear of the Saint Valentine's Day Massacre? In Chicago, two groups of gangsters had an all-out gangland-style war that day. One group lined up the other family against a brick wall and mowed 'em down using handguns, shotguns, rifles and machine guns. Ours could be remembered as Saint Valentine's Day Massacre II! I look at the VA as if they are gangsters, taking our money against our will, you know what I mean?"

The other two thought this over for a few moments, letting it soak in, and Murdit finally agreed, "You hit that nail right on the head, buddy. The mob is running the VA, and it is past time to clean house!"

Before Ben called it a night at about nine thirty, they drank a couple more beers and moved on to lighter subjects for a bit as the bar was becoming more crowded. At that time, Ben assured them they would stay in touch and get this thing rolling, and they all departed for home.

Based on the information shared that night, the next day, Jackson called Washington, advising him they needed an opportunity to talk. Washington shared that he and the wife were considering a trip to DC, as she had never been, and maybe in July?

Gerald told Mike that they had a very long talk and decided that they needed a chance to try to regain their closeness and were hoping that they could do so by doing things together. They had fallen into the trap of not doing anything as a couple.

"Sounds good to me. We have an extra room here, so no need for a hotel, and when the girls go off, we can powwow with the others. Talk to the wife, and let me know what week is good for you."

RAOUL HEADS WEST

SARGE REACHED OUT TO RAOUL, advising him of travel dates, restrictions for carry-on, and the need to have a doctor's note for his insulin needles, and that he would be flying into Colorado Springs and could pick up his ticket at National on the day of travel. After profuse thanks from Raoul, Sarge asked if he liked salmon, especially catching them.

"I'll bite. Far as I know, salmon don't run in Colorado, but maybe you are privately stocking a pond or two?" asked Raoul.

With a laugh, he replied, "Don't I wish. But Rice and Ellis are in Idaho, and maybe once we finish our work, a road trip is in order! Little business, little pleasure... Sound good to you?"

"Oh yeah, see you soon, and thanks again!"

Raoul then let Tom and Hawk know about his trip, both the working trip in Colorado and the pleasure portion in Idaho. He really did not have to explain. They caught on right away to the scheme of things, wished him the best, and did admit to a bit of jealousy but were both happy things were progressing. Raoul reminded them to keep in touch with Ben and let him know if they needed anything.

The next morning, Raoul decided he wanted his plane ticket in hand (to be sure it existed), so he headed out to National to pick it up, stopping by the gym to update Ben. Ben informed Raoul he was pleased things were going so well, offered Raoul a ride to National, and told him to keep in touch, get things rolling, but enjoy himself too.

The flight was an early a.m. flight next day (Sarge had moved quickly), so Ben dropped Raoul off first thing with one last word of advice, "Be very careful if you call me or anyone. This is when we start practicing caution. I have all your flight details to pick you up, and you can fill me in on the rest then! I will keep your stuff in a locker at the gym, no worries there, as I see you pack light."

"Ben, thanks again. Yeah, I have always been a light packer. Figure they can't lose much that way! If the summer stuff I brought isn't warm enough, I know I can borrow a jacket or coat, so away I go."

He took a walk around the airport before they called his flight then settled in getting lucky enough to have a window seat. And also the flight attendant still had a pillow left, so he got comfortable and went to sleep, only waking up when they announced touching down in Dallas. As he woke, the guy next to him said, "Man, I envy you. Wish I could sleep like that. Flying is so boring and now uncomfortable, the nap would make it fly by!"

"I am lucky. Can sleep anywhere! Once I actually feel asleep on a DC bus and only woke up when they checked in at the final station. Had to find another way back to where I was going. You have a good flight on, bud." And with that, he rushed to get to his gate for the Colorado Springs flight. Wondering if any airline ever made connections easy.

As it was a very close connection, he was down to the wire when he boarded and, with a big sigh of relief, fell into his seat, which for this leg was an aisle. Thinking to himself that as this was about a two-hour flight, window sure would have been nice. He sighed again and settled in, waiting for takeoff.

Finally they boarded everyone and taxied down for takeoff. The flight attendant did the safety pitch, and everyone settled in, getting as comfortable as possible. Raoul looked at the magazines in the seat pocket in front of him to kill some time. The guy across the aisle was nice to talk to. He was going out to meet his fiancée's family and was a bit excited, so Raoul tried to be nice and help settle him. They finally brought the snacks (boy, how generous, pretzels and half a can of soda).

When they landed, Raoul wished Mike good luck with the inlaws, grabbed his backpack from the overhead, and rushed out. Sarge was waiting right outside the terminal. They had decided a drive-by was the best way to go, so Sarge had to keep driving by the terminal 'til Raoul got out, but it saved parking, at least.

Raoul threw his pack in the truck, climbed in, and before he could hook up his seat belt, Sarge was rolling.

"Jeez, Louise Sarge, no hug, no handshake—"

"Nope, no hug patrol on duty! It's about an hour drive, if traffic cooperates, and once I get out of the Springs, I am so much happier. I've been stuck on 115 for up to three hours going home from here. And if you aren't hungry, I am gonna be very surprised. American, like all airlines, doesn't believe in food anymore."

"Yeah, I am getting a little hungry. Ben made me eat a real breakfast before I left DC and gave me crackers and a candy bar to carry in case my sugar level tanked."

"So do we need to stop now? I sure don't need you comatose halfway home," asked Sarge with a smile.

"No need to stop yet. I really am fine."

By this time, they had left the airport area and were turning onto Highway 115. Raoul had never been out to this part of the country and was staring at terrain, in awe of the beauty. Then he felt them accelerate and looked over at the speedometer, which was at ninety miles per hour.

"Sarge? Is there a speed limit here?"

"Huh? Oh yeah, there is, but if I go it, I get run over. Look around, we aren't passing everyone. Some are blowing us off, and my radar detector is on and functioning," he replied with a grin.

"Okay then, I think I will just close my eyes, if you don't mind?" said Raoul, figuring Sarge would never know he had a three-hour nap already.

"Wake you up when we get close."

There really was no need for Sarge to wake Raoul. It seemed like no time at all when Raoul felt a change in the road and realized they were now on a dirt road and going a normal speed.

"Wow," said Raoul, realizing they had entered the foothills and he could see down into a valley that looked picture-perfect, with a farmhouse, gorgeous green fields, a barn, and miscellaneous out-buildings. "This is incredible!"

"I love this place. Alfalfa is in and doing well, couple of cows for milk and hens for eggs. All good. Let's go get you settled. Your room is ready, private bath and all. No mini bar, however, so drinks in fridge in kitchen always cold."

They walked into the house, and Raoul let out a whistle. Sarge gave the grand tour and ended up with Raoul's room, telling him to take his time, settle in, then head into the kitchen for a salad and sandwich late lunch / early dinner.

Raoul checked out his room and bath, shocked at the plush-ness of everything. The queen-size bed had three thick pillows and a beautiful comforter and looked like something you could live in. The bath had towels and washcloths that looked like they had never been used, along with new razors, a toothbrush, soaps, and shampoos lined up. He quickly unpacked his stuff, showered, shaved, changed into clean clothes and headed down to the kitchen.

"Sarge, I noticed clothes in the closet and dresser. Am I getting a roommate?"

"Wish I had thought of that, Raoul. Would have confused ya, huh? But no, no one else. Hopefully I got the size right, 'cause I knew you would be traveling light, and at Casa Lewis, we do our own laundry, right down to bed linens, and I didn't want you to have to do that every two days! Make sure the sizes are right before you pull tags, though, 'cause if need be, we can head into town to do an exchange. Same with food, fridge is always stocked, so if what I feed you isn't enough, help yourself. I did buy light beer. I know with the diabetes, you have to be careful, but from experience, I also know you do imbibe now and again."

Raoul, trying not to let Sarge hear the emotion in his voice, said, "Sarge, this is way too much. One of these days, when and if I get what the VA owes me, I will pay you back something. And what-ever you need help with here, I'm your man."

"You may regret those words. Ever pull fence?"

"No, but got a hunch I am going to, right?"

"Oh yeah, did you notice those heavy leather gloves? Hopefully one pair will do the job."

They enjoyed the meal and took a walk around the farm, and Sarge explained what the fence needed. Apparently some of the posts had rotted, and they needed to reset those and restring the barbed wire; hence, fence pulling was born. Sarge figured two to three days to fix that, and along with helping with the animals, that negated any debt Raoul owed. Raoul thought about protesting, remembering past trips he had taken thanks to Sarge, but figured a better time might come along to discuss this.

They headed back to the house, sat on the porch awhile, and Raoul looked at Sarge around 8:00 p.m. "Sarge, I know its early, but I am still on East Coast time. Gotta hit the rack. I know we cleaned the kitchen earlier, but is there anything else before I go cut some zzzs?"

"Nope, I always do one last walk around to tuck the animals in, and you are not that far off on bedtime anyway. Sleep well."

When Raoul heard a knock on his door, he opened an eye, looked at the alarm clock next to the bed, then heard, "Up and at 'em, soldier. Busy day ahead!"

A smile broadened Raoul's face, remembering past times those words came from that mouth while in the Army. Even if all the days weren't good, the friendship that bonded them endured, and Raoul felt very lucky to be here. With a "Be right down," he threw on some clean clothes and headed for the kitchen. When he got there, Sarge had a breakfast in front of him that would put Denny's to shame. Sarge informed Raoul that he wasn't sure if Raoul was a big breakfast eater or not, but to check the fridge and fix what he liked.

"I think today, coffee and maybe toast. I see apples on the table, and they look really good too. Thanks."

"Good. Once we finish, we can go feed the animals. They like having feed by eight a.m. Then I was thinking a little sightseeing is in order."

After the kitchen was cleaned and both their rooms straightened up, they headed outside. As Sarge filled up water containers for the stock, he asked Raoul to go into the chicken coop and, using the basket hanging inside the door, gather today's eggs, which get cleaned up inside and placed in the fridge, and the basket must be back in the coop. Raoul missed seeing the rabbit hutch when they walked around last night but was introduced to them when he went out to feed them. Then hay and grain for the two angus, milk the Holstein, and done.

While they were doing this, Sarge explained, "A couple of families in town split the initial outlay expense for the animals and their feed, and we split the meats, eggs, milk. My brother, who you will meet, comes out every few days to get some of the eggs and milk 'cause I sure can't use it all. Then, of course, when we butcher, that also gets divided. Then there is pheasant trout and deer to catch. Oh yeah, and one guy on the edge of town has enough room to have the pork on the hoof there. Everything as natural as possible. Now for some sightseeing!"

They walked into the barn, and Raoul noticed a big tarp covering something in the back. Sarge walked over to it and, with a flourish, pulled it off, revealing a red WW2 Jeep with a black star on its hood.

All Raoul could say was, "Nice, very nice."

As they left the barnyard, Sarge traveling at his usual fast clip, Raoul advised him he would never be allowed to drive in a parade. Sarge, with a baffled look, wanted to know why not.

"Sarge, could you ever drive slow enough to follow other cars? And if they let you lead, it would be over before it even started!"

They both laughed, and Sarge responded with one good punch of the gas pedal. All of a sudden, they were off the road crossing a low plain area, heading for the mountains straight ahead. At the base of the mountain, the Jeep was put in four-wheel drive, and away they went. Sarge appeared truly in his element, weaving in and out of the trees, bushes, and logs in his path, seeming to know where they all were. When they finally slowed down, they were in a flat area that had a small waterfall and stream running through it that originated up the mountain they were facing. At the mountain crest, Raoul could see snow and, with a small gasp, exclaimed, "Breathtaking! Looks like something out of a fairy tale!"

When Raoul turned, Sarge was taking two fold-up chairs from the back of the Jeep, placing them carefully in the line of sight of the waterfall and mountain and majestically waving Raoul into one of the chairs. He then pulled out a cooler with beer and water, apples, and premade sandwiches in it, sitting that in the middle of the chairs to act as a table as well.

"This is my getaway spot, sometimes for a day, sometimes up to a week. Gives me space to clear my head and be nowhere."

"I get it, really, I do. But who keeps the farm going when you run away?" asked Raoul.

"Remember I mentioned my brother in town? He and his wife own a fourplex in Cañon City. He retired from being a guard at the prison—Cañons claim to fame, you should know—and they look for excuses to come out to the farm. Sometimes even when I am home. But it is so nice to have someone trustworthy to watch things when I am not there. We were always close, but bonded even more after the folks died."

"Can't wait to meet them," responded Raoul. "Now, about the VA. I noticed you haven't said a word yet. Does that mean you are having second thoughts about being involved at all? Because, especially after seeing this all, I would understand. From a selfish standpoint, I would be upset, because we work together well, past history has taught us that, but I would respect that choice and still help you fix that fence."

"Raoul, don't worry, I'm in. However, we are not gonna discuss this at all until we go to Idaho in a couple of weeks. Here we work our butts off to get everything done. You get yourself a normal life for a while, take a break... then in Idaho, we all talk!"

"You're right, Sarge. I'll try."

"I know we brought the sandwiches, but they will keep in the cooler 'til later or tomorrow, because I want to take you into town for a local treat at a local bar. Are you getting hungry?"

"Sarge, if you remember me correctly, I am always hungry. You all accused me of having a tapeworm back then, and I still can eat

24-7 if available. Have to be a bit more careful, but hey, sugar isn't the only food in the world. Gonna tell me what the local treat is now?"

As they loaded the chairs and cooler back into the Jeep, Sarge grinned and advised Raoul he would just have to wait to see what was for lunch. Then they headed down the mountain, and Raoul was eternally grateful lunch had not already been served. A couple of times he knew if he had a full stomach, it would now be empty.

When they were in town and Sarge had to slow down, he looked at Raoul and asked, "Do you like oysters? We have one good bar here that serves 'em Rocky Mountain style."

"Oysters in Colorado? Must be really expensive to ship 'em in."

He didn't catch the grin on Sarge's face, but Sarge said, "Here we are. Bring your appetite and let's go!"

As they walked in and took a table, the waitress met them as they seated themselves. "Bill, it's been a while. You doing okay? And what would you like?"

"Sarah, I am good, thanks. Meet Raoul, an old service buddy. He came out to check out God's country. A pitcher of light, please, two glasses, and two orders of Rocky Mountain oysters with onion rings."

Before they could say anything to each other, Sarah was back with the beer.

Raoul was flabbergasted, both with the quick service and the familiarity Bill was greeted with.

"Come here often?" he asked.

"Raoul, you did notice how small this town is, right? I can't go out on my front porch and fart without everyone knowing about it. I am actually surprised Sarah didn't mention you as my guest and ask for an intro before I gave one."

At that moment, two heaping plates appeared in front of the two of them. Raoul looked at the amount of food in awe then told Sarge he would probably need some tartar sauce.

Sarge responded, "You don't put tartar sauce on these oysters, Raoul. Try it, and then if you think they need anything, the local choice is ketchup."

After the first bite, Raoul had a somewhat puzzled look and stated, "They don't taste anything like any oysters I have had in the past, but, man, they are good."

And on that note, both men cleaned their plates, finished the pitcher of beer, and when Sarah came over to give the bill to them, Sarge asked her to please tell Raoul what he had eaten.

With a straight face (she had done this before), she said as solemnly as possible, "Sir, you just ate a plateful of bulls' nuts, and there for a moment, I seriously think you considered ordering a refill."

Raoul replied, "Really?"

Sarah said, "Really and truly."

Raoul said, "I was contemplating more, but... next time?"

They all laughed as Raoul and Sarge left, with promises of another plate of oysters in their future.

Back at the farm, they cleaned the Jeep up, placed it back under its tarp, checked all the livestock, then settled on the porch for coffee and discussion about the great day. Raoul really enjoyed Sarge's version of sightseeing, but should they not spend the next two days fixing that fence?

Which was exactly what they did. There were only about four spots that needed fixing, and Raoul learned a whole new trade, using muscles he hadn't used in years, but realizing he needed to get in better shape for the mission. It was a resolution he made silently, because they were not discussing plans at this point.

After the fence was done, two very long, hard days behind them, Sarge advised Raoul they were going to his brother's for the afternoon. They both cleaned up, put on clean clothes, and headed into town. Raoul was introduced to John and Carol, and they spent the afternoon becoming acquainted. Carol had prepared a great dinner, salad, lasagna, and fresh fruit for dessert. Raoul felt right at home with them and received a warm kiss on the cheek from Carol and a hug from John when leaving.

As they were getting ready to leave, Sarge advised them that he and Raoul were planning a fishing expedition in Idaho with Tony. Neither one of them appeared surprised by this. They had also met Tony Rice when he had come into town to see Sarge. Carol asked him to check the pantry so she could restock what might be necessary, and they parted for the evening. Sarge said he would call with what details he knew and e-mail the pantry info and, of course, would contact them while in Idaho to tell return date.

They returned to the farm and settled on the porch, as they had done every evening. Raoul, looking around very content, asked Sarge if he ever tired of this place. "I doubt very much if I could ever tire of this all. The peace, the beauty."

"Not tired if it, no, but need breaks to keep it all in perspective and be sure my mind stays clear and right. If you get too complacent, you stagnate then forget what you have or are working for. Plus, sometimes being alone gives you too much time to think, and there are things I would rather not dwell on, so I go, hang with family, or fish with buddies, or just go where it is different, then return to my spot."

"Yeah, I can relate. I did notice something that I am curious about, Sarge. I noticed you and John both have your flags upside down. What's that all about?"

"Actually, my brother did it first. He was four years Navy, Signalman. Hoisted flags for a living on ships for that time and had to know what flag meant what. It seems flying the flag upside down told others the ship was in distress. We do it now because we feel the US is in distress and really needs help. We really need politicians in office that want to make things right and turn our country back into what it should be, a superpower, with respect from others," replied Sarge.

"Have to agree, Sarge. America needs repair bad. And even though we are not supposed to discuss anything yet, I can't help but wonder if what we are planning will help wake up people to that fact."

"You know, Raoul, it may help," Sarge said after a moment's careful thought.

The next few days, they checked all the fences and the food for livestock and pantry as Carol had requested, e-mailed her details and firmed up the departure date, caught up all the laundry, and started prepping for Idaho.

Day before departure, camper top was on truck, and everything that could be packed in advance was loaded. In the morning, all that was left was to fill the cooler, have breakfast, call John to remind him the farm was his for a while, and go.

Raoul actually beat Sarge up that morning, had fed the animals, brought in the eggs, and was finishing preparing breakfast when Sarge entered the kitchen.

He informed Sarge of what was already done. They sat and ate breakfast, cleaned their dishes, and filled the thermos for the ride.

"So, Raoul, guessing you are a bit excited to see Idaho, huh? You have not been up before me at all yet, and today... not only up, but some chores done, and breakfast? I did notice you used the last of the sausage we had in the fridge, and your eggs were perfect, so thanks."

"Sarge, if I could think of more to do for you besides saying thanks, believe me, I would. Words are nowhere near enough to tell you how appreciated you are for all you do, not just for me, but I know you help everyone you can."

"Okay, enough. I do what I can only 'cause I want too, and you are worthy of this all. Now, let's hit the road. There are a few surprises still waiting for you," Sarge stated as they loaded the last things in and locked the door, and Sarge quickly called John to tell him what was left to be done.

"Carol is loading the car now. Once she is done, we go. Thanks again, bro. I look forward to your travels as much as you do," said John with a chuckle.

IDAHO BOUND

As THEY HOISTED THEMSELVES INTO the truck, Sarge broke out into a very bad rendition of "On the road again, just can't wait to get on the road again!" At that point, Raoul broke into a howl and asked him what he had done with the money momma had given him for singing lessons. "Or was she aware that was a lost cause and gave ya no money at all? Please promise me that was first and last time I get that pleasure! Please, please!"

"My feelings are hurt, Raoul," stated Sarge, trying his best to look sad faced. "I was part of a band in high school. Well, actually, I had a truck, so I was the driver. You know, they wouldn't let me sing either." At which point they both laughed outright.

Then it was pedal-to-the-metal time, and of course, Sarge did just that. Luckily Raoul was now used to his style of driving and felt somewhat more comfortable. He still caught himself occasionally trying to brake when going around a curve of down an incline but overall felt okay. Stopping in a few towns for gas, pee breaks, and leg stretches, Raoul was seeing more beautiful country than he knew still existed. Sarge had an incredible digital camera and, as they were leaving the farm, had handed it to Raoul, letting him know all pics he took would either be saved on a jump drive or CD. "Have fun. The card in their is thirty-two gig. Should cover a world tour, not just our little road trip."

Because they had stopped for the necessities, hit one bad stretch of traffic (for what reason, they never figured out), and stopped for some photo ops, it had taken them about eight hours to make the four-and-a-half to five-hour drive. Pulling into a campground area around 3:00 p.m. that afternoon, they were waved in at the gate, at which point Raoul advised Sarge he was really impressed he was that well-known.

"I guess I've been coming here long enough now that they all know me. It used to be that only some of the guards recognized me, so it is kinda nice to just zip in and out. Makes the travel that much nicer."

They stopped at the main office to check in, were told what campsite to go to and offered coffee, picked up some bait, and headed over to set up. The decision was made to eat what was in the cooler for dinner that night and fish in the morning for that day's food. They had been put on a site not only near the water but also near the fish cleaning station the park offered. It was decided that it was too nice out to sleep in the camper, so sleeping bags came out, and the campfire was banked early.

"Hey, Sarge? Are we safe out here from bears and stuff?"

Sarge could hear a bit of fear in Raoul's voice and couldn't resist. "Shit, knew I forgot something. The darn rifle and the bear repellant. But I think we're okay. No one's been eaten here since about '97."

Raoul heard the snicker and said, "Bear repellant, huh? I was born during the night, but it wasn't last night! And kinda hard to miss your rifle, so guess I will trust you to protect me."

Early the next morning, they had gotten up had a quick cup of coffee, and before the sun was over the horizon, they were at the fishing spot Sarge said was primo. Enough fish were caught for lunch, and once those were cleaned and stored in the cooler, Raoul fired up the camp stove and made bacon and eggs for breakfast.

At that point, they headed for the office. Once arriving there, the key that was hanging right by the desk was removed by Sarge, and he informed Mike behind the desk, "Have this back to ya in an hour or so."

"Thanks, Bill. See you then," Mike replied.

As they got into the golf cart with the trailer attached, which was in the back of the office, Raoul looked at Sarge with a raised eyebrow. "Are we special here, or do you pay extra for privileges?"

Pulling in next to his camper, Sarge said, "Grab our garbage, throw it in the back, and I will explain. I have been coming here for years now, and when I first began, money was tighter than it is now. Here and at a few other campgrounds, I spoke to the owners and/or managers and worked out deals. It's all become habitual now, and sometimes I stay longer than planned if something needs attention, but at the very least, I help with something. And they give reduced and/or free stays. So today, the trash needed gathering, and this time that is our job. And also give an update to the office if anything looks out of place or does need extra attention."

"So you bartered for camp space! Good idea."

"And occasionally, someone from one of the grounds is passing through town and stays at my place. It all eventually balances out."

Continuing around the grounds, Raoul learned where everything was. There were a few cabins for rental as well, two homes that were permanent, and a couple of bathhouses, as well as Porta Pottys scattered. In one spot was a waste dump spot for people to clean out their trailers, and Sarge did make a note to tell Mike that area needed some extra attention.

As they swung back to the office, Sarge told Raoul, "If you head to the bathhouse or to hit a Porta Potty after dark, bring a wooden spoon and metal bowl just in case you run into a bear."

Raoul's responded, "And if that doesn't work?"

"Well, then, guess it was nice knowing ya!"

By this time, it was almost lunch, and the fish was fried, along with home fries with onion and garlic. Raoul informed Sarge that if they kept eating like this, sweatpants would be in his future.

They both were ready to bed down early, asleep by eight thirty in front of the safely banked fire pit.

Falling asleep that early made for two very early risers. At 4:30 a.m., coffee was brewing while Raoul rolled up the bedding and started loading and straightening the camper. Filling both mugs with coffee, being sure the fire was completely out and sand was scattered, they were ready to hit the road.

Sarge spoke first after they got out on the open road. "Next stop, Southern Cross, Montana. I have a friend from Cañon City who lives out near there in Anaconda, but love the fishing there, the friendship, and the fact the man is a gourmet cook helps too, not to mention the cool ghost town Southern Cross is. I always stay there at least a week and always, always enjoy. Les has more stories to share than any human I know. And at his age, he does repeat 'em sometimes, but it doesn't matter. And yes, I know you are concerned about the time frames and the mission, but, Raoul, I think you will realize this time and break will give better perspective as things do fall in place, and you deserve a great vacation before the real work begins."

Raoul thought for a moment, nodded, and stated, "I think you are right, Sarge. Even though thoughts come into my head at times, this is giving me time to weed through what is probably all the bad ideas, and maybe then only the good stuff will be left. Hope so, anyway. Let's enjoy, and thanks again."

They headed on down the road, again with Raoul making them stop occasionally for pictures, the obligatory pee stops, and once at a burger joint, where the order was a to-go so they could continue on. Raoul had offered to drive a few times and finally gave up offering, realizing that Sarge could only travel if going ninety miles per hour or better. The thing that amazed Raoul, though, was the fact that he never got stopped or had tickets out his wazoo already piled up.

Late that afternoon, they drove into a long, beautiful curving drive, being met by two gorgeous dogs barking maniacally, but tails moving so fast they seemed invisible. The black Lab stood at the passenger door, while the wolf-looking creature stood at attention by Sarge's door.

"And I was worried about bears! These two look like they want to eat through the door for a bite of us. Is that an actual wolf. Sarge? Is the rifle loaded?"

Sarge roared with laughter. "Raoul, meet Black Dog and Wolfie. Once they know you are okay by Les and that I am here, they will be your best buddies. And FYI, Wolfie is only one-half wolf. His mom was a malamute."

About this time, a slender elderly gentleman came off the porch, whistling to the dogs to stand down, and Sarge opened his door and managed to get both feet firmly planted before the two dogs realized it was a friend. They proceeded to dance around him, both doggie talking, and he gave ear rubs and back scratches then solemnly shook hands with both of them. Raoul slowly got out of the truck, was formerly introduced to Les and the two dogs, and received an apparent seal of approval from them all, when he wasn't eaten for a snack.

"Bill, got the back cleared for the camper. If you don't want to completely take it off the truck, the Jeep is yours while you are here. *Mi casa* is *su casa*. And I planned dinner for us. How does spaghetti and salad sound?"

"Raoul," said Sarge, "you are in for a treat. This guy makes it all from scratch, from the bread to the pasta. Did you bring those stretch pants?"

Dinner was great. Raoul had never eaten so well in his life. After, they went out to the deck and sat around telling history and learning one another's past. Wolfie and Black Dog settled nearby, and before they headed into bed, Les advised them the campsite was all theirs. They could take the truck or just load their supplies in the Jeep as the manager knew they would be coming.

Les closed the evening with, "Great to see you, Bill, and meet you, Raoul. This is someplace you should feel welcome always now that you have been here once. Please be aware, my campground is not the deluxe KOA type. Hopefully Bill had given you the rundown."

Raoul stated, "Les, you do not know what this whole trip has done for me. I would be happy if I had to sleep under your porch!"

GERALD AND KATHY VISIT DC

MEANWHILE, BACK IN DC, MIKE Jackson, with his wife, Jean, was getting the house ready for Gerald and Kathy Washington's visit. Jean was the type who loved meeting new people and made friends very easily, so when Mike had told her about the potential visit, she got Kathy's number and had assured her it was okay. Today was finish-up day for them. Mike got stuck vacuuming while Jean finished putting clean sheets on the bed and clean towels in the bath and just being sure all was as she wanted it to be.

Just as they finished, the doorbell rang. They looked at each other, and you could see them thinking that it was way too early for the couple—maybe it was the mailman? Mike did speculate out loud as Jean opened the door.

"We're here," said Gerald, trying to play it sinister.

Everyone laughed, greetings and introductions made their rounds, and Gerald and Mike went out to the car to get the bags.

"Man, I appreciate your hospitality, Mike. Not only can we guys get some time together, I think the wives are going to get along great, and this trip is doing us good too. I apologize for being so early. We actually left yesterday and spent the night in Richmond."

"Hey, glad we could get together like this. Cleared my calendar for the entire week, and Jean needed to burn some vacation time, so this is great for us too."

By the time they got back in, the wives had coffee and the light lunch out for the guys. They ate while all got better acquainted, and the ladies took the dishes into the kitchen once done and advised the guys the house was theirs. They would retire to the patio.

Gerald and Mike were happy for the opportunity to speak of things the wives need not know about.

"Mike, do we know where we are going from here?"

"First," said Mike, "I know you only drove the last two hours today from Richmond, but… you guys can settle in today. We want to show you DC and enjoy some of the city ourselves. It is nice now and again to vacation in your own town and relearn some of the things you may have forgotten exist. But aside from that, the more knowledgeable we all are about the city, the better things will go later."

"Makes sense. I am not familiar with DC at all, so the logic to learn as much as possible is definitely a good idea. What about the other guys? Will I meet any of them this trip?"

"Yup, the locals anyway that are here now. Sometime along the way, we will do a boys' night out, or afternoon, whichever seems to work best. Should we see if the girls would like a walk around the neighborhood to stretch their legs?"

The girls were all for the walk. It was nice to get out and see some of the area they were in. Everyone chatted back and forth, building new friendships on the ladies' behalves while the guys renewed theirs.

When they got back to the house, Jean and Kathy went into the kitchen to finish up dinner. Kathy was in awe over what Jean pulled out of the oven, stating, "Oh boy, this could mean you never get Gerald to leave."

Jean replied, "So he likes apple pie and/or chocolate cake? And what do you think of them? Hoping you like roast with all the trimmings too, that Crock-Pot over there just beeped to signal it is done."

After dinner, with everyone complimenting Jean (Gerald proving his love of both desserts by eating a piece of both), Kathy offered to help clean up, and Jean insisted they go settle into their room as she could handle it. They headed into the room to do so. Mike went into the den with beer in hand, and Jean spent the next hour or so in the kitchen.

When she finished, she headed into the den and, in a bit of a huff, said to Mike, "Little help cleaning up woulda been nice."

He informed her that she could have asked for help and headed to bed.

Jean decided to make sure the coffee pot was ready for morning and then followed Mike into bed.

When they all awoke the next morning and were having coffee, and had leftover pie and cake for the guys' breakfast, Gerald informed the ladies that it was a balanced meal, eggs, sugar, fruit, with the "C'mon, Mom" look and smile. They gave up, shaking their heads and chuckling at the way men behaved. Jean and Gerald informed the Jacksons that today they would like to take them out for lunch; however, the Jacksons would have to pick the place for obvious reasons.

Jean stated, "We want you to know how much we really appreciate this. And, Kathy, thank you especially. I really feel I have found a new good friend."

Kathy blushed and responded with, "I feel the bond too, Jean. And, guys, not one word. Be grateful we get along!" The grin came back on her face, and she added, "There is this great little place about ten minutes from here that serves wonderful food. Mike, you agree we do Maria's for lunch?"

"Great idea, hon. And isn't that little touristy place near there that has the maps and stuff for DC and the surrounding area? Maybe we can head over there early and pick up some stuff to help plot our sightseeing trips out. Want me to help you clean up this stuff?" he said, feeling a bit guilty about last night.

Jean had already started gathering cups and plates and assured Mike they could handle it, so the guys went off and decided it would be a good idea to go make the beds and straighten up the rooms. "Brownie points always pay off, my man!" said Gerald with a wink.

Once all the chores were done, they headed out. The strip mall that housed the restaurant had a bodega that carried all styles of Mexican products, and the girls had to check out the line of food available. They were contemplating doing a Mexican dish one night to perhaps try something new. It was fun to watch them. Even the locals were enjoying watching the gringas check out real Mexican foodstuffs. As this was just an opportunity to waste some time, the guys finally pulled them out after about forty-five minutes, and they headed over to the shop to get maps and info on tourist things. Then lunch, which they all agreed was fantastic. Back to the house for an afternoon of pouring over maps and brochures and even heading for the Internet to determine the finer points of seeing all they could.

As we all know, you can't just go tour the Capitol, and they weren't sure of dates far enough out, so they contented themselves the next day with just walking the entire parameter of the White House, realizing the expanse of the property and looking to see if maybe they could glimpse someone while walking. Jean took pictures. Lots of pictures! Even Kathy and Mike had not realized how much walking it took to circle the entire building and grounds, but once they had made the entire circle, they knew the rest would wait for another day and headed back for the house. Even though it was only a five-mile drive to Cherrydale, the Alexandria suburb they lived in, it could take a half hour or more to get there, and the parking area they had parked in was about another ten minutes from where they started the White House circle. As they headed over to the car, Jean yelled out to a guy she passed, "John Denver! Oh my god, I am one of your biggest fans!" Kathy was ready to speak, and Gerald placed his hand on her arm while he offered to get a picture of them together. "If Mr. Denver is okay with that?" He was, and Jean was on cloud nine the rest of the day. They headed home and finished the pot roast for dinner that night, all going to bed fairly early so they could head back into town the next day.

The next morning, they woke up to rain. It seemed if they were to see anything that day, it would require more energy than they wanted to expand. Between deciding if public transport or the car and parking issues were worth the effort, it eventually came to pass that they would relax, maybe play pinochle, and nap... oh yeah, nap. They decided they were at the age a nap was a treat, not a punishment. Sandwiches for lunch, pizza delivery for dinner, ending the evening with a recheck of tomorrow's plans, and all was quiet in the house by 10:30 p.m.

Smithsonian, in all its glory, was on tap for the next day. Jean and Gerald had not realized how many museums there actually were as part of the Smithsonian and decided to hit the ground running to see at least the American History, National History, and if time allowed, the Castle. They had discussed prior to this using either the Metro system and not worrying about parking at all or driving in as Parking Panda always seemed to have something in the area needed. Kathy also stated that if Parking Panda had nothing, they could always park at the Ritz she worked at, which was not too far from the museum. Leaving the house by seven thirty, they got to the area where the museums were by eight fifteen, and as usual, Panda had a spot near there with space available. Gerald asked what people did who worked in the city about parking, 'cause fifteen to twenty a day could sure rack up at the end of a month, and he was informed that those that weren't fortunate enough to have dedicated parking either built the cost into the pay they requested or more often than not used the public system.

Somehow they managed to see all three of their desired locations of the Smithsonian, grabbing lunch at the Stars & Stripes Cafe at the National Museum locale, and then going to the Castle, which surprised everyone. No one realized the magnitude of the information and artifacts the Smithsonian had custody of nor the architectural history it encompassed. They did not leave the museums 'til almost five thirty, in awe that it was an eight-hour day to visit them and still not have seen all. The Washingtons vowed to come back to see what they might have missed.

Another day hanging out at home was in store for the next day. They decided to hang out, catch up on laundry, have at least a home-cooked dinner, and again maybe that nap, or cards?

Everyone slept in. Jean and Kathy coordinated a huge breakfast, and Kathy impressed Jean by making the best sausage gravy for the biscuits. Jean told Kathy she needed to learn that North Carolina was considered the South, and it would look bad if a Yankee came down to visit and showed her up. "You guys will come down to our place for us to return the favor, right? We can send the guys fishing, and there are quite a few discount malls nearby."

"Sounds great. Probably a bit cooler there when the temps here go to ninety-five-plus humidity. Let's see what we can plan. Now, we need a shopping day here too. You guys have to head back Wednesday, right? I know we have to go back into the city and see the monuments and Arlington area. How about girls' day Monday?"

"Now that sounds like fun. I cannot believe how much there actually is to see here. I am still so glad we got to go to the Castle. That really summarized all the Smithsonians stand for. I never realized just how extensive their collections and influence were!" stated Jean. "Hey, guys! Do you want a break from us gals Monday?"

The guys were hanging in the den and winked at each other before Gerald came around the corner with the hangdog look on his face. "What? You two wanna desert us? Well, guess we can survive a day without you."

He walked back into the den. They high-fived each other, and Mike asked, "Got a clear credit card for her? 'Cause if they are going shopping, watch out, world! Good news is, we can get the guys together to meet and greet at the VFW. They do great wings and, of course beer. We will need beer!"

Mike followed up by going out to see the girls and letting them know what they would do while the ladies were shopping. Kathy had informed Jean there were two other ladies they could meet for lunch that she would enjoy.

Back in the den, Mike called Durham and explained what he had in mind, and Durham was all for it. "Great idea. We need to meet and know each other, sooner the better."

"So wings and beer at VFW Monday? No work conflict for you?"

"Nope, you said around two, right?"

Then he called Ben and spoke with him. He seriously contemplated telling Ben one o'clock instead of two, thinking maybe he would arrive on time, but because Ben would be bringing or advising others of the meet, he kept it to the 2:00 p.m. time. Ben was good with the time and date, advising Mike he and Tyrell could be there, and they would let one of the coaches have the keys in case they ran late. He explained there were two or three employees he could trust absolutely and completely.

"Would you mind going by the shelter and letting Hawk know, and he can pass it on to Tom and Ron?" Ben asked Mike. "I would, but have some things to take care of here the next couple of days, and I know you are spending time in town."

"Not a problem. We are going in tomorrow to do monuments, and Jean knows I know some guys at the shelter, so if I just pop in, nothing will be thought odd."

"See you then," said Ben, and Mike and Gerald headed into the kitchen to check on the wives. The day had turned gorgeous, and the girls were getting antsy, so the dishes and laundry were done. Two sets of hands did make quick work of it all.

"Mike, I know we said Monday was girls' day, but that is gonna be city shopping. Unless you two want to do something else, I was thinking about going over to Crystal City and look around there."

"Know what, you two can do that. I think we guys need a Home Depot trip. Maybe Gerald can help me pick out an edger. Seeing as how we had a big and delicious breakfast, how about we guys grab some snacks for later and meet back here when we are done."

The ladies wholeheartedly agreed to that plan, Kathy advising Jean there were plenty of places they could grab a bite if need be, and they went their separate ways.

As the guys got into Gerald's car, Mike looked at Gerald with a grin and stated, "Two of the best things God allowed creation of are credit cards and shopping malls! Let's go enjoy Home Depot and then run over to the shelter today to let the guys know what's up."

They walked through the store, discussing what they already owned and what they would like to own later, looked at the edgers, got names and model numbers to compare, and headed into the city. Hawk was not at the shelter, and Mike informed Gerald that he hung out often at a nearby park, so they headed over there.

As they walked over (of course they had to park elsewhere—Panda to the rescue again), they noticed an ambulance and EMTs were in the park standing over someone lying on the ground.

"Jeez, hope that's not Hawk," exclaimed Mike as he rushed to get closer. He sighed with relief as he got to where he could see, and the guy was gray headed and probably seventy years old. "Whew, but sure hope he will be okay."

He continued to look around for Hawk, finally spotting him standing over near some trees, and waved to him as they started over that way. Mike introduced Gerald to Hawk, explained why they had stopped by, then asked if Hawk had not eaten at the shelter today, following up with, "We were just gonna grab a bite. Would you like to join us?"

Hawk responded, "Some days there are just too many people in there, and an occasional skipped meal can't hurt ya any. But yeah, without the crows, lunch sounds good, and we can get better acquainted."

They headed over to an English-style pub nearby and settled in with lunch. "Best Fish and Chips on this side of the pond," touted the banner over the bar.

Gerald opened the conversation with, "Mike told me you were SEAL, Vietnam. I was Green Beret there."

"Sounds like we were the same bird flying with different flocks there. I like you already!" Hawk replied.

After a moment's thoughtful silence, Gerald said, "I agree."

Mike then asked if Hawk could also get Tom and Ron together for Monday's meet.

"You said two p.m. at the VFW, right? Sure can get those two. For beer and wings, we would all travel to Maryland," Hawk responded with a laugh.

The three of them spent the next hour and a half talking about their history, their lives, and the VA, the VA conversation sparking a lot of animosity. Mike finally summed it all up by saying, "Guys, I really wish we were the only ones with issues with the whole situation. Sadly though, there are thousands fighting this battle as well. My hope is, what we are trying to do helps everyone out there who is on their last dime, their last prayer," and as his voice faded away, the other two hung their heads and actually stated in unison, "Amen." With sheepish looks all around, they decided it was time to call it a day, Hawk determining an afternoon park nap in order, and the other two having to decide what they could do for this evening's snacks, 'cause they knew that for them, it would have to be dinner as well.

"We can hit Safeway on the way home and pick up a sandwich platter, cheese platter, and fruit platter. Got beer and wine already, so that should please everyone, right?" said Mike.

"Sounds good. Let's go," Gerald replied.

They beat the wives home, put away the food, and settled on the patio to discuss the day. It was decided unanimously that the team they were putting together seemed to fit well so far, and hopefully things would continue to fall into place.

Pinochle cards came out again. The girls trounced the guys well and had one double run and another hand with double kings, with final score being 624–442. "We are the champions," they sang in unison and sat back to discuss their plans more fully for the weekend and upcoming Monday. They pretty much knew the weekend plans—back into DC to see the monuments and Arlington on Saturday, with Sunday being reserved for a ride through the countryside surrounding the area. And when the guys mentioned that they had gone to the pub, Kathy said, "Aha, I know where we are gonna go Monday to eat after shopping!"

Saturday, they headed out early, walked DC yet again to see the monuments they could, and then took a walk through Arlington National. Jean looked at Mike and Gerald, noticing they seemed a bit sad as they entered the cemetery, and asked in a very quiet tone, "You guys know some Vets that are here, don't you?"

"Yes, and more that aren't," responded Gerald. "'Gotta admit, not my first choice of sightseeing places, but it is humbling to see, and realize, how many lives are lost during wars."

They all agreed, headed over to see JFK's site, and left the cemetery, all somewhat quiet, thinking their own thoughts. This was their last stop before home, and it was a very reserved evening for all.

Sunday was the day for a country drive. Kathy and Mike had determined that Fredericktown, Maryland, would be a good day's drive, go through a couple of covered bridges, maybe stop at a flea market or yard sale, have a meal on the water there, and return. Which they did, and a good time was had by all. That evening, everyone collapsed for the night. Everyone had relaxed that day to the point of total meltdown. Jean made the comment, "I didn't think it was possible, but this pair of sneakers I just bought before we came are done. I can feel the lining corroding now! Thank God I have a good pair of sandals for tomorrow." And on that note, those sneaks disappeared into the trash bin.

The next morning, everyone was still calm and relaxed, and knowing that it was girls' and guys' day, they eased into Monday. One of the stops they had made in Maryland coming home was at this little donut shop that did more than just donuts, and they had picked up some stuff for today. The men literally attacked the donuts, while the women truly enjoyed the croissants. By about 10:00 a.m., Jean and Kathy were ready to head out. They blew the guys a kiss, and with the comment, "See ya when we see ya," they left.

Mike looked at Gerald and with a wink said, "Should we go get a topper for the car?"

Gerald replied, "Nah, betcha she only replaces those sneaks. She is more a window shopper unless it is time for replacement clothes. Then it's time to watch out. No lie, one year I ended up with twenty-four pairs of skivvies and forty pair of socks. Yes, it was time to replace them, 'but they were on sale,' she cried."

"You lucky dog. Mine doesn't quit!" Mike said with a big sigh.

VFW, DC

THEY PROCEEDED TO MAKE SURE their cups were rinsed and coffee pot off before heading into DC. They did leave a bit early because the post they were meeting at did have a small banquet room that was a first-come, first-served space to hold. When they arrived at twelve thirty, they were informed it was all theirs, and being a Monday, they probably shouldn't be too concerned with someone wanting to step in. They did inform the manager they would leave by seven and called this an informal reunion. About one thirty, Mike placed an order for wings, figuring one hundred would get 'em started, and if anyone wanted something else, they could order it. Gerald got two pitchers of beer for now, but as the guys rolled in, they'll add accordingly.

When Tom, Ron, and Hawk arrived at about ten to two, Mike said, "Hmmm, you guys are on time, but my question is, how late will Ben be?" At that point, they all laughed, except poor Gerald, to whom they had to explain Ben's one-half-beer-behind issue. So when Ben and Tyrell walked in at 2:02 p.m., they all stood and gave a standing ovation.

"Aw, shucks, guys, didn't know you cared that much!" Ben responded.

They all had a good laugh, and everyone was introduced and provided some background on themselves. More food and beer were ordered, and the first hour or so was friendly and calm with no mention of the VA.

At one point, Ben got up to head for the men's room, and Hawk followed. Ben took advantage of the time away to ask about Tom's and Ron's intentions because he had had the impression that they were not interested in coming on board.

"Trust me, Ben, they are in it with us. Some things happened personally that turned them around. They want to see changes too and think this is probably the only way that will happen."

As they sat back down, the realization that the conversation had turned serious was obvious.

Ron waited for them to sit down then, with a deep breath, asked, "So are we it for the team, are there more that aren't here, or are we recruiting?"

Ben knew at that point it was time to get the ball rolling. "There are more. Raoul Martinez and Sarge Bill Lewis are either in Idaho now or on their way to meet up with two others, Tony Rice and Robert Ellis. One other, Durham Murdit, couldn't make it today. He works for the city, but I will keep him in the loop."

Gerald spoke up then. "My neighbor James Becker may join us, but if he decides not to, I trust him implicitly to keep it quiet."

Tom said, "Everyone is exmilitary, I assume?"

"Yes. We got Vietnam, Iraq, Iran, Afghanistan. Army, Army National Guard, Green Beret, Navy SEAL, Marine, Infantry, and Ranger. We got 'em all, and both urban and jungle warfare. As to the Vietnam guys, just 'cause there is snow on the mountain doesn't mean there isn't fire in the furnace! Once you've been on that bike, you never forget how to pedal!"

Ron then asked, "Was it planned that we have all branches and forces for this? If so, hats off to the genius who tracked everyone down."

Mike thought a minute before he answered, "You know what? No, it wasn't deliberate. Guess we got lucky when we started looking for and at people we knew."

Tyrell piped up after everyone agreed that it was interesting it was playing out the way it was and stated, "Look, guys, you have noticed we are looking at a team that is about the same size as the teams on squads in the various forces. We figure twelve to fourteen is a great number, easy to work with, and as we are hoping for little resistance when this all goes down, based on the element of surprise!"

Ron said, "When is this all gonna happen?"

Ben replied, "Thinking January or February. Be kinda hard to hide stuff during warmer months, but heavy winter coats, great to hide things in."

"Next meeting would be when and where?" asked Tom.

Ben responded, "In August, we can reach out to everyone and see when in September works for everyone. At that point, I think it makes sense to have at least four days, better a week, but we can fine-tune that as it goes. What I am thinking is this: I have a lot in back of the gym, and right now I keep my camper there most of the time. There is a small building back there that has plumbing to it, and I was thinking the local guys could help clean the lot up, put up a privacy fence, and get it ready for our next reunion. Tom, you, Ron, and Hawk would be able to make a little money as well, and Raoul too when he returns for helping out. We could add a bath and kitchen to the building, and there is enough square footage to add bunk rooms with bedding for anyone who needs a place to crash. And of course, there is a dumpster there as well as a septic tank—yes, I had it checked out, and it is good—so if we needed to do so, the campers could hardline into the septic. That way, anyone and everyone could be together to plan."

Hawk jumped in with, "Wow, you are definitely a planner, aren't you? Very impressive and well thought out. Now I see the beer and wing tray empty."

Gerald said, "Be right back. I will get us refills. I am impressed also. Nice to know someone has this lined up so well."

The rest of the day was spent with more idle chatter. Occasionally someone commented on the VA, but for the most part, they were just moving around to acquaint themselves better with one another. By about six thirty, those that could had thrown money on the table and left, and Mike and Gerald settled the bill and left for home.

Jean commented to Gerald when they got back that she could understand why they liked the pub so well and asked if he liked her new sneakers. Laughing, he looked at Mike and said, "Told ya," and looking back at his wife, he said, "Love 'em, hon."

Then the evening was spent enjoying the breeze that blew across the yard and discussing plans for another get-together and, perhaps in the future, Kathy and Mike visiting North Carolina. Tomorrow would be packing day and loading the car, filling it up with gas, then Wednesday, they'd head for home. Both Jean and Gerald thanked them profusely for opening up their home and showing them an incredible time.

Kathy emphatically stated, "We enjoyed it too! Sometimes it does people good to remember what is in their own backyard, and often when you live somewhere, you forget. As reservation manager, I don't often take calls, but now I remember what the things are that I told people they really need to see in DC, and I will remind the agents when I go back."

Kathy was always an early bird, and Tuesday morning was no exception. Coffee was ready when everyone else headed into the kitchen, and breakfast was leftover donuts and fruit that was already there. When everyone had drunk their share of coffee and eaten the donuts and fruit, they headed for the patio before starting to pack and get ready.

Mike looked at Kathy and said, "Gerald and I need to go off for a bit. Can you two handle things for a while?"

Kathy glared at him. "Really, Mike? You can't stay and help and enjoy the last day the four of us will have for now?"

Jean sensed this was going down a bad road and said, "Kathy, it's okay. I always pack the bags, but Gerald has to pack the car. As long as he is back then, it is actually easier on me."

"Thanks, Jean, I really wanted Gerald to meet Durham, and he is off work today, so we can go, grab a quick cuppa, and be back long before the car needs loading. Kath, do you want us to grab KFC for lunch on our way back?"

With a sigh, she said, "Yes, can you do the rotisserie and fried combo please."

"Any other special requests?" responded Mike.

No one wanted anything else extra, and the guys left. Arriving at Durham's, they gave a complete update on the VFW meeting, had the cup of coffee, and as promised, grabbed chicken and headed back. Gerald saw Mike was a bit downhearted looking and asked what was up. He could tell Mike was hesitant to talk and waited patiently.

Finally, Mike took a deep breath and said, "Sometimes I wonder as long as Kathy and I have been together if it will continue. She gets so snappy at times, and I never know what to say or do."

With a chuckle, Gerald responded, "Mike, has menopause been mentioned?"

"No, why?"

"'Cause, my friend, the odds are that is the whole reason for the mood swings. She may be unsure of how to tell you. Luckily Jean is an open book and tells me everything, about that, anyway. Talk to her, okay?"

When they got to the house, it looked as if someone was being kicked out. There were suitcases and a duffel bag sitting on the front porch. Gerald laughed. "Looks like Jean got things done quicker than usual. Take the food in. I will get this stuff loaded."

Mike walked in, Kathy greeting him with a peck on the cheek, taking the food, and proceeding to take it into the kitchen. Mike advised her Gerald was loading the car, and then a beer on the back porch was in order before eating. She said that they would join them with some wine, and they could all relax the rest of the day.

They headed in to bed about 10:00 p.m., and the next morning, everyone was up and gathered in the kitchen for a final breakfast by 7:00 a.m. It was decided they would not rush the departure time, because one, it would be rush hour, and two, silly as it sounded, they were going to do a two-day drive. So french toast and canadian bacon were truly enjoyed by all. About 11:00 a.m., the Washingtons were ready to go, with hugs and kisses around. Kathy said, "Call when you do get in, please." And Jean assured her she would. Gerald thanked Mike for introducing him to the guys, and with a "See you soon," they were off.

When they got to Durham, North Carolina, and stopped for gas and a bite to eat, Gerald said to Jean, "Hotel and a good dinner?"

"Sounds good. Shall I call and see if the Marriott has rooms? Then we can either eat there or head to one of the nearby places and leave the car parked."

Which they did, having a relaxing evening and discussing how much they enjoyed DC. Gerald told her about the menopause discussion, and Jean responded, "I wondered about that. Kathy seemed a bit reserved though, so I kept out of it. But now maybe I can mention my issues and open her up. It is hard, I know. And I really have enjoyed our time this week. We really are back on the right track, huh?"

The next day, they didn't check out 'til 11:00 a.m., proving it pays to have status with hotel chains, and after a meandering drive home and a stop for dinner and groceries, they arrived there about 7:00 p.m. While the groceries had to be put away, the rest of the stuff could wait, and Jean called Kathy as she was doing so. They then settled in and were in bed by ten.

Both were up by 8:00 a.m. the next morning, and as they were drinking coffee, they slowly started unpacking the bags they had brought in the night before. Luckily the laundry was minimal, so it was a quick job, then Jean was going to dust and sweep while Gerald checked the yard. As he went out front, James walked over with his mail. "Good time up there?"

"Yes, we saw a lot, and I met some great guys!" And Gerald gave James all the information that had been provided concerning the mission.

"Sounds like a well-organized team," said James, "and the planning seems as organized as what it was for us in Vietnam. We Green Berets had to do that a lot!"

"James, been thinking that too. It is like planning those missions. We had to set up our team, look at any and all eventualities, and then go with it. But hearing you today, are you considering joining the team?"

"I'm always thinking about it. But I am still on the fence. Rest assured, when I decide for sure, you will be the first to know. And on that note, I need to go back to the house and get something done today to make the witch happy. Some days I wish I had gotten a job and let her stay home. I may still do that, and maybe this mission will be my job!"

"Hang in, pal," said Gerald as they both went their respective ways.

THE TRIP TO IDAHO CONTINUES

MEANWHILE BACK AT THE CAMP, Raoul and Sarge had spent a glorious week fishing, checking out the nearby ghost town, Southern Cross, and even doing a little panning for gold. Raoul had gotten so excited when he found flakes, and Les had a vial he could place them in so he could keep them as a souvenir. They spent the last night at Les's house so they could do laundry, clean themselves and the truck up well, and have one last great meal cooked by Les. Les had spent time with them at the campsite too, and when the next morning came and it was time to leave, he handed them their cooler, which was packed with traveling food.

"There is sandwich meat, bread, packets of mayo, mustard, and catsup, lemonade and tea, cookies and brownies made with Stevia—so, Raoul, thanks to you, I have tried new recipes safe for diabetics or just those watching calories—and a few other goodies. See you on your way back?"

In unison, Sarge and Raoul thanked him and said they would let him know for sure when they would pass back through. Even if only as a one-night stop, for sure.

They finished loading the truck and started out. Sarge informed Raoul, "Okay, here we go. It's about three hundred miles to Cascade and mostly state and county roads. So you should be happy to know ninety mph is not gonna happen. Probably won't get in 'til about seven. It seems there is always construction somewhere along the way."

And he was right. What actually slowed them was a boulder that fell across the road, and it took the crew about two hours to clear it. Luckily that happened around lunchtime, and there was a spot to pull over and eat until they could move on.

Pulling into Cascade, Raoul commented that the place was bigger than he expected. Sarge advised him he had felt the same way first time through, and it had grown since.

They continued on, and when Sarge saw the sign "Donnelly 15 miles," he told Raoul, "Seven miles and we are there!"

They finally pulled up to the cabin, and Sarge jumped out of the truck ran to the door and, without knocking, threw the door open. Tony, with raised eyebrow, said, "I am not getting up for you two. You know where the fridge and beers are. Help yourself, then we can talk."

Raoul noticed light beer and knew Sarge had advised Tony of his dietary restrictions, and he voiced his thanks immediately upon entering the living room.

"Not an issue, and you made good time. Usually its about a month from when you leave home. Fishing musta been bad, and apparently you didn't stop in Salmon to see the hussy, right?"

Laughing, Sarge agreed, and they moved on to other things, Raoul showing off his gold and some of the pictures he had taken. They unloaded the camper and ate the rest of the food Les had provided (he did overstock and there was plenty for a light dinner for three). They talked a bit more, but all had their showers and hit the racks before 11:00 p.m.

Raoul and Sarge didn't crack eyes open until about nine. They could smell the coffee and headed for the kitchen, where Tony was waiting. Raoul stated he could not imagine having an actual lake in one's own backyard.

"I never get tired of this," Tony responded. "Just sitting here looking out over the lake takes a lot off my mind and really relaxes me."

"It must be nice to have an outlet like this, Tony. Sarge has his farm and incredible mountain views, you a peaceful lake. Stuck in DC, I can't find anything to ease my mind when I feel pressured or depressed. But I will tell you, working on this mission to attack the VA has helped. I feel like I did when I was in the Army, and we had to get ready for our mission to destroy the enemy. I feel useful again!" stated Raoul with conviction.

"Tell me all, you two," said Tony.

Sarge looked Tony straight in the eyes and said, "Because of the way the VA is not supporting our Vets with medical help and then denying compensation to those who deserve it, we are going to take action. They claim they have a cure for Vets with PTSD, so please explain to me why twenty-one Vets commit suicide a day? Our Vets are burning out, Tony. You heard about the guy in Texas who shot his doctor, right?"

Tony was able to nod his head yes, and Sarge continued, "Now on top of all that, the VA claims lack of money. I'm thinking it could be because of the fraud and embezzlement they have perpetrated themselves. White-collar workers are making money and receiving gifts at our expense."

At that point, Tony broke it to ask what he was referring to. "I don't watch the news much and missed all this."

While Raoul sat quietly, letting Sarge do all the talking, his head did do a steady yes nod.

"Let's see if I can shorten this a bit. Apparently the workers were entitled to bonuses in the form of debit cards and/or gifts worth any amount from a few hundred to many thousands. It totaled millions. And I just found out the medical field has had issues too, which all takes away from the same pool. Clinics were buying equipment and reselling it and pocketing the money! Now here is the crux of the matter. It seems our illustrious government can't or won't address this. As there is no media coverage anymore, I am thinking they also put out a gag order to keep it all quiet. Meanwhile, who ultimately pays? You got it, the Vets! And if they won't prosecute and try to make it right, it is time we make a statement and do something that they will never forget. I think they feel there is nothing anyone can do to change or correct this, but I want them to know that I am one Sergeant who is more than willing to prove them wrong."

At this point, Sarge needed a pit stop and looked at Raoul with a questioning look.

Raoul gladly took over and outlined what he knew at present about the plan. Tony was nodding his head both yesses and nos throughout the whole discussion, showing shock at times as well.

Sarge by then had returned from the head and looked at Tony with a questioning look on his face. "Think you and Robert or anyone else you know may want to join us?"

"I know Sarge has mentioned Robert to you. Robert Ellis and I belong to a group but have extensive contacts throughout Idaho. None of us are happy with the way our country is being run but 'til now have not considered taking action. I definitely understand the thought process and reason for this, but as you can imagine, would be a big decision if we decided to help. Could bring any one of a number of federal agencies down on us if it all fell apart. Robert comes in day after tomorrow. Let's talk to him, get his take, and go from there. Fair enough?"

"Sounds like a plan," said Sarge. "And how are the rainbows doing now?"

Tony advised they were just the right size now, and if the guys wanted to get a load of laundry in first, they could head for the dock to catch some dinner. Surprisingly within a half hour, there were enough trout caught for dinner. Tony lit the fire in the outside pit and threw some potatoes in while the other two cleaned and filleted the fish, Raoul advising the two of them that he was more than willing to stay at either one's property and work for food if this was what the food always looked like. They all laughed, and the evening passed with stories of days gone by being shared and beer disappearing from the cooler.

Early the next morning, Raoul was up and took a walk around part of the lake, just enjoying the calm and quiet. Living in a city, moments like this never happened, and he planned to store every moment he could. Back in the cabin, he found the coffee pot ready to switch on and decided to see if he could figure out where everything was and make Tony and Sarge breakfast. By the time they got up, the bacon was crisp and french toast was being kept warm in the oven.

"Hmmm," said Tony, "maybe you should plan on moving here. Can you do dinner too?"

"Token of my thanks, and if you like spaghetti, I make a mean sauce."

"And I could freeze the leftovers, right?"

"If you had any… My sauce is good!"

They sat, enjoyed the food, and spent the day hanging out. Sarge and Raoul took the boat out around two to try for some fish for dinner, and Tony made a potato salad and prepped the flour to bread the fish, knowing full well some kind of fish would come through the door. Which of course it did, and with extras that were prepped and frozen. It was an enjoyable evening. They lit a fire in the fire pit and sat out 'til about ten, Tony reminding them as they headed in that Robert would be in about 10:00 a.m.

And he did drive in at the stroke of 10:00 a.m. As he got out of his truck, the long hair and rugged, mean look put Raoul off at first. All he could think of was, *Wrestler or hit man*. However, once they were all introduced and he realized that you couldn't judge a book by its cover, or a man by his appearance, he relaxed.

Throughout the day, they discussed the situation with the VA. Sarge and Raoul told Robert about the fraud and embezzlement and could, of course, explain various situations that the Vets encountered, such as not getting benefits they were entitled too and waiting for appointments for doctors and hospital tests and procedures. Robert did a lot of head shaking with a look of disbelief on his face and asked quite a few very good questions, one of which was, "Why a VA affairs office and not hospital?"

The response from Sarge after about a thirty-second pause was, "We feel anything and everything that the VA does is sanctioned by the VA head honcho. Therefore we need to go to the top. Kinda like going after the queen bee, more impact in a quicker time frame. You can try to kill off the nests one by one, but that can take way too long!"

At that point, Robert was bobbing a yes nod, then he stated, "I think we can help. Let me call a couple guys and be sure all is clear with them." With that, he walked away, pulled a cell phone out of his pocket, then came back over. "You guys wanna meet tomorrow at Yellow Pines? Tony, I know you can find your way there. How about around eleven?"

They let Tony respond and shook hands, all going their separate ways. Tony explained as the started back to the cabin that Yellow Pines was where they met sometimes for privacy.

After they had their coffee the next morning, they headed out to Yellow Pines. Tony provided a running commentary on the cabins and homesteads they passed and some history on the surrounding areas once they headed into the more isolated areas. He made sure Raoul put the camera away long before they reached the actual meet spot.

When they got to the locale, Robert, who followed them in, said they were clear no followers. Tony knew when Robert had fallen in behind him. This had been protocol for so long to be sure no one was following them. Then they walked over to where three guys were waiting, standing by two four-wheel-drive trucks. Again, introductions and handshakes around, and Robert provided the quick version of the upcoming mission.

One of the guys, Ted, said, "What exactly are you looking for and when?"

Robert turned to Sarge and Raoul and asked, "What do you have already for weapons and manpower in place now?"

Sarge looked at Raoul. Raoul nodded to go on, and Sarged responded with, "Approximately ten men in place at present. No confirmed weapons known as of now. I am thinking Glocks, nine millimeters, and final count for men, twelve to fourteen probably."

Ted, looking at Robert and Tony first to see if they did nod yes, then responded with, "Hard to get Glocks, but what about .38c revolvers or .45c semiautmatic pistols. Either would be possible."

Raoul was nodding and spoke up, asking, "Okay, I am thinking you guys are really connected, right? Can you get grenades too?"

Ted smiled and said, "We can probably come up with some for the cause! And I know the two standing behind me agree this is our contribution to the mission, as well as the rest of our group, who will give 100 percent support." As they all looked around, the two heads in the back of Ted were nodding in agreement.

Sarge and Raoul looked at each other, and the others could see the shock in their faces. Neither knew what to say, and finally Tony broke the silence, saying, "So I guess we are set? I know you all need a final count for guns and ammo, and I will be sure you know in plenty of time to get the stuff to us. Thinking by the first part of September, we should have this all in place as far as the supplies being delivered. Ted, gentleman, you are all appreciated more than you will ever know, and I know that if Sarge and Raoul could talk, they would confirm that."

At that point, everyone shook hands and got ready to depart. It was decided Tony, Sarge, and Raoul would go out first. Robert told them as they pulled out he would meet them at a small restaurant that he and Tony frequented then maybe have some drinks at a nearby bar. And later when they met at the restaurant, where dinner was good, drinks were better, and nothing related to anything important was discussed, they shared some fish stories and headed home. This allowed Robert and Sarge and Raoul time to become better acquainted and bond with one another.

Over coffee the next morning, they discussed Raoul heading back to DC. Sarge had gotten him an open-ended ticket, so he called American to arrange a flight out of Boise. Raoul then called Ben with flight details so he could pick him up when he landed. Sarge planned to spend a few more days at Tony's before heading home but promised Raoul he would tell Les thanks again.

RAOUL UPDATES BEN

When Raoul finally landed in DC (weather delay in O'Hare), it was so late, Ben said, "Crash at my place. Gonna guess no beds available this late. Then we can catch up in the morning."

Raoul did update Ben on all that transpired, and by the time they got to Ben's, both were yawning and went straight to sleep. Surprisingly, Raoul was up early the next morning as well as Ben. Ben stated, "Did not expect to see you up so soon. Time change doesn't have you confused?"

"I think it is a case of being wired, Ben. The whole trip was incredible on its own as a vacation. But realizing what has been accomplished as far as the mission, not much to compare that too."

"I get it!" and Ben went on to explain progress at the gym. Tom, Ron, and Hawk had worked very hard to get things done. Two dumpsters had been filled with trash, and the crap in the building had been emptied out. The plumbing and necessary electrical wiring changes were made. The new walls were framed, and Sheetrock was being done now. "Your buddies could form a building crew. Everything looks so professional." He advised him then that paint, hopefully with one guy working inside, the others out, have the privacy fence on the front and chain link down the sides and back done, with a gate that could accommodate an RV, would be next.

Raoul said, "Can't wait to see this! Those deadbeats can work, huh?"

And with that, they finished their coffee and headed over to the gym. Ben went in to open up and get the day started while Raoul walked around the back.

BACK TO REALITY AND
AN UPDATE FOR HAWK

Hawk was leaning against the building smoking a cigarette and saw Raoul come out the back door. "So vacation over and you ready to get to work, boy?" Hawk questioned as he ground out the butt and shook hands then hugged. "Good to have you back."

"Good to see you too, Hawk, and let me tell you, vacation? Wouldn't call it that. I worked hard! Catching fish is work, hard work. Plumb tuckered my arms out. Living conditions were horrible too. I had to sleep on the ground, in a tent, in the middle of nowhere, and worry about wild cats and bears if I had to go pee."

"Buddy, my heart bleeds for you. If we do meet your pal Sarge, I can't wait to hear the truth."

"Yeah, well, I have pictures. I will get the camera later to prove it. Ben is gonna keep the camera for me for now."

"I can't wait to see the pics! Now time to do some work. Ben told you, I hope, to go to the snack bar when hungry, right?"

When they got inside, Tom and Ron took a quick break from hanging Sheetrock to welcome Raoul home and ask if he was good at mudding and taping. He said he was, and they set him to work on the other side of the room that was complete and ready.

Ben showed up about twelve thirty, very impressed by the amount of work that was done. Instead of the snack bar food, when they walked outside, a platter of sandwiches from a nearby deli and a cooler of drinks were on the picnic table.

As they settled in to eat lunch, Raoul was wondering if he should say anything with Tom and Ron sitting there and just listened to them all updating him on their activities while he was gone. Finally when they took a break and were eating their sandwiches, he questioned Tom, "I am confused, Tom. I get you're helping out here 'cause I know Ben is paying and that would make going home and being a priest or whatever easier and get back with the wife. But it sounds like you are in, so what is it?"

"Well," responded Tom after a brief pause, "not long after you left on your trip, I spoke to the wife. She made it very clear it was over, asked for an address to overnight the divorce papers. Ben was kind enough to let me use this address. They came, I signed, and I would guess by now I am a free man. Then I thought the whole thing over about the mission you guys were planning and decided that it was something I wanted to be a part of. You good with that?"

"Welcome aboard, Tom," and he finished updating them all on what had transpired on his trip west. He had noticed when the conversation first began, Ron was nodding his head yes and did reconfirm with Ron as well that he was in 100% in.

"Lunch is over!" stated Ben after about an hour. Amid groans and growls, they all thanked Ben for lunch, and everyone headed back to their work. Knocking off about 5:00 p.m., Hawk asked Raoul if he was going with them. Raoul advised him that as some of his stuff was still at Ben's, and Ben had told him to stay that night too, so he would see them in the a.m. With a snicker, Hawk asked him if he was getting too used to having a private room. "Enjoy, my friend," he said as he Tom and Ron headed back to the shelter.

Raoul headed into the gym, showered, changed clothes, and found the sandwich that was left from lunch and Ben had told him would be in the fridge. Ben came up to him and asked if he was ready to go.

When they got to Ben's and had settled in (Ben had also eaten at the gym), Raoul asked Ben if he thought it would be okay if he did stay at the gym in the RV Ben already kept there.

"You know, Raoul, good idea. We had talked about you guys staying there later, and it seems like a good idea if you all filter out of the shelter rather than all disappearing at once. And plus, you could be security. I like. Good thought, Raoul! And water and electric are hooked up because I wanted to make sure everything worked right. We can check in the morning and see what is needed to clean it up though. No one has been in it to stay for about a year."

"Thanks, Ben. Let me know what I need to do. I can run to Safeway to get anything we may need to clean."

"I have cleaning stuff in the gym. Only thing you may need is a broom and/or mop. But we can hit a dollar store for that if need be."

The next morning, Raoul made sure he had all his stuff. This would be the first time in many years he had been in a place by himself and was truly excited. He knew he could eat better in the camper than what they fed him at the shelter. His three hundred a month would definitely cover that.

As they got to the gym early, Ben and Raoul did go check out the camper, and later in the day, Ben walked by with a bucket full of cleaning supplies with a mop and broom in hand as well.

Ron noticed him and yelled, "We having company?"

Raoul heard this and advised they guys that he was moving in now. Ron looked a bit upset by this, and Raoul took full credit for asking but reminded them they too would end up there and promised a dinner or two home cooked prior to that time.

Tom chimed in, "I guess we are being a bit pissy, and I apologize for thinking ugly thoughts, Raoul. It all makes sense. If we did all leave the shelter as one group, that could look a little funny."

Hawk said, "And as security, I like that, I would be really PO-ed if all our work was damaged by punks who come by bored and decide to ruin it."

"Appreciate it, guys. You all like spaghetti?"

And on that note, they headed back to work. Before they knew it, it was lunch. Ben came out carrying pizzas and envelopes. He advised them that the work they were doing was great and told them to let him know if they felt it was not enough money—200 cash in each envelope!

A shocked look settled on each face, and Hawk finally spoke up, "I don't think we expected this, Ben. We were in it for the mission. But rest assured, it is appreciated. Probably will be needed later to dress us or something. I know I don't own a winter coat, and that is an important part of what goes down later. So thanks! Now may I ask you to keep some of it for me? I will keep 50, but can you hold the 150?"

The other two also thanked Ben profusely and asked him to hold some of their money, which of course he did.

Then it was on to work details. Ben told them the cement and fencing posts would be in this afternoon, and they already had wheelbarrows and shovels. However, he had noticed no post hole diggers and ordered three of those to be delivered as well as new hoses that would be enough to reach pretty much the whole perimeter of the property to make the job easier.

"You think of everything! We got this. Gonna kind of trade-off so no one ends up outside all day every day to finish this all," Ron said.

"Again, thanks, guys. Better get inside. Just so you know, staff inside thinks this is all for a gathering of Vets who know each other from various places, kinda a mini reunion. Don't want you blind-sided by weird questions later."

GERALD CALLS MIKE

MIKE WAS SITTING AT THE kitchen table, coffee in one hand, paper spread before him, when the phone rang. He looked before he answered, saw Gerald's name show up, and answered with, "What you doing up so early?"

"Fishing trip details. You want 'em?" was the statement made.

"Tell all. I am ready."

"Okay, Mike. Got us a week at Lake Marion resort. Ninety-five to Santee exit, go through town, but don't blink, five miles out you will see the sign for Lake Marion resort, turn left. For this Sunday as we discussed."

"Nice. Do we have space for one more? Durham is ready for a break too."

"That works. I did get the two bedroom. James Becker, who was the POW in Nam, is coming too! So see you then."

A little more discussion followed about who would bring what groceries and beer and booze, and they said their good-byes.

Mike then immediately called Durham and asked if his fishing gear was ready, 'cause if not, he better get it ready and be packed and ready to hit the road by 8:00 a.m. Sunday morning.

"See you then, and probably at least once before. Thanks for inviting me."

SANTEE, SOUTH CAROLINA

Sunday rolled around, and of course, Gerald and James got in first, arriving about 10:00 a.m. They settled in and headed over to the dock to fish. Once they had enough for dinner, they went to the cleaning station and cleaned and prepped them. By the time, Mike and Durham showed up around 4:00 p.m., everyone was ready for fish, potatoes, and beer, lots of beer.

Getting to know one another took time. As was guys' way, the stories had to flow to know one another's personalities and character. By the time dinner was cooked and eaten and cleaned up after and beers on the porch consumed, it was late. No one heading for bed until after midnight. So the next morning, no one crawled out until about 9:00 a.m. By the time they gathered their gear and walked over to the office to get the keys for the pontoon, it was about 10:30 a.m. They then picked up ice at the office and filled the cooler. They quickly loaded the pontoon and headed east along the lake shore until they saw and pulled into the state park for information. The Ranger told them where the best spots were to fish, made sure they paid for and received a license to fish, and sold them bait. They then headed out for the day.

Heading west on the lake, they were entering a swampy area, and Gerald asked if anyone wanted to take a swim. The response from James was to ask Gerald how he felt about being gator bait 'cause the fourteen footer there looked like he could definitely make short work of him.

Mike asked, "Isn't he licking his chops as we speak?" At which they all laughed and decided swimming was out, unless it was in the pool at the resort.

Swinging in an eastward direction, they headed toward the locks, which would allow them to go down to Lake Moultrie, which they hit right on the half hour, so no waiting was necessary. They enjoyed the experience of riding down to the lower level and were excited to see Lake Moultrie. They cruised the lake for a while then noticed a marina and stopped to get gas, and the attendant advised them the restaurant on site had a special on a steak dinner, which everyone said sounded great. They felt they would get enough fish to eat on their own. The steaks were cooked to perfection, and everyone drank just a couple of beers before heading back to the pontoon to ride back up the lock and then back to the cabin.

They did fish once they got back up on Lake Marion, catching more than enough for their dinner, Mike saying that if Dee was still at the office, they would offer her some of their fish. She was and gladly took the leftovers off their hands.

Everyone knew what they had for dinner that night—it was bluegill that night—saving the cat to have with grits in the morning. Discussing the day, James made sure they all knew and remembered his fish was the biggest.

Gerald came back with, "You may have caught the winner today, but I predict for tomorrow you see nothing bigger than a minnow compared to my catch of the day!"

Again, they had beers on the porch and went to bed at a reasonable hour. Fresh air made sleep come early and easy, and they all took advantage of that.

The next morning while they were drinking the last of their coffee on the porch, Gerald questioned Mike on how things were going. Mike could update him on the DC project at the gym and getting the guys out of the shelter (which Ben had updated him on before he came down to the lake) and the gun/ammo situation out west. They all had looked around before starting this conversation and realized that any of the cabins occupied near them had no one in them at present, everyone either going off in cars or being seen heading down to the lake to fish. Durham added some additional details concerning time frames, and everyone watched James to see if he showed any indication of his mind-set but did not feel the need to not discuss things, regardless of his decision. Later, Mike actually said to Durham, "I really feel James is a stand-up guy, but wish he would come in. He could be a real benefit." Durham agreed wholeheartedly, and they decided not to push for his decision.

There was no clear winner on the fish contest. Everyone caught some nice-sized ones and a couple of nights gave fish to some of the neighbors who had not been so lucky. And they even cleaned them before, even the catfish! Time lounging was also in the plans. Thursday night, someone cracked the Beam open, and by midnight, it was a dead bottle. Durham awoke on the couch, with a minor hangover, while the others didn't fare much better, so Friday was a complete washout. Saturday, final fishing day, everyone had enough extra to pack coolers the next morning with dry ice so they could all prove fishing was the reason for the trip.

Sunday morning was packing trucks and making sure the cabin was clean and garbage taken care of. Gerald and James offered breakfast in town the night before as thanks for introducing them to this fantastic place, and they headed in.

At the local Shoney's, they all ordered breakfast and coffee, and while waiting for the food, James looked at everyone and said, "Guys, I know you have all been patient waiting to hear my decision, and a bit scared that if I say no, I may turn you all in, so… I do want in. The reasons to do this are too compelling not to be a part of it, and if the rest of the team is as smart and focused as you three, well, count me in."

The three others looked a bit shocked, Gerald thinking to himself, *Wow, didn't think he had the cojones to do this, but I am glad he did it*, at the same time holding out his hand to give a congratulatory handshake and a "Welcome to the team, brother," which led to woo-hoos and congratses across the table with more handshaking. Breakfast was served, and they discussed things in general, recapping their distaste for the VA, but not discussing any of the plans that had previously been talked about. They managed to finish three pots of coffee before everyone finally headed out. As they walked out, Gerald asked, "So a meet in DC next, right?" And with more handshakes and teasing about fishing abilities, they all headed out.

Mike called Ben once they got back to DC and updated him, letting him know about James and that he had some fish for him cleaned and ready. He knew that Ben had been seeing Mary and razzed him a bit, asking if he had cooked for her yet.

"Nope, haven't. But I can fry a mean fish. Can you drop 'em off later, and I will call her and see when we can get together? Sometimes it is hard with both our schedules, but I do enjoy her company. And glad to hear James signed up. That makes thirteen, lucky thirteen, I am thinking. What's your thought, Mike?"

"I like the lucky thirteen concept. Now what's next?"

"Let's see if we can get all of us in DC together for a powwow. We have the area behind the gym all cleaned up, fenced, and I would like you all to come over for a picnic. You let Durham know, and I should be able to get to everyone else. Tuesday be okay?"

"I will check and let you know for sure later today."

FIRST MEETING AT THE COMPOUND

By Monday afternoon, everyone knew about Tuesday. Raoul, Ron, Tom, and Hawk would be sure the area was ready by four for the others and start the fire for the barbecue then as well. Ben had picked up burgers, hot dogs, and all the necessary sides, and Raoul had made some potato and mac salad, telling Ben it was his chance to try out the stove in the camper and see if he could remember how to cook.

Tyrell had grabbed some chicken and brought that as well, and everyone was there by four thirty. The grill was smoking, and Mike and Durham could not resist teasing Ben, telling him that the only reason he was on time was because it was in his backyard.

Ben noticed the fifth of Jack on the table and looked at Hawk. "I'm betting that was your contribution, Hawk."

"Somebody had to invite Mr. Daniels, so I assumed it was up to me. I might be persuaded to share, though," he responded with a laugh.

"Thanks! Although I hope none of the die-hards who work out inside find the back door and see us out here like this. Beer, Jack, and all the unhealthy food, they may report me to the workout police," said Ben, too which they all laughed, and Ron said, "Yeah, well, I would bet you quite a few of them are here sweating out last night's beers and steaks themselves!"

After a few moments, Ben advised everyone that if they would get a plate ready and their drink of choice, the new and improved building in the back had a table set up so they could talk with some privacy. Tom turned off the gas grill after being sure all the meat was in place to keep warm and the rest of the food on the picnic table was covered or brought in with them.

"First off, let me thank Hawk, Ron, Tom, and Raoul for all this, 99 percent of this was done by them. They cleaned this out, redid the Sheetrock, plumbing, and electrical as needed, added the kitchen and bath. Painted the outside and in, did the fence as well, and Raoul is checking to be sure the septic is okay by using my camper facilities."

Tom spoke up, "Honestly, we all have talked, and it felt good to work like this. As you guys may or may not know, before the economy crashed, I had a handyman business, which worked well for me, because with the small crew I had, if I had a bad day because of the PTSD, they could handle things for me. When the economy dropped and the wife bailed, I decided I was tired of the bugs and heat in the South, and assuming I could get my VA bennies quicker being in DC… you all know where that got me."

Ron and Hawk also thanked Ben for the opportunity to help, and Tyrell questioned Ben, "So I get the feeling you have a pretty good idea where things stand, boss, am I right?"

"Let me recap what I know for now guys. There are eight of us here now and five more in the mix that will be here later to set things up and be a part of everything."

"Do we have names and info on them?" Tom asked.

"Let's see. Sarge Bill Lewis in Colorado, who was with Raoul in Nam. Tony Rice is in Idaho, and he served with Raoul and Sarge, so Raoul knows both of them well. Robert Ellis, also in Cascade, Idaho, who Tony has worked with was in Nam too. Then in Charlotte, NC, we have James Becker and Gerald Washington, Mike and Durham having spent time with them."

Raoul spoke up then and advised, "Guys, I just spent time with Sarge and the two in Idaho. They know some people, and all I can say is this: I have a hunch if we asked for more than just guns, ammo, grenades, and vests, they would be found and available. We who can't contribute monetarily need to really thank those who are, 'cause I can tell you, this shit is expensive!"

Hawk asked, "Grenades?"

Raoul replied, "Yes, grenades, Hawk. I know you. You want those all for yourself, don't you?"

"Raoul, you know I share… but only if I have to!"

They discussed the logistics of getting the stuff into DC and decided it was a good thing that those that would be coming in had trucks and campers and that if they staggered in and/or came in at different times for a visit to old military buddies, there shouldn't be any questions later.

Mike said, "Good points, all. Just so you all have some background, Gerald was Green Beret in Vietnam and James was also Beret, but spent a long time as a POW. I know both of them they understand why we feel the need to do this, and they will be an asset to the mission."

Ron asked, "Might we be recruiting anyone else?"

Everyone thought a moment, and Ben spoke up first. "I personally think the amount of people we have now is perfect. I know from what we currently know about everyone, we can mesh well and work together. Anyone else got a thought?"

Hawk chimed in, "I agree. Thirteen feels right for this mission to me."

Durham then asked very solemnly, "Does this look like a suicide mission to you all, or do you think we will be able to have an escape plan?"

Ben again spoke up. "Wish I could answer that clearly. Will there be opportunities to get out alive? Possibly. Will we lose guys? I say yes. This is a government office, and once the attack starts, hard to say just how they will respond and how quickly. Will we try to spare anyone? I am thinking we will be trying not to harm any of the Vets that are there for appointments, etc. Could you conceivably slide out with them? Possibly. Will there be SWAT out there by then and you get shot anyway? Also possible. My mind-set? I am going to be sure my affairs are completely in order before I go in there."

Tyrell then said, "Ben, I agree. At this point, we are somewhat speculating what can or will happen. Even though we can't tell people what we are up to, you are so right. We all need to have our affairs in order just in case it goes either way. One thing to keep in mind, should you survive, it is either prison or you get lucky and totally disappear, so keep that in mind too."

Everyone agreed with all the points made, and Mike then questioned the five that weren't local. "Aren't they at a definite disadvantage not being familiar with the building? Puts them at a higher risk, doesn't it? Of either being lost or…"

Ben prefaced his answer with the disclaimer, "Guys, I don't want to seem like I am running this show, but my thought is this, because that is definitely a concern. We start with six two-man teams to sweep the building. No one is without someone from DC. We know the building, each of us there often enough to say that. And we will be mapping moves as well, pooling our knowledge to be sure we know who and what is where. So homework, due in two weeks. Each and every one of you knows an area of that building, as I said earlier. Use that knowledge to plan your attack, document the rooms you see are always empty, where people congregate, whatever you know to make it all feasible. If you know where the cameras are, note them. Are there guards? Document it. There are pads and pens over there in that drawer for you guys that hang here, and the lockers will be in tomorrow for you to have a space of your own. Maybe someone knows where the central camera monitoring is done, and we can have that info too. Duplicate info is great, so let's not sweat that at all. Now enough work. Let's finish the food. One more thing that I will do, and that is to check news broadcasts and/or other channels to get you guys the knowledge of what the head honcho looks like."

They headed out to finish the food, but Hawk stayed in and looked at Ben with a grin, pulling the Jack bottle out from behind his back. "I just want a minute to toast you, because officially or not, you are running this show as far as I can see, and doing well."

"Thanks, Hawk. I consider it all a joint effort, but for a shot of Jack… I'm in. And one more thing, do you think you and Raoul would do okay as roommates? I think its time, if you want to."

"Okay, now we need another shot. I really don't have much at the shelter, but if you mean it, I can be in tonight. Raoul approved me too?"

"Of course he did. He actually suggested it."

Raoul was asked for more detail on the guns and ammo and said, "Rest assured, these guys have our back. I am so surprised and impressed to see how well run the survivalist and Militia groups are out there, but that is all I can say. Of course, most are Vets, so that explains a lot I think!"

Just as he finished that statement, Hawk came flying out of the building, walked up to Raoul, clapped him on the back, and said, "We are roomies again! Woo-hoo."

Raoul just smiled and said, "One thing, though, you can't hog the john!"

"Won't have to here. In the shelter, the toilet stall was the only place to have privacy," responded Hawk.

When the food was gone and the area cleaned up, everyone who had someplace to return to left. Hawk did head over to the shelter to get his few items that were there, and Tom and Ron knew they would also eventually leave there too, so they congratulated Hawk.

RAOUL SCOPES OUT THE TARGET AREA

THE NEXT MORNING, RAOUL HEADED over to the VA. His goal today was to see Randy and check out some things. As Ben had paid him for his work behind the gym, he had a tactical move in mind.

"Randy, long time no see. Thought I would drop by and, if I timed it right, buy you lunch!"

"Well, you did time it exactly right. Let's go to the cafeteria, but there is no need for you to pay for mine."

Raoul replied, "Nope, I insist. Came into a bit of green, and I really owe ya. Please let me do this."

With a nod of approval, they headed into the cafeteria. People were scattered around the room, and Raoul unobtrusively surveyed the room. They got their trays and food and headed over to corner table. Randy asked Raoul how things were going and if he was staying out of trouble.

"Depends on what you mean by trouble," said Raoul. "An old buddy offered me a vacation to head west and camp and fish with him. I may never be invited back 'cause I whooped his butt on fishing. Caught all the big ones! He has an incredible place in Colorado. It was the next best thing to heaven!"

"Now I am jealous. Fred would be too if he knew."

"It was so quiet. Not like here. I notice this gets loud, and there are only, what, about fifteen people in here. Each floor doesn't have a break room?"

"You would think so, wouldn't you? Eight floors and one cafeteria. I don't stay here and eat often. Usually grab the food and go elsewhere."

"I'm gonna bet you go through that door marked Security and hide out there, I would."

"You win! Would take ya in there for the quiet if I could, but with the monitors for the cameras, no can do."

"But I bet you could tell me some good stories though, especially from the muckety-mucks' offices on the upper floors?"

With a laugh, Randy said, "Not them. They won't allow cameras in the offices. But every now and again, an elevator gets interesting!"

"Stairwells too, I bet."

"Believe it or not, no cameras there, but if the stairs could talk! And I probably should head back. Don't need another black mark on me."

"Those jerks still giving you problems?"

"Yup, but after income tax time next year, I may look for something else. That money would give me the extra cushion to cover."

As they walked out to Randy's security station, Randy said, "Hey, I just realized, I am off tomorrow. Would you like to come over and hang with Fred and I?"

And it was decided.

Raoul headed back to the gym and updated Ben, who thanked him profusely for working so quickly then went over to the trailer to document all he had learned and talk to Hawk.

FIRST NIGHT FOR RAOUL AND HAWK IN THE NEW DIGS

As the RV only had one real bedroom, they had decided they would take turns, and this week being Hawk's first week there, he got the room to himself. Raoul had told him not to be surprised at how strange it was to sleep by oneself in a room and not hear the night noises of everyone that they had become accustomed to.

With a wry smile, Hawk responded, "My friend, you snore loud enough to make me feel right at home, even with you in the next room. But I will survive!"

Raoul replied, "Okay, Hawk, let's see who snores loudest! Sleep well, my friend."

LUNCH WITH RANDY (AND FRED)

THE NEXT DAY, RAOUL SHOWED up at Randy's right on time. When Randy answered the door, he was almost plowed down by Fred, who was so happy to see Raoul he almost knocked them both over.

"I am guessing he remembers the steak bone he got last time I was here and is hoping I have something today. Hmm, hey, Fred, what's this in my pocket?" And as Fred danced around, Raoul pulled out a dog bone treat, telling Randy as he did so that it was all natural and made in the USA. "Hope you are okay with this."

Randy laughed and said, "Yes, he gets his share of goodies, and I thank you for being cautious with the manufacturing place."

"Heard on the news food made in China has killed some pets. Can't risk Fred. He is too cool and well-behaved to ever suffer!"

They then got sodas, and Randy sat out some snack foods while they shot the breeze. Randy was happy to hear about the change in Raoul's living quarters. It was explained that he got free board for keeping an eye on things at the gym. "Ben is a great guy, and I think really wants to help everyone he can," stated Raoul.

Randy had realized that Raoul was homeless quite a while ago but, out of kindness, never let on he knew. When Raoul opened up about how long he had been on the streets then going from shelter to shelter, he knew Raoul trusted him and felt the same.

He was told about some of the guys Raoul had met and their stories, most of them he had probably seen pass through the doors at work, trying their damnedest to get something to help let them have lives. Raoul wound down by saying, "It is really frustrating and sad. We all did as we were asked and told when in the military, with the promise made that we would be taken care of! When and how? Please tell me, 'cause I don't see it. I get my meds, three hundred a month, and were it not for this opportunity with Ben, a place at a shelter to sleep. Some life that is!"

Randy was shaking his head the whole time Raoul spoke. He was very quiet for a few minutes and then said, "Yes, Raoul, know what you are saying. I have a buddy in Florida, and let me tell you his story. He had prostate cancer, was advised he should apply for VA because of the Agent Orange, Vietnam tie-in, and did so. They gave him compensation at 100 percent permanent and total, sent the letter granting that and because the letter did state that the VA could not request a review, he did call the main office, which I think in Florida is in Tampa, and they did confirm what the letter said. Twice he got the same answer, 'Yes, sir, we cannot take that away from you, nor do you need to worry about us reviewing your status.'

"Great news for him, huh, Raoul? Well, it was, for about a year. Then a letter comes telling him they are lowering his percentage without an explanation. So as they tell you to do, he puts in for a hearing. He drove down for that hearing, and they advised him he didn't have one. Poor guy is still trying to get this straightened out!"

"Question," said Raoul, "they really sent a letter with the words *permanent* and *total* and are still pulling this crap?"

"Yup, and there is more! Cecil is the kind of guy who won't just go down one road at a time. He will try different avenues and see what happens on those. He had previously involved government offices in other issues and gotten results and figured the whole VA issue should be seen by the White House from a Vet's standpoint. So he drafted a letter to the president and sent it. I got a call a few weeks ago with the update on what that letter generated."

"Don't know if I can stand the suspense… Tell all, Randy."

"Ready for this? Let me tell ya, fiction writers would have a ball with this part of the story! He sends the letter, and in it states he is well aware the White House can't help one Vet but perhaps can help them all by addressing the issues at the VA administration. Tells them it may be time to replace the people who do work there, from the top down, with Vets, who will help their own. Says it is a sad world that allows people to embezzle monies from the VA and then be able to walk away, no ramifications at all, and didn't one person get two mil or better!"

Raoul let out a gasp at this point, and Randy stopped for a moment to let this all sink in. Raoul looked at him and said, "Can we send this guy a medal? Or at least a bottle of Beam or Jack?"

Randy chuckled. "You ain't heard it all yet. Sit tight, my friend, and listen! The letter also mentions PTSD. The VA claims he doesn't suffer from it. However, his therapist is treating him. So in the letter, he states that the VA claims they have a cure for PTSD, and yes, the twenty-one-suicide-a-day figure is also mentioned, which is what the Vets consider the solution to PTSD. He says he has heard the cure is that the VA will give a voucher for a gun. Yeah, Cec was a bit riled but never expected what happened next. Apparently some numb-nut at the White House felt Cecil may be contemplating suicide and forwarded the letter to the VA crisis center. They in turn called him and offered help. He advised them that they were no help, and when they questioned him further about suicidal thoughts, he made a crack about the VA giving vouchers for guns and ammo to those who wanted to commit suicide."

After a quick look to be sure Raoul hadn't fallen over yet, he continued, "About forty-five minutes later, the cops arrive. In Florida, if it appears to someone, i.e., the VA, you are a threat to yourself or others, they can commit you for up to seventy-two hours. So kinda like maximum security for those three days, checking on you every fifteen minutes, no shoelaces or belts and therapy! How does that grab ya for helping our Vets? Oh yeah, and they make your insurance pay out for the medical!"

"You know, I have heard similar stories from Vets, but it still seems crazy that they would handle things this way. I know the reports say twenty-one Vets a day commit suicide, but I would be willing to bet that is not an accurate figure. How many others don't look like suicide but are. It really makes me want to grab a gun and go clean house. You?"

"Only if I can be sure to get my lieutenant first," said Randy, and Raoul noticed a bit of a grin when he said that. "And on that note, enough serious crap. I promised Fred that next time you came we would have steak, so let's light the grill. Snacks are okay, but when dinner rolls, we need real food."

By the time Raoul left, everyone was happy and full. Raoul told Randy before he left that he never knew a dog could belch, but Fred was a pro, or so it appeared, and as he said good-bye, Randy advised him to wait 'til Fred graced him with a fart.

COMPANY IS COMING, SARGE HEADS EAST

RAOUL RECEIVED A PHONE CALL a few days later from Sarge. "I hear there is some good fishing on the east coast, and Tony, Robert, and I are ready for a road trip. We actually found and set up a charter in Maryland and will stop by to pick you up on our way if you can spare the time. Of course, as you know us, we will be fishing our way across the states, so be sure you have freezer space for any bait and/ or fish we have left."

"Sounds like fun! You guys bringing a camper, right? I know a place you will be able to park it. When you are on the road, we can give you directions."

"We will call you when a day away. Thanks for the info on parking it. Can we stay in it as well?"

"Yup, sure can. See you soon."

Raoul went in to update Ben and Tyrell on the trip out. "Maybe it would be a good time to get everyone together for a meet and greet and start really setting up stuff. They did say they had a charter planned over in Maryland, but maybe a real fishing trip, say, two or three days at a camp as well. Thanks to you, Ben, I can help with the cost as well."

"Good idea, Raoul. Let me touch bases with Mike and let him talk to Durham. I can call Gerald and James and check their calendars too and see if we can coordinate this one. Will you tell Ron and Tom as well? And I think it is time to bring them over to stay here as well. With the furniture coming on today, let them know to get their stuff over here. Perhaps best to stagger a day or two for that, but let 'em know!"

"Will do, boss. Let the furniture guys know the back gate will be open."

REMODEL CONTINUES

THE BUILDING IN THE BACK, being about 1,200 square feet, had basically been turned into a small house. Three rooms were bedroom sized and would house a bunk bed each plus a big dresser (no closet, however), a desk, and nightstands plus lamps. Living area housed a nice large sectional, three easy chairs, end and coffee tables and lamps, and a nice big area rug to make it look cozy. The dining table had been a donation from Tyrell, who ended up not needing his, and it was already in place. Miscellaneous pictures that came with the packaged rooms Ben had bought were left to the side to place later.

Earlier Ben had headed over to the Ikea in College Park, Maryland, and bought everything needed to stock the kitchen as well as had Raoul find the best prices he could for bedroom and bath linens. Also Mary had donated some stuff. He and she had dinner together at least once a week, and while she knew he was letting some of the guys stay on property, she assumed Ben was just giving those he could a leg up, never having a clue what was going on. The guys had all determined that those that they loved or cared for had no need to know what was going on. It would protect them later.

When Ben went out to check on things about one o'clock, everyone was moving around, making sure everything looked as they wanted it, and Ron and Tom had each claimed a bottom bunk in different rooms. Hawk and Raoul had given them the speech about the odd feeling of sleeping alone, and they both stated that that was fine; they would definitely deal with the weird feeling just for the pleasure.

"Sorry I couldn't get all the deliveries today, guys, but the appliances and washer/dryer will be in tomorrow. I was lucky enough to get those at a used place, but they are gently used and look good. Was funny, I was waiting for the salesman to give the little-old-lady-only-used-'em on Sunday speech. They looked so good!" said Ben.

Everyone was kind of milling around while they ate the sandwiches they had made, looking at their handiwork. The place was an open-floor plan. They had kept the industrial look and painted the walls light gray and kitchen cabinets a medium silver gray. They bought inexpensive wood and painted it themselves also doing black countertops as well as black sink and hardware. When Ben went to get a sink for the kitchen, Home Depot actually had a black sink with the correct size of countertop on markdown, so it really looked professionally done. All the wood pieces were a light wood, and the furniture was gray, black or maroon. If you looked up, you saw the exposed heat and air ducts, which were left metal, but the ceiling itself was painted black. They had put in drop lighting, spaced throughout the living and dining area with no covers, but had Edison bulbs and dimmer switches. The bathroom had a double sink, urinal and toilet, shower, and tub.

The bedrooms followed suit in colors, light wood furniture, rugs to be put down later, but all there for them to place.

When Raoul got up the next morning, he knew it would be a busy day. They needed to get the bunks actually put together, arrange everything in its final spot, hook up the appliances, and then pool their monies for a grocery store run. They had decided that was the fairest way to go stock up on basics and then fill in as needed. So Raoul fixed himself and Hawk a breakfast of eggs, bacon, and toast, and they sat out at the picnic table eating breakfast and discussing how well things were going.

"Kind of sad, isn't it?" stated Raoul. "Here we are, actually in a home, working, comfortable, and look at what is going to come down to end it all. Guys in prison on death row have it rough, but they put themselves in that spot by doing wrong. We, on the other hand, did all we could to serve our country and are ending up in a situation like this! Don't get me wrong, Hawk, I am not going to back out of this. It is way too important to so many, not just us, but talk about irony."

Hawk contemplated that for a moment. "Yeah, know what you mean. I haven't had direction in my life in a very long time, and all this does makes me kinda wish things had gone down different, but like you, I am committed fully."

They finished eating and cleaned up the RV, and Ron and Tom came strolling in, both carrying their backpacks. Raoul told them it might be easier to leave those in the RV for now then bring 'em home later, and they agreed. By the time they finished their coffee and discussed the day, the appliance guys showed up. There was a flurry of activity to get all the appliances in place and hooked up, including the TV and stereo.

They also then realized that the bedrooms all had a different theme, so they placed the correct rugs and lamps accordingly, one being beachy, one looking like stuff from a bunkhouse on a ranch, and the third one having a total fifties look.

When they finished, Raoul looked at the other three and, with a big grin, asked if they thought Ben needed to come see it all. They concurred, and he headed in to get him.

Ben walked in and was absolutely speechless. Finally he spoke, "Wow, we are a great team. We all had ideas and suggestions and did this! I could sell my condo and live here very happily. Can't wait to show Mary! She was so excited when I told her what I was doing—the other version, of course. After dinner tonight, I will let her see our work. Don't be surprised if you hear her scream her approval out in the RV."

Raoul and Hawk shared a smirk, and Hawk said, "Scream of approval? Thinking maybe a scream, but for another reason. Do us one favor, though, not the dining room table, please! Let's tell Ron and Tom they need to bunk with us tonight."

"Jeez, guys," Ben retorted with a telltale blush over his face.

BEN SHOWS MARY THE CHANGES

HE HEADED HOME SOON AFTER to clean up and get ready to pick up Mary. They went back to the Italian place this time, where they had become pretty well-known as a couple, and while seated at their table, Ben updated Mary on the progress of the building.

"Ben, what you are doing is so great. I know it won't make the VA process any better, but for those who get to stay there and try to rethink what may help or even be able to look at their skills and find a place to apply them, that is incredible."

"I know. I wish I could do more, but you are right. If a few guys find their paths and life gets better for them, that is what counts. Now, I do have something for you, and before you consider a no, read it over. I really trust you to know what to do with both the gym and the Vets if anything happens to me. We will spend some time together getting you to know my accountant and lawyer as well. And the lawyer has copies of both the will and power of attorney too."

He reached into his pocket and pulled out an envelope that he handed to Mary. She hesitantly took it and looked at Ben with a somewhat baffled expression. "Ben, no family member or perhaps Tyrell would be better suited for this? I… I don't know what to say."

"Mary, I know this seems strange. But having spent time with you, I trust you implicitly. You have good business sense and read people well. All the talks we have had about life make me sure this is the right decision. And I really don't plan on going anywhere soon, okay?"

"Let me mull this over, Ben. I don't want to even think you may disappear out of my life anytime soon, but I get the need to be sure things are okay. And let me also thank you for your vote of confidence on my skills. And while I am thanking you, I also appreciate having you to talk too concerning the hospital issues. You never judge, let me vent, and I feel very supported."

"You are welcome. Now ready to go see if you approve of my building-design skills?"

"I was gonna ask for dessert, but let's go! Can't wait."

Ben drove around back rather than going through the gym, and as he pulled up to the gate, there was a sign attached to it: The Goodmans' Veteran Resort. Mary grinned as she turned to Ben, and he said, "No idea. It wasn't me!"

They proceeded to park and walk into the resort after saying hi to the four at the picnic table. Inside, candles were lit, and there was a bottle of inexpensive champagne on ice, two glasses next to it, and a note that said, "Enjoy your evening."

Mary was wandering the kitchen and living area as Ben popped the cork and poured the champagne. She had opened a few cupboards and drawers in her travels and stated as she took the glass just how impressive this all was.

"A toast, a toast for good things for any and all Vets who stay here," said Ben. Mary seconded the thought. They tapped glasses and drank.

Ben gave her the full tour, and when the reached the bathroom, she laughed out loud. "Guess there won't be any ladies staying here, huh?"

"Well, guess you need to plan the ladies' quarters."

"Seriously, Ben, that may come down the road. You did such a great job here. We may need to collaborate on that next. There is nothing here I don't like."

"I may have had the idea, but those four outside put it together. They actually are the lynchpin for this whole thing and honestly can stay here forever as far as I am concerned."

"Well, then, the only thing I can think of that would end a perfect evening is if we could finish it with breakfast in the morning together."

"Your place or mine?" Ben asked as they walked out and said good-bye to the guys, Mary being sure to compliment them profusely on their work.

PREPARING FOR COMPANY

THE NEXT FEW DAYS WERE spent waiting. Everyone was on hold for the guys from out west to come in. There was some speculation over where the goods would be stored, but what the guys had done when remodeling was to fix a spot that was dead space and would contain the guns and ammo. It was a spot about five by six, so fairly large.

At Ben's request, Raoul had picked up at the local WalMart some folding chairs and a white board and dry-erase markers to have on hand. They had also stocked up on throwaway cells so as not to be obvious and bought a few at a time.

No one missed any appointments at either the VA hospital or the VA admin, all trying to glean any information they could when they went over. However, no one's situation changed. Those that were trying to instate VA benefits still awaited something to happen. When they spoke among themselves though, they reiterated their commitment to the mission. Raoul summed it up perfectly. "Even if they gave me one hundred thousand dollars in back pay and stated I would get my money for life. That wouldn't make it right for everyone, and that is what I would like to see happen." Everyone agreed, and life moved on, awaiting the next phase to begin.

Durham did call Ben and advise him he would come in Saturday and bring his camper to give them more space. Ben advised Raoul that Durham would be dropping by Saturday, and sure enough, at about 11:00 a.m., in rolled Durham. Raoul shut off the mower, showed him where to park it, help with the hookups and opening the extensions, then gave him the grand tour. Raoul told him how he had forgotten how nice it was to not be in a room with twenty or more others, and he was so grateful to everyone for this opportunity. Durham, who had been very fortunate after Iraq and started a consulting firm that netted him a nice chunk of change that allowed him some freedom from worry and the money to have things like this RV, and to know when he retired from the city, he would be very comfortable, said as they all worked together to get things in place, "I do wish this mission weren't even necessary, but we do what we can and pray it does what we want."

As he said that, Ben came out, and they traded handshakes, and Durham congratulated Ben on a job well done. Ben thanked him and again told him to applaud the guys as they had done all the work. He then headed back in, and Durham looked at Raoul and asked, "Do I get a beer?"

Raoul advised him he would go in and grab him one and he could sit and relax at the coffee table. Hawk, Tom, and Ron came in from their various locations and joined them as well. They sat around for a couple of hours, sharing stories and talking about the upcoming mission, when Durham said he needed to let his wife know she could pick him up anytime, explaining she had some shopping to do in the city and should be ready. He pulled out his cell and dialed her, she confirmed the location, and they hung up. He told them he had one-more-beer time and that he would be right back for that. Walking into the gym, he found Ben in his office, told him what was up, then handed him the title to the RV, explaining, "That thing will do you a hell of a lot more good here than growing cobwebs in storage."

"Man, you sure? Thanks so much. Will let you know as soon as I hear from the western contingent. Barbecue then?"

"Looking forward to that. You mentioned fishing too, right?" Durham said as he headed out.

A couple of days later when Raoul's phone rang, he answered, "Hey, Sarge!"

"Hey back at cha. Ready for company? And fish, lotsa fish. You did say there was a place you knew of we could park at, right?"

"Got one saved for you, under the tree! Made sure of the three left you got the prime one," said Raoul.

"Only three left? Out of how many? I really don't want to be stuck in a crowded park, Raoul."

"Sarge, let me tell ya what's up here," and he went on to explain the setup and locale, advising him Ben had done it all by the book, permits and all. Then he explained that even though they referred to the gym as being in DC, it was actually in Reston, Virginia, and provided the address so Sarge could GPS it.

Sarge then asked about fishing close to the gym. "There are places really close," Raoul advised him.

In closing, Sarge said that they would arrive late Wednesday or early Thursday and that it would be great to see each other and hung up. Then Raoul went in to update Ben and waited for the other three to come in from there various pursuits to update them all.

They strolled in separately, all arriving by about five thirty, knowing Raoul would have dinner ready by then. He enjoyed cooking and, when he wasn't there, knew Tom, who had done some short-order cooking, could take over, so meals were not an issue any longer. The one thing they had decided on was to not become invisible to those people who were used to seeing them around town. So they did explain that they had all disappeared for a while helping a friend do some odd jobs, but all kept a presence in the parks and shelters they had always frequented.

Raoul had gone into the gym, and Tyrell was there, so he told him what was going on, and he said he would let Ben know as well as get with everyone else to let them know they should keep an open schedule.

Ben did reach out to Mike and Durham that day once Tyrell told him what was going on, and Mike would then contact Gerald and James and arrange for them to come up.

The next day, Gerald called Mike and advised him they could be there Sunday but needed to be back in Charlotte by the following Saturday. Gerald told Kathy a buddy needed help with a remodel up by DC, and James just told his wife he was taking a break. Kathy did question not seeing Mike and Jean this trip but knew Gerald would be so focused on the remodel he wouldn't even call him. She offered to pack for him, and all was a go. Gerald was sure to call Mike when Kathy was not nearby and filled him in so he would not tell Jean Gerald was in town without Kathy. KISS was the best way to go when fudging a story—always keep it simple, stupid.

WEST MEETS EAST

THURSDAY ROLLED AROUND, AND LATE afternoon, there was a horn heard at the back gate. Raoul looked out, recognized one of the trucks from the meet in Idaho, and went out to open the gate. This time there was an actual camper topper on it, and after introductions and handshakes all around, they set up the camper and hooked up the power and water. Hawk went in to tell Ben that their guests were here. "Great. Once I am done here, I will come out to say hi, please let them know."

He did break away from the gym as soon as he could, the guys already having been given the tour, and after his intro, he advised them that once the gym closed, they could come tour it, and of course, if they all didn't come in as a herd, to please feel free to use the facilities.

Robert spoke up. "Thanks for your hospitality. As a small token of our appreciation, we would like to feed you dinner this evening. Yesterday when we stopped just east of Columbus, we found a spot that had great fishing, and we are on overload with the fish. Was thinking fish fry for all."

"Sounds great. Tyrell and I will have to stagger coming out to eat, and you can find all the beer and booze you need inside as well as hopefully anything else required for the fish."

The rest of the afternoon was spent, as is usual when guys meet, telling the stories and getting acquainted. Then dinner was prepared, and everyone enjoyed, Tyrell and Ben breaking away to taste some of the best fish they had ever had. After dinner, more stories went around, and Sarge really embellished the bear stories that had occurred, making sure Raoul's hackles got raised, and he finally defended himself by saying, "Look, never dealt with bears before, think I did well, and do we not have some business to attend to now that it is dark? Let me show you guys this."

They went inside, and in the hall by the bathroom, Raoul moved a picture and showed them how to slide the seam that moved the whole piece of Sheetrock opening the secret room. They had put in some metal shelving, knowing they couldn't sneak in gun racks very easily. Sarge and the others were impressed. "Not only is this place incredible on its own, but this little goodie... icing on the cake. And there will still be room if you need it."

Tom spoke up next. "Yeah, we all figured extra storage was a good idea. The little box over there has cell phones. We figure closer to time we all should have those in case we need to talk and play it safe. Bought them in pieces at various stores, so no one noticed."

"How many do you have now?" asked Rice.

"Twelve to fifteen right now," was from Tom.

"Sarge, we can grab some heading home too!" stated Robert.

"Good idea. So then we are covered all around on that... Use them for one to two calls and trash them!" said Sarge.

Then the guys went to grab their bags from Robert's truck. As they finished unloading those bags, Tony grinned and flipped open a toolbox that sat in the back of the camper. He then moved something else, and they realized a false bottom hid what rested under the bed of the camper. "Now I know why Sarge's truck was left behind. You think our room is awesome. Well, I think this beats us by far."

Robert then said, "Did you think we forgot why we were here? You all know better, don't cha? We have sixteen .45 cal. tucked away here, six .38s, a shitpot of ammo for all, and thirty grenades. Ammo-wise for each gun, three hundred rounds per person should cover ya. Let me tell you, guys, my gas mileage sucked coming out here. Poor truck was maxed out! Let's fill up that room of yours and call it done for now."

The guns all had a spot on shelves and had been in cases, so everyone knew they all had been safe on the trip. One of each was opened, and everyone got to touch and feel the stock and heft so they could know what they were working with. Ammo was in ammo boxes and the grenades in flak jackets to protect them while traveling.

Robert grinned a bit as he pulled out a large duffel back from another hiding spot in the camper. "A little bonus, guys. Hoping no need for these, but twenty .25 cal. to carry in case of close contact. Just call them back up! And a few tear gas canisters as well. Yes, there are masks too. We talked and figured not being sure how and what this mission may require, we would supply a couple of things that may or may not be necessary as planning occurs."

"Wait 'til everyone sees this. Thank you, guys. This is really gonna happen, isn't it?" said Raoul. "I wondered at first if we could pull it off, but every day, it seems more possible. Let's wrap this up. Got the makings for sandwiches in the fridge if anyone needs a snack."

"Beer?" was asked in unison by all.

"Duh, did you think that would be forgotten?" said Raoul with a chuckle.

One beer later, they were all yawning and decided hitting the rack was the best idea anyone had. Robert was planning to sleep in his camper, and Sarge and Rice would bunk with Ron and Tom and leave the other room for James and Gerald.

Sarge was up first. He just had coffee brewing when Rice joined him. They took their cups out to the picnic table and awaited everyone else. Luckily there was a twelve-cup pot in the kitchen, but also one of the large ones was found in the laundry area, and Sarge was smart enough to know that was the way to go. Forty cups might make it through the morning with seven guys. Or they might need to do it all again. Everyone was awake, and Ben had dropped off donuts, bagels, and other pastries before Raoul finally rolled out.

"Raoul, I see all that beauty sleep just isn't working for you, sorry," said Sarge.

"Nope, you haven't gotten any prettier since you left Idaho," added Rice.

"And good morning to you all too. Thanks for the warm welcome," said Raoul, going in to get his coffee. Walking back out, he asked, "Is this the designated pick-on-Raoul day?"

In unison, the response was "Yup," and everyone laughed and finished their coffee and breakfast.

The rest of the morning was spent learning where things were, laundry being caught up, grounds being patrolled by campers, and RVs being straightened up. By lunch, everyone was done, and Ben and Tyrell came out to join the guys for sandwiches and potato and macaroni salad Raoul and Ron had made earlier. When they went in to see the storage room, both were in awe. Neither had realized the amount of stuff the guys from Idaho were bringing. They headed back into the gym to finish their day, and the guys settled to watch some TV and chill. Football season was getting ready to start, so they decided to catch up on the NFL channels season's highlights from last year and got into a discussion over who would win this year's Super Bowl.

Sarge emphatically declared the Broncos would get rings this year, and Robert informed him that even if they made it to the game, Seattle would kick their butts.

"No way, Jose!" responded Sarge.

"Not enough horsepower to pull it off, Sarge. Wait and see."

"Well, when Denver wins, we will have Seahawk Stew and Coors for the victory dinner."

"Thinking a slightly different menu in the cards, Sarge. We shall see!"

A few of the others considered chiming in but were enjoying watching the show so just let it go on. When they finished catching up on last season's games, dinner was barbecue hamburgers, and all settled in for the evening.

As things were winding down, Ben popped in to let everyone know the gym was theirs for the duration as was the cafe. "Should anyone question any of you, we are working on the rest of the plans for the assistance program we are setting up for Vets! And if we can all meet here Wednesday at two p.m., that would be great! I think our cover is secure with the nonprofit line we can use for questions from anyone."

FIRST OFFICIAL MEETING

It was 2:00 p.m. on Wednesday, and everyone was there. Ben had become the unofficial official leader, so when everyone fell into rank, he chuckled and started the roll call.

"Tom."

"Here, sir."

"Ron."

"Here, sir."

"Hawk."

"Here, sir."

"Sarge."

"Here, sir."

"Raoul."

"Here, sir."

"Rice."

"Here, sir."

"Robert."

"Here, sir."

"Tyrell."

"Here, sir."

"Mike."

"Here, sir."

"Durham."

"Yup! Sorry, couldn't resist!"

It made everyone laugh, while Gerald and Becker tried to keep a straight face, also with a "Here, sir" once the laughter subsided.

"I know we have spent some time together before this, but I think we need one last gathering not for the mission per se but to be sure we all can get along and are in this for the duration. I hope you all agree with me 'cause I closed down the gym at two p.m. when I headed out here, and we are going to eat, drink, and be merry tonight. We can pretend we are celebrating a birthday, retirement, and whatever else to make it all happen. So let it rip, you guys with wives. If you have not already done so, time to either call 'em and give an excuse now or plan for what you are gonna tell them tomorrow."

With a loud cheer from everyone, they settled in for some serious food and drinking. Everyone was amazed at how much they all meshed like a perfect pair of shoes or that tight-fit glove that just felt right. At one point, the different branches of the military deemed it necessary to have a wrestling match and to determine which branch was the strongest; however, no one knew or cared who won when the matches were over.

By the time everyone was ready for some serious drinking, it was getting late, and as men were prone to do, military or non, someone suggested a drinking contest, probably to end the evening! Sarge said, "Not that beer pong crap, right? We just chug 'em like real men 'til no one's left standing!"

Ben, with a chuckle, stated, "If we were doing side bets on who would survive, I would win it all from you guys, but hey, let's go!"

Raoul knew he couldn't take part in this. He had had his two beers but also knew watching this could be an absolute blast, so he did get out his camera, and videoed some of the antics as they progressed, and he already had footage of the wrestling, which he advised everyone could potentially be used for blackmail later.

At about 8:00 a.m. on Thursday morning, when the area looked like a war zone, with bodies strewn all over and debris cluttering the area, Becker awoke to see Hawk sitting on a picnic table, doing what was probably his hundredth rendition of ninety-nine bottles of beer on the wall and clutching what should have been the last bottle of Jack to him.

"Are you kidding me? Shut up now and hit your rack," said Becker.

Hawk tried a salute, failed miserably, stopped singing, chugged the rest of the JD, and fell off the table into the grass, snoring within twenty seconds.

Becker went looking for coffee, finding it in the house. Raoul had gotten some sleep and made the big pot so that as people came back to life, coffee would be available. There was also some food left from the day prior, and that was available for those who wanted any breakfast.

Hangovers do kinda quiet you down, so today was again learning about one another, taking stock of yourself and others, and being sure that everyone was on the right track and in this 'til the end. Even though the discussion was not had at this time, everyone knew this was the time that you had to decide—in or out.

By the time Hawk surfaced at about 5:00 p.m., the others had cleaned up the yard debris and pretty much had the area looking like a yard again. Hawk went inside, did find one more bottle of Jack, hit it for one swig, then went to the coffee pot.

Becker walked up to him and stated, "I have never seen anyone pass out that quickly. It was like the switch was turned and away you went!"

Hawk's response was, "Sorry, I don't pass out. That was sleep mode, pure and simple. Gotta be drunk to pass out, my friend, and I was just tired!"

"Yeah, right!" Becker said with a laugh as he refilled his coffee.

Ben and Tyrell had been in and out all day, going back and forth to the gym, and by about six thirty knew they needed to finish the day working, so they headed back inside, thanking everyone for coming and being sure they all were on board to be back Saturday at twelve to start officially planning Operation Dirtbag, the name that surfaced while drinking and somehow stuck. They had actually mentioned a few other potential mission names: You're Gone with the Wind, Kiss your Tush Good-Bye, and Embezzlement Gone Bad. After some discussion, some of which was rational, *dirtbag* won!

FIRST OFFICIAL PLANNING SESSION

COFFEE WAS READY AND DONUTS were on the table by noon on Saturday when everyone rolled in. Hellos, backslaps, and handshakes were all around as everyone settled in and grabbed coffee and treats.

Ben began by asking whom everyone felt should conduct the meeting from this point forward. It was decided a vote was in order, and they asked for names of whom everyone would recommend. After a few moments of silence, Robert offered Sarge's name, followed by Mike, who offered up Ben. Prior to any voting on the spot, it was determined what the conductor's job was to be.

As a group, they decided the following:

1. The conductor couldn't make decisions. All decisions made were by the whole group.
2. Conduct, not lead. Job was to be sure all were heard and considered.
3. Keep notes and keep track of things.

Much as they all hated to admit it, no one would be able to remember all the finer points discussed, and someone needed to be able to keep track of everything. The reason that it would be one and the same person, i.e., conductor and secretary, would be based on the less hands in the pot theory and having only one person maintaining control.

At the end of this discussion, the vote was done by ballot. Everyone was handed a slip of paper, and Ben won, hands down. After the vote and tally, Sarge spoke up. "Thanks, you all. I really didn't want that job. First of all, I can't write for shit. Second, not organized enough."

They all chuckled, and Ben then stated, "Well, I do have a solution to the penmanship issue, 'cause mine sucks too. I will be right back."

And when he walked back in, he had a small pocket recorder, stating, "Between meetings, this can also go in the secret room. I use them a lot at the gym to make notes and remind me of things, so… shall we get started?"

There was a bit of clapping, and Hawk gave a loud wolf whistle and followed with, "We got us a leader. Let's get ready to rumble!"

"Remember, Hawk, I am not your leader. All decisions are made by the group in total. Something else weighing heavy on my mind as well as probably a lot of yours is this: is this a suicide mission? Personally, I am hoping not. We may all go to jail or not get out of that building at all, but based on the two-man-team concept per floor we have discussed, I am in hopes that everyone manages to escape and disappear quickly. As we fine-tune the mission, hopefully we will find other contact points and ways to know what is what when all is said and done. Questions, concerns about this at this time?"

Everyone thought for a few moments, and finally Ron spoke up. "I am good at present with what you just said, Ben. It does make sense, so unless anyone else has anything to say about this, what is next?"

Ben replied, "We have had some guys inside the VA office, and I think they can provide some really good intel. Let's see who has what info, and here are pads and pens for notes and questions for you all to wrote down as needed. Can we let whoever is speaking finish before we ask questions? I think you will all agree this is the hardest thing we have done in our lives, and we need to focus and allow everyone the best chance to make this mission successful."

Again, handclapping and cheering. They knew, to a man, the seriousness of this mission, and the commitment level showed, each and every one knowing what this would require, a 110 percent buy in, and damn the personal consequences.

Raoul spoke up then. "Would you like me to start?"

All nodded respectfully, knowing this was a beginning.

"I have spent a lot of time at that place, and not much of it for fun. However, I have made friends with one of the guards, Randy, who you all may remember that attended Mary's barbecue. He really isn't a fit for this mission, believe me, it crossed my mind, but he has been unknowingly helpful. So I can stop by occasionally without an appointment to see Randy, and last time I did that, I took him to lunch in their cafeteria as payment for his dinner he had me over too. As we sat at lunch, I was able to question him. I had noticed cameras at the main entrance and at each end of each hallway. There was also one of those ball-like ones you see in department stores hanging down from the center of the cafeteria ceiling. I have been in quite a few of the offices for one meeting about my bennies or another and had never seen a camera in them, but they do have them in the elevators."

As he stopped to take a drink of coffee and a breath, Ron must have thought he was finished and spoke up, "So it appears there is no way we would not be on film and, if lucky enough, to escape all over *CNN*, *Fox*, and whoever else shows up, right?"

"Right, in theory, but there is a room that contains all the equipment for the system, and we just need to be sure that that is taken down first."

Again, a pause, and this time Sarge questioned, "This room? Does it have easy access, or like Fort Knox, and do we know where it is?"

At this point, it crossed Ben's mind to remind them of the "wait 'til the speaker finishes" rule, but he realized they were finding their own rhythm and gathering the correct info, so he sat back and waited.

"Let me tell you about this room. High-tech security... not so much. As you walk into the facility, as you all know, the guard station is first. You pass through that, and if you look off to your right, there is a door, ironically an unmarked door. I see heads nodding. You all get it, huh? Main question now is, is it locked? Well, no, it is not. Apparently that is the place the guards go when they don't feel like sitting in the cafeteria for a meal or are just bored and want to see if there is any action on any cameras. One guy does monitor regularly, and then there are the variables. Usually no more than three at the most hang in there together. Randy took me in there. The room is about twelve by twelve. There are computers set up on two sides, four total, with each having split screens and dual monitors. When I showed surprise that the room wasn't secured, Randy chuckled, saying, 'Think a minute. We at the guard station are watching. What do you think would happen if someone attempted to open that door?' Comments, questions, points I may have forgot to make?"

Tyrell said, "I know you have been through more of the building than the rest of us. Have you noticed any other break areas or spots where guards may congregate?"

"Thanks for that question. In areas I have been, no other designated break areas. I did ask Randy, 'cause it seemed odd that there wouldn't be a couple areas, and he said nope, technically just the cafeteria. And that brings up the other thing that I do know. There is a guard assigned on each floor to walk the floor and monitor movement and things, only one, however, per floor. So if you go onto a floor and see no guard, he could be in the restroom or hiding out in an empty office. That is definitely one of the variables we need to be careful of."

Tom replied, "If necessary, Raoul, as you stated, Randy is not with us. Could you take him out, friend or no?"

After a moment's thought, Raoul responded, "Without hesitation, our mission is what is the most important."

Durham then said, "I am thinking we need to really review our plans for starting this. Being an office building, we need to start as quiet as possible, perhaps having knives and guns with silencers to allow us time. Think about it, if we go in blasting, people will have time to react or run, causing chaos way too soon. We need to at least shut down the security room and main guard station before anyone catches on to have a chance."

Tyrell stated, "Good points. I may be able to get ahold of one or two guns with silencers and knives. I have a few old Ka-Bars I have collected from yard sales, etc., 'cause I thought they were cool. Never thought they would come in handy, but let me look and tell you how many I have. I do keep them in good shape, will tell you that now, so they will be useful."

Hawk interjected, "I can get guns with silencers. I have friends in low places. Let me talk to them and get an idea of prices and let you all know. Also, when I go to the VA, I take the stairs. Elevators creep me out. I can draw up where the cameras are I noticed, and if it seems all floors are standard for set up, can add the ones you guys know about so we all are aware of the set up. Before you all rag on me, when I was in junior high, I wanted to be an architect, so yes, I can draw."

Mike chimed in next, "Walking hallways three times I have been there, I took note of where the cameras were as well. I peeked in some offices acting like I was looking for someone, and no one seemed concerned when I did so. A few people in the hallways did ask if I needed help but took my 'No thanks' response and walked away. It seems some of the rooms are set up differently than others, with some having waiting areas and then another internal space, apparently for the person to whom that office belongs. Some are actual conference space, and some are just offices with a desk and a couple of chairs or file cabinets. I really don't think there is a method to the office space, so as we go on, we will need to check each room on each floor.!"

Ron asked, "Was it obvious where the Vets would sit versus where the VA employee would be?"

"Oh yeah. The rooms that had the chairs on one side would also have the computer facing where the employee would be. Plus, as you all know, if you work at the VA, you have to wear a badge, kinda like this one," and he threw a woman's badge on the table.

Ben gasped and asked, "You got this how?"

"Well, I opened the door to one office. No one was there. So I said hello just in case anyone was nearby who saw me. Looking around, no one was down the hall, but the camera at the hall end was obvious, and not knowing if it recorded sound, I said, 'Let me leave a note letting you know I did stop in as promised' and walked in. Marsha had left her purse on her desk, with that badge attached to the strap."

"Crazy move, Mike, but love the guts. Please tell me you did not look right at that camera, and we are good. Now, pass that badge around so we all know up close and personal what they look like. Enough for today, all? Hawk, I will see to it you get drafting paper and pencils. I think there is a pot of spaghetti sitting in the kitchen for lunch and perhaps some garlic bread too if we are lucky. Let's all try to become more familiar with the building and even perhaps try to find out who is who before the big day. Memorize faces when you can, but remember, we do not need to be so visible that we are questioned about why we are there."

All enjoyed the food and talked a bit more about plans. Prior to everyone leaving, Ben asked if they all liked to fish. The resounding yesses brought a smile to his face, him saying, "Thursday, seven a.m. departure? I have a buddy with a twenty-eight footer, and I think we could catch some killer dinner. All in? Followed up by camping one night at the state park, with dinner included."

And it was agreed. It was decided that those in the area could come by the night before and be ready at 7:00 a.m. rather than fighting traffic, and of course those on sight would be ready. Wednesday, everyone was at the compound, as they all lovingly referred to the area in back of the gym, and had settled in by 10:00 p.m., knowing morning came early.

FISHING EXPEDITION

THE NEXT MORNING, WITH BEN, Mike, and Durham as drivers, they were ready to roll by 7:00 a.m. It took about an hour allowing for traffic to get to the marina just outside Woodbridge, and by 8:45 a.m., they were on the water.

They headed down the Potomac, and the captain came over the PA system, announcing, "It will take about three hours to get to the open waters of Chesapeake Bay. Continental breakfast is now being served, and around twelve we will have a light lunch with cold-cut sandwiches, tea, and soda available."

During the pause, the captain heard grumbling—he didn't mention beer! He finally came back on and said, "At about one p.m., we are out far enough that the fishing should be good, and there will be some coolers found lying around that I think have some beer in them." Amid the applause and happy screams and whistles, he added, "Please enjoy the ride, enjoy the view. I will keep you posted as to our progress, and Jimmy, my first mate, will tell you where the john is and life jackets. Oh, and one last request. Should you get seasick, please do so over the side of the boat. Makes it easier to clean up later. This is Captain Long John Silver, and knowing who you all are, let me thank you for your service."

As they cruised the Potomac, they all enjoyed the history and having the captain point out things of interest. A couple played craps, and one group set up a card game, using olives and peanuts to bet with.

Once they got out on the open water and popped their beers, it was only about 4:00 p.m., and the coolers were full. Someone was overheard stating they didn't realize one could catch that many fish in about three hours, and Sarge responded with, "Done it alone in one-half that time! If they are biting well, oh yeah, entirely possible."

"And on that note," chimed in the captain, "let's head over to Kiptopeke State Park. Tents are set up, the New England boiled dinner should be about ready to go in the pot, and we can clean our fish and have fried fish with that for dinner."

Hawk looked puzzled, asking, "What in hell is a New England boiled dinner? You boiling Natives?"

Tyrell looked at him and, as seriously as he could, responded, "Yup, three to a pot with Old Bay seasoning and lotsa hot sauce, 'cause the older New Englanders are tough, especially if you get 'em down from Maine or Vermont, but the seasoning makes up for it."

Captain John interjected, "Okay, give him a break. For Hawk and those who haven't had the experience, it is clams, shrimp, oysters, and/or lobster, sometimes all four, others times whatever is available, with potatoes and corn on the cob, boiled together."

A few had kind of shocked looks on their faces, trying to envision this conglomeration as an edible dish, but everyone determined they had to at least give it a shot.

Once they docked, everyone helped unload the boat, and Sarge and a couple others helped clean the fish. The smell of the dinner and fish being fried had everyone drooling, and by six thirty, everyone settled in to eat themselves pretty much into oblivion. Universally, they decided that the New England dinner was a hit and would definitely be eaten again if given the chance. Settling in after dinner around the campfire, the captain handed out cigars, and they listened to the waves and told some great fish stories, everyone avoiding military history. No one said it out loud, but they all knew from this point forward, every meeting they had had to focus on Operation Dirtbag, so this was going to be enjoyed and immortalized by all.

When they awoke the next morning, it was perfect weather. Hawk was sitting staring over the water as others came to life, and when asked how long he had been up, he stated, "It was still dark, but quiet and peaceful."

They left him to enjoy his solitude, sensing this was rare for him, to actually have that peace, and helped load the boat for the ride home. When all was in place, Ben called Hawk. "Hey, time to ride some more waves. You ready?"

"Can't I just make this my home?"

"You think it's cold in the city in the winter? Try a breeze off that water and no heater in sight."

With a really big sigh, Hawk got up off his log and headed for the boat. "Okay, you win."

Once on board, continental breakfast was served, and they all settled in for the ride. They stopped for fuel at Bay View and followed the coast, fishing sporadically and discussing what they had seen and tasted, oh yeah, and caught! At Harborton, the captain changed course, turning northwest across the bay back to the mouth of the Potomac, then eventually backing into the marina.

With many thanks to both the captain and first mate, Jimmy, everyone was finally ready to head back to their respective homes. Back at the gym, after securing the supplies and determining how much fish needed to be left out for the going-away party on Saturday, everyone went to take showers and prep for trips home. Gerald and James needed to head back to North Carolina on Sunday, and Sarge, Rice, and Robert figured they would head out on Monday. Rice advised the others that he had checked the news and snow was already hitting the higher peaks. Sarge then said, "And I have to drop you yahoos off then drive my butt home, so yeah, guess we should head out then."

So Friday evening was cleaning clothes and vehicles, packing loading, and getting some rest. On Saturday, there was some discussion over coffee about not only the great fishing trip but also firming up the plans for the meets in January to finalize the mission. It was determined they would meet in mid-January and stay together 'til it was done. That evening, fish was fried, beer was drank, in moderation, of course, and good-byes were said.

Sunday morning, everyone was up by 7:00 a.m. (amazing how early you arise when not hungover), and Raoul and the others had coffee ready and did offer breakfast, which was declined by James and Gerald but accepted by the others. By 9:00 a.m., with thermoses filled with fresh coffee, the two headed out for Charlotte.

Sarge and the other two spent the day checking out the truck for the long drive home, doing an oil change, and checking the antifreeze levels as well as the tire pressure and all else they could think of to be sure all was well for the drive. They then spent a little time in the gym, using the pool and sauna, enjoying the moderate temps. Dinner was served at about six, with Tyrell and Ben joining them, and bed by ten so they could head out by 6:00 a.m. Again, on Monday morning, breakfast was offered, and this time was accepted. At 4:00 a.m., it was amazing to see everyone there to see them off. Even Ron and Tom staggered out for coffee and good-byes.

As they all headed out to see the three off, Sarge smiled a sly smile at Rice and Robert and winked. He then threw back his head and opened his mouth, "On the road again, just."

At which point Raoul looked over and let loose a howl, followed up with, "Good luck, you two. You did notice he can't carry a tune in a bucket, right?"

Robert responded, "Holy crap! This is a new development. If he tries it again, we will truly take his keys and throw his butt out of the truck. Trust me on that!"

HOME AGAIN (FOR A WHILE)

They did take their time going back. Fishing was always good in the fall, and they had the camper with heater if the nights got chilly. They did have a few discussions concerning the operation, but it only reaffirmed their commitment to it.

Once they got to Cascade, Sarge did spend a few days with the guys before heading back to Cañon City. While he knew all was well taken care of regardless of how long he stayed away, he needed his fix—his home, land, animals, and fishing and hunting spots as well as family time with his brother and wife. He did periodically think over his next DC trip and checked in with Raoul no more or less then he had before. The one thing that made him happy at this point was seeing how content Raoul was having a home and being settled for a while.

Ron and Rice spent their time fishing and hunting as well, also hanging at their favorite watering hole at times. They would also see the Militia group now and again and came to realize two of the guys (who helped set up the initial weapons drop) were interested in the DC plan, asking really good questions and making Ron and Rice wonder if more bodies would be beneficial to the mission. And also wondering if they might be wanting to flip and turn them in for some odd reason. Ron finally said at one point when they were speculating, "I don't think that is even a concern. I really believe it is concern for our mission and being curious as to how and how well we do this. Remember, these guys are mostly military and/or have a military connection, and I feel they may also want to see a change for the better for the Vets regardless of the loss to the VA."

Rice thought that over and responded with, "Good points, and of course, we can potentially pick their brains for more info. Also, I think after what you just said, if we needed help, or more stuff, they would be willing to contribute." And winter rolled in.

Rice did mention Isaiah and Wane to Ben, who did contact them periodically, and they had quite a few conversations about the mission. It seemed Isaiah's dad had been in Nam and did end up committing suicide, and Jon had been in service also, and they were more than willing to provide additional bodies as well as arms. Ben and the two of them had a few things up their sleeves that they decided to keep quiet about until the time was right. On one of the last calls on the throwaway phones they were currently using, Ben said, "I may get my butt in a whirlwind, after all the talks about any decision being made by all, but with you two, I think the surprise element could be a bit more fun. And yes, I know that really sounds strange with this mission, but I will take the heat if it comes down. Guys, I appreciate you and all you are doing. Now throw away that damn phone!"

PLANS MADE IN DC

BACK IN DC, BEN AND Tyrell were keeping the gym running smooth and monitoring the guys at the resort. Ben was seeing Mary, but they had decided not to move in together, both loving their times together but also enjoying time alone. Mary summed it up perfectly one evening, stating, "I think with us, because we deal with people all day, every day we both need to decompress, and part of that process is solitude. If you can enjoy time alone, you are never truly lonely."

Ben mulled that over and said, "You know, you are so right. I think that is one more reason I love you and love being with you."

Raoul, Hawk, Tom, and Ron kept things on an even keel at the resort, taking turns cooking and keeping the grounds and property neat and clean (and being winter, shoveled, even doing the front walk area of the gym). They did head into DC for appointments at the VA or to check in at the shelters and keep up appearances, not forgetting to find the Vets who really needed a break from street life and offering them a short stay at the resort. They soon realized that quite often, being in a new locale without the pressures of being on the street or in a shelter changed drastically the attitudes of many, and most Vets ended up gainfully employed or getting their benefits soon after moving in.

Hawk commented, "Maybe if we didn't have plans, things would flip for us too."

Tom looked seriously at him and stated, "But this is such a small percentage of Veterans in crisis. You aren't thinkin' about droppin' out, are you? We need to take and make that stand, Hawk."

"Nope, ain't losing me! This is for all, not just the handful that come through here. Sorry if I sounded otherwise, but I do hope we have the effect we are wanting and no Vet ever is out on the street or feels suicide is the only out."

This conversation was had while all four were sitting together at the table, alone in the house, and as Hawk quit talking, everyone's hands went up for multiple high fives, and a quiet "Amen" was heard mouthed by all.

Raoul did still go to Randy's for the occasional dinner or would meet him for lunch at the VA office. Raoul had given up trying to speak to someone about his benefits, realizing that they truly did not care and that it truly did not matter, because once the attack took place, he would probably be either in prison or six feet under, and the VA money would no longer be a concern. But those trips to the VA gave him more opportunity to check out more of the building. It really wasn't hard to just go around and check things out. One security guard per floor left a lot of unpatrolled space!

And Randy was seeing someone. That made things a bit awkward, as she also worked at the VA. While she seemed nice, Raoul saw a bit of a bossy person, and that helped him decide that no more mention of the attack would ever cross his lips to Randy.

Hawk had spent a lot of time on the drawings of the floor layout. He would periodically question Raoul on what he remembered in certain areas and felt he had a good grasp on the major layout and location of security cameras, stairwells, exits, etc. It was a feeling of satisfaction that he could do this, hopefully to help all go very smooth when the time was right.

The decision had been made that they needed a full month together to formulate and finish the plans and be sure they had everything necessary.

Tyrell had surprised Ben and the four in the compound by bringing in knives, fifteen Ka-Bars, and ten miscellaneous switchblade and others. With a sheepish grin, he admitted to Ben, "I have more, but it seemed this would be a good mix for people to choose what they are more comfortable with. And these are nontraceable. They came from yard sales, flea markets, places like that."

Tom looked them over. "I don't think I have ever seen knives sharpened this well. Sure they are not brand-new?"

Tyrell grinned and retorted, "Good, aren't I?"

And into the secret room they went.

Hawk had had a few powwows with Ben, and some other ammo boxes and wrapped items had also shown up in the room, everyone assuming that was the batch of guns with silencers, but no one asked, knowing full good and well all would be revealed at the appropriate time.

GATHERING OF THE CLAN

So WHEN JANUARY 14 ROLLED in, Ben asked Raoul if he wanted to ride to the airport. Sarge was the first to arrive, and as they rode back to the gym, he commented on the cold, amazed that in a city, it could feel worse than out on the open plain. Ben laughed and advised him he had apparently never been to Chicago in the winter, 'cause that place would make Siberia feel warm when the wind whipped off the lake. The only response to that was, "No thanks!"

When they got back to the resort, Hawk, Tom, and Ron had a light lunch ready, and they all said their hellos and updated one another just on the general stuff. Sarge told them that his brother and wife pretty much kicked him out when he told them he would be gone for about a month to help a friend back east with a new business. He closed with, "They actually told me that I could stay 'til spring thaw if I wanted too."

"Interesting," responded Ben. "Now before I head back inside, a favor, if I may. Do you feel you know your way to the airport when the others fly in? None of the guys here drive, and I can't be leaving the gym all the time, or things would look odd."

"Not a problem! GPS is a wonderful thing if I think I am off course."

"Great, let me go in and see how things are. Raoul and the others can catch you up for now while you settle in."

And they did just that. Raoul advised Sarge that while he spent his days in the building if not out and about, at night he went back to the camper. Hawk also was sleeping out there, and because they periodically had Vets staying temporarily, it left one room always open, plus the couch was a hide-a-bed. So that meant Sarge would be sharing a room with someone and they would actually have a full house once everyone came in.

As Mary did know about the boarding facilities, Ben had told her that even though the timing kinda sucked, he couldn't room anybody from mid-January through the end of February. She knew he had friends coming in but thought it was a deal where different people would be in at different times, not questioning the whole situation. So she would not be offering space to anyone she might have normally done so for.

Sarge settled in. The guys updated him on things. He was favorably impressed by Hawk's drawings, stating, "Nice, it really gives those of us who couldn't spend as much time there a great sense of where everything is. Those drafting skills really paid off. I for one thank you... a lot!"

Hawk, who was not used to compliments, blushed, smiled, and responded with a very subdued "Thank you."

The other thing that impressed him were the knives. He knew the age of the Ka-Bars and was shocked that Tyrell had so many in such excellent shape. With a shrug, Tom stated, "I really think that man has a fetish about knives, but he really contributed to the cause, so let him have it!"

Until the other two came in on the eighteenth, it was pretty much hanging out. Raoul and Sarge went into the VA one day to have lunch with Randy, Raoul stating that it was time his two buds met up. He knew that would give Sarge a bit more intel on the area, and he got to see the monitor room as well, because the day they went in was a very busy day and the cafeteria was packed, so Randy offered the quiet place, and of course, they took advantage of that time to recheck details on the computers, monitors, and setup of it all.

The eighteenth rolled around, and Rice and Robert arrived. The group determined that they needed to spend a bit more time at the VA, and as the guards never asked for proof of why someone was there, they determined that those that had not been in would go at least once and, if no further, at least hit up the cafeteria area. That and Hawk's drawings, as well as everyone's notes and feedback, should help everyone feel more comfortable when the day came!

One night they all met at the VFW, including the locals. Everyone was happy to update one another on the general stuff, day-to-day details, but no mention of course of anything related to the mission. Knowing the guys from Charlotte would be flying in, they had also planned to do a dinner that night at the VFW before knuckling down to business. So when Sarge met James and Gerald at the airport midafternoon the twenty-fifth, they immediately headed over to join the others.

Amid hellos, handshakes, and backslaps, everyone got reacquainted and updated, but as before at this point, only on the day-to-day usual stuff, like weather, jobs, etc. They all knew the nuts and bolts info would come soon enough, and while anxious to begin, this was not the time nor place. After food and a few beers, it was determined by all that they needed to move on, and the unspoken spot to move to was the resort. Ben quietly recommended those that had cars to park in unobtrusive locations so it was not apparent that many people were back there, and amid groans (because the local guys knew that meant a walk to get in, especially going in the back way), they headed out.

By the time they all met up back at the property, it was about 7:00 p.m. Ben sent Tyrell out, who reminded everyone to have a reason for being there if needed. "The four that are always here, everyone is so used to. They are part of the landscape, and I really doubt anyone will realize others were here before, but just in case you guys could either be waiting for a ticket home or a shelter to open in town, just be prepared. Also, no ordering of food. That could look suspicious. Make sure too that if you need a grocery run, it is not a full stock up. There should actually be enough here to last twice as many people three months or more."

On the calendar in the kitchen was a note penciled in for the twenty-sixth, saying, "House meeting, 6:00 p.m." Everyone got it and settled in to continue their evening. Raoul and Hawk updated them on the knives and drawings, and they did all peak at the other items in the secret room, feeling better that the guns and silencers were in place. Everyone departed by about 10:00 p.m. knowing that tomorrow and the times thereafter would be busy and they all needed to be fully prepared to go forward with the plan.

The next evening, the guys from around the city were all in place by the 6:00 p.m. start time. Mike complained he had to park six blocks away, and Durham laughed, explaining to everyone that he did manage to score the last parking spot on the street within a two-block area and that he had waved cheerfully at Mike as Mike flipped him off and drove away to his final parking spot.

SERIOUS PLANNING BEGINS

LASAGNA WAS PULLED FROM THE oven, along with loaves of garlic bread. The smell alone let everyone know that the food was edible and the guys admitted it was a true joint effort, everyone remembering different things that had to go in the sauce and sending Sarge to the store for ricotta cheese to finish the dish. Once everyone was finished, the table was cleared, and everyone settled in for the scheduled house meeting.

"Grab a drink, all, and I pulled the notebooks we all have out of the room. Get yours and grab a pen. Also before this, I made a copy for everyone of the drawings Hawk did, and I think those will help us as we go forth. Thanks again, Hawk, great job! Now, tell me if you all agree, those of you who have not been around should probably do at least one last pass through the VA and also recon the outside areas as well. Agree?"

There was a chorus of yesses, and Ben spoke again, "I want you all to know how appreciative I am of everyone here. I have spoken to all of you as a one-off prior to this meeting, and based on the info you have given, here is my initial thought for the mission. Again, feedback and thoughts welcome. Thinking five two-man teams with one three-man. The three-man will take out the guards and destroy the monitor room, effectively killing the cameras as well as everyone there. Cafeteria next and any offices on the ground floor. While that team is cleaning out the ground floor, everyone else should be headed for their respective floor. They can of course take the elevator for sake of speed and wait 'til time to attack. But be sure you all either take separate elevators or not be an obvious pack. Some will carry backpacks, and some will not to be less obvious.

"The three from ground floor will then hit the stairwell and prevent anyone from going up or down. You will have the guns with silencers, knife of choice, be picking those out later, and grenades to hopefully save for SWAT or use earlier if really necessary. We do need to synchronize our attack, so we all begin at exactly the same time. Once we know morning routines, i.e., are the guards in place at exactly eight, or is it eight ten, we will be able to coordinate that time frame."

Ron questioned the need to hit all floors, starting at the same time. "Is that really necessary?"

"Once the guns start going off, you can't be sure it won't be heard on the other floors. If we hit them simultaneously, there should be no chance for the guards on those floors to react. And if there is a lockdown procedure, hopefully we can negate that going into play."

"And what if a door is shut and locked?" asked Rice.

"Well, I think the C4 with primer and fuse should fix that. Just remember your Bic!" Ben came back with.

Rice, with a smile, said, "Hiding any other toys, Boss?"

"Depends on your definition of toys, I guess. How about two M79 grenade launchers and a .50 cal. machine gun?"

There was a whistle heard from Sarge, and Tom spoke up, "So we found John Wayne and the Calvary before we even attack? Guess that is the answer to how we get that .50 cal. inside. Never mind the fact, never seen anything of that size used for indoor combat. Bring it on, John!"

Everyone roared, and Ben finally gathered his composure enough to say, "You are absolutely right, John Wayne will have control of that .50 cal., but also right, that cannot be used inside. Hang tight, details will follow at our next gathering in a week. I would like two volunteers to head over to the building early a.m. to scope out schedules as we had discussed earlier."

Durham advised he needed to be in the area one morning and it would be no problem to head in early and review the situation, and Tyrell said he could also do so. At this point, they all took one of the throwaway phones from the stash, still leaving about thirty in the room for future use.

They also discussed for the next meeting determining who would team up with whom and what floor they would take, knowing they would make the final decisions at that next planning session.

Sarge then asked, "So dinner at six again followed by house meeting?" Wink, wink. "And I volunteer to make some chili."

AFTER-MEETING MEETING

AND ON THAT NOTE, THOSE who had homes to head for did so, while those staying cracked one last beer and cleaned up the dinner dishes and put away the notebooks before heading to bed. However, as Ben headed out the door, he pulled Sarge aside. "Favor to ask, please. Would you go pick up one of those ten-foot-by-twenty-foot closed-in canvas garages tomorrow?"

"The ones with PVC framework, right? And what should I do with this once I get it?"

"You know what I am wanting. Yup, that kind. We need it to set up before we get together next time. Here is a map of the area we are in, and you can see I penciled in the corner it goes in."

"Got a hunch if I ask you what it is for, you will blow sunshine up my patootie, but I gotta try, maybe even just a hint?"

With a grin, Ben responded, "Nope, no clues. If anyone asks, storage is the answer. Sometimes Vets do have stuff that needs to go somewhere while they try to get back together, and this may be necessary. Of course, even if a vehicle shows up, in this weather we would want to protect it till the Vet can use it again, right?"

"Ah, think I see the light, and that vehicle needs its own space, doesn't it?"

"Just remember, don't touch, don't tell. What you don't know can't bite you! This one is on the QT from everyone right now, 'cause if it goes south, only I am implicated, and you guys can still proceed."

Mike walked out to have a smoke before bed and questioned the two, "You guys don't smoke. What's up?"

"Nothing, Sarge actually had a question about the gym. He noticed the lighting out front seemed brighter and better, and I was explaining the new halogens we put in."

And with that, they did all depart for their respective beds.

SETTING UP A GARAGE

THE NEXT DAY, SARGE HEADED for the store, got the garage, and came back to start setting it up. As he was laying out the pipes to get a feel for how it would go together, Raoul came out and questioned him on the build.

Sarge stuck to the story that Ben put forth last night, potential van, no touch, etc. Raoul thought that over then said, "Interesting. Aren't four hands better than two?" And they were, and it went up fairly quick, with only a few expletives expanded.

ADDITIONAL MEMBERS
(AND FIREPOWER, MORE FIREPOWER)

THE MEETING BEGAN AFTER THE chili was inhaled by all. Gerald actually belched, apologized profusely, and said, "You could can that and sell it!" The rest of the guys agreed. Then it was time to get down to business.

Ben started by asking if everyone knew who they wanted to partner up with and said that he and Tyrell would go on the fifth floor.

Ron stated, "Good idea. You guys work out the most, so you should have to head up first to the highest floor."

Mike claimed Gerald and the fourth floor, to which Gerald nodded approval. Durham stated Becker and third floor. Rice advised he and Robert would take the second floor. Sarge and Raoul chimed in almost simultaneously, claiming each other and the first floor.

As everyone looked questioningly at Hawk, Ron, and Tom, Hawk spoke up saying, "I think you know we have all discussed within ourselves where and what we wanted to handle when the time comes. Let me say we three want to go in and be the first attack. We can secure the ground floor, wipe out the security cameras, then prepare the entrance for the arrival of the police and SWAT team."

Everyone was in awe over the way it all fell into place, and a few moments was spent with everyone explaining the conversations they had had with one another that led up to their choices. They decided as a group that there could be no better way to team up. The history each team had made it very logical to all why and how the decisions had been made.

Ben at that point started by saying, "Thanks, you all, for the way you all handled this. Now for the details. You guys need to know your floors like you know your selves. Hawk has the drawings he worked on, but you also need to head over there at least once more to be sure nothing is left unknown. We need to be sure down and dirty is the operative action here, as well as quick and painful, but only for them, we hope. Okay, so now I have to turn this meeting over to Sarge. I do apologize for keeping you all out of the loop and allowing only one person to know what is going on, but until we could be sure this was gonna happen, we wanted safety in silence. Sarge, the floor is yours."

"Thanks, Ben. Okay, here goes. When we were in Idaho talking to the Militia guys and Robert and Rice, one of the guys pulled me aside and asked if we could meet. Of course I arranged to meet with him. We talked, and he explained himself, telling me this mission really spoke to him. He felt compelled to see if maybe he could help. Then he told me about his experiences as a Ranger in Iraq. It seems he was in the urban warfare areas and had experience in driving the vehicles that ran interference when al-Qaeda was attacking those areas. I did mention this to Ben, and now it appears we have Jon Wane willing to play Calvary for us, bringing a .50 cal. to the table that he knows how to shoot."

From the table, Sarge noticed some really interesting looks going around, and everyone was trying not to laugh. "Do we have Zorro coming too?" was heard.

Sarge, gaining control, started speaking again. "Maybe if all else fails, we can try for that, but for now Jon and Isaiah are willing to help, Jon as another marksman, and Isaiah, driver and potential lookout."

Ben then interjected, "And, guys, even though Sarge and I sanction them and hope you all do as well, we still need to agree as a group to let these two in. Questions, concerns, then a vote. Fair enough?"

Raoul did remember seeing the guys when they met in Idaho and, with the memory of their attitudes and demeanors, knew whichever two of the three may be the ones felt fine with that and said so.

Mike questioned the safety and security of bringing new people in this late. "Can we really bring two new members up to speed at this point and feel comfortable with them?"

Sarge answered, "These two would be in a slightly different category for learning their roles. Being outside, it is basically street, locale, and entrances they need to be familiar with. I really don't feel uncomfortable with that at all."

Ben then said, "And even though I have not had a face-to-face meet, both talk the talk, and I have no qualms about their ability to also walk the walk with us all the way! Anyone else with a question or issue, or can we vote now?"

"Let's do it!" Ron said.

"Hand-up vote okay?" asked Ben.

"Yup" was said in chorus.

And so the two new members were voted in unanimously. At which point Ben advised that the two of them had planned to arrive on the fourth with the equipment, and everyone said they would also drop by. With a laugh, Ben said, "Curiosity did kill the cat, you know!"

"Like that will change anything," chimed in Gerald.

So they had changed the scope of things somewhat with the new members, and while everyone was excited to figure out how this all played out, everyone was ready to call it a night. First, however, they did address what had been discovered by scoping out the morning routines of those that they could.

Tyrell started, "I actually was able to go by twice. Once I just hung out across the way and observed. It seems that the back entrance may be where cafeteria staff and guards come in first, starting at about seven fifteen. By seven forty-five, the front area is manned by the guards, and then it appears the staff only uses the front door, because between seven forty-five and eight a.m., that door is almost non-stop open. You can tell they know the staff 'cause no one appears to show a badge. The second time, pretty much the same, but I went in myself about 8:02, told the guard I had a meeting with Sam Thrift, who I knew was on the seventh floor so I could wander about, and realized by hitting the floors going up that not all the guards were in place 'til eight ten. Durham, anything to add?"

"Pretty much noticed the same patterns. However, it looks like Mondays may be a staff-meeting-type day. When lotsa people carry in doughnuts, that is usually why. Gotta keep everyone happy, and sugar is one way to do that. It may be worth it to consider Monday for the mission, because by eight a.m. on that day, I think more people would be in place, and the guards may also be on their floors. Is it possible someone can go over on a Monday before to see if we are right?"

Tom said, "I have an appointment at the hospital next Monday. I can swing by after to drop off records."

"Good, we are heading into the homestretch, guys. Need to meet on the fifth with potential escape plans and, of course, dinner. Who is cooking then?"

"Soup?" asked Ron. "I do make a great vegetable soup."

"You got it. Six p.m. for dinner, meeting at eight Feb. 5? If we are good with that, you all be safe out there."

With a bit more discussion among themselves, everyone eventually headed out. Ben and Tyrell did help clean up before leaving.

By about 7:00 p.m. on February 4, everyone had gathered at the resort, and speculation was running wild. Ben and Tyrell had not come out yet, so they waited. At 7:30 p.m., a horn was heard at the back gate. Hawk went out and opened the gate, and the van proceeded to head into its new garage. It was kind of hard to look at everything and not be able to touch, but they knew the importance of no prints on van or contents. Like kids in a candy shop, they oohed and aahed and then helped carry in the flak jackets and bags for the two new members.

Durham had stayed inside with Gerald, knowing they could get a look later, and that with the amount of bodies out there, they couldn't have seen anything anyway. When everyone finally walked in, Durham was in the head. As he walked out of the house, he heard a gasp and a familiar voice saying, "No, that cannot be who I think it is!" Jon exclaimed loudly. "Sergeant Murdit?"

When Durham realized it really was Jon Wane and could speak, he said, "You know, when your name was mentioned, I truly thought it had to be coincidence, Jon. I really thought you had gone to South America to join the mercenaries."

Jon replied, "I tried the South America thing, too damn hot down there. Had been in touch with Isaiah off and on. He offered a place to stay in Idaho. I fell in love. Have lived up there off the grid for a while now. Good to see you. Do I have to salute and sir you still?"

"Nah, we are all considered equal in this squad. Ben is our conductor, but only so someone keeps the meetings in line. I am so happy and surprised to see you."

Isaiah spoke up then, "Never expected a reunion here. Guess that six degrees of separation is true. You never are far from someone you know or knew. Can I be honest and say this makes me feel even more comfortable about this whole mission?"

Jon grinned and asked, "Would you like a tour of the new toys out back?"

The three headed out, and when Jon opened the back of the van, Isaiah almost bit his tongue when the two (Gerald and Durham) gasped a very loud gasp. Durham then asked, "You said toys. I like seeing this .50 cal. sitting here, but what else ya got?"

Isaiah interjected, "See those two boxes? Those are not one but two M79 grenade launchers. And if you look around some more, there are some extra grenades and more ammo."

They then headed inside, agreeing as they walked in this could add some interesting twists to the mission.

As they joined the rest of the squad, Tony Rice made the comment, "You know, guys, this mission is looking more and more like My Lai in Vietnam. Do you think we should perhaps change the mission name? You all do know about My Lai, right?"

They all admitted knowledge of the attack at My Lai and the ugly outcome with women, kids, and elders being slaughtered. It was a no-mercy kill. After some discussion, James, who really had been quiet throughout most discussions, said, "How about We Lay You All Down? Bit wordy I know but kinda sums it all up. And should we ever slip up and say it in public, it sounds like a man's club!" He added this with a laugh.

Some further discussion about the change, and even though everyone enjoyed Becker's take, it was decided that should they change the name. It would probably just be My Lai. It was decided to table that discussion until tomorrow at the meeting.

And with a collective sigh, everyone settled in with sandwiches and beers to get better acquainted. Two new men made for new stories, and the evening progressed with everyone becoming more comfortable with one another. Knowing tomorrow would come soon enough, everyone had left by 10:00 p.m., and after being sure the new guys knew where everything was, those at the resort settled in by 11:00 p.m.

They had adjusted sleeping quarters earlier in the evening, Gerald and James taking one camper because Raoul and Hawk had one already. The two newbies offered to take the couch and chair in the living room. Jon claimed his back gave him fits if he lay flat to sleep and the recliner there looked even better than his at home. Tom and Ron in one room, Tony and Robert in another, and they all informed Sarge he could be the single because his snoring was incredibly loud and he would live longer if in a single.

"Hey, you guys are mean! I *do not* snore!" he claimed emphatically.

However, once they threatened to tape him, he gave up and moved into the single.

NEWBIES TOUR THE CITY

EVERYONE CONGREGATED ABOUT 9:00 A.M. the next morning, and Jon and Isaiah asked if they should perhaps head into the city and check out the target before tonight's meeting. It was decided that was a great idea, and with explicit directions for what bus and train to take, they were off. Public transport was the way to go, they had all decided, and they made sure the two looked like they would fit in. "Just two more Vets checking out the facilities," they would tell anyone if asked.

So the two headed out, and there was some discussion over this addition. Ron summed things up pretty well. "It really seems this whole thing is coming together. I know I had doubts, a group of people storming a government office, but the more things pull together, the more confident I feel we can pull it off and make a difference for our fellow Vets."

Unanimously they agreed and went about their day, getting ready for dinner and tonight's meeting. When the guys came back from the city, they told everyone they were glad that they had taken the time to recon the area. Even though they knew it was only a brief overview, it helped to have a start at familiarity of the area. "And we will go back, as well as get a lot more detail from all you guys, I know that," Isaiah said.

And they settled in awaiting 6:00 p.m. and the later meeting. Some played cards, the TV was on NFL network, and for the rest of the afternoon, no business was discussed.

The soup was smelling really good by 5:30 p.m., and everyone kept trying to get a taste. "Just to be sure it is good" was the statement they all tried on Ron, who threatened to remove fingers or more. He had discovered some garlic bread in the freezer and threw that in the oven to have it ready with the soup at 6:00 p.m., informing those drooling already, "You can wait and eat with everyone, children!"

CATCHING UP THE NEWBIES AND MORE PLANS

As THE OTHERS ALL FILTERED in, Ron provided everyone with a bowl of soup, and the breadsticks were sitting on the table. It was agreed that a restaurant could be opened just with the soup, lasagna, and chili they had had here. Jon asked, "Chili, lasagna? When? Where? How did I miss those?"

Tyrell informed him that there were freezer packs of both labelled and in the large freezer. Apparently no one here understood portion control so those could be eaten for lunches. They all praised the chef for tonight's dinner, and by 8:00 p.m., the table was cleared, and everyone had notepads and drinks of choice in front of them. Yesterday, Ben had provided Isaiah and Jon with the tapes from previous meetings so they were caught up on all phases of the project to date.

Ben opened the meeting with an official welcome to the newcomers and, after a round of applause, asked if anyone had thought about escape routes.

Rice offered the opinion that he thought it might be best if everyone headed out a back door as SWAT and the cops would probably be congregated out front. And if the .50 cal. were also being used at the front to distract and do additional damage, that would give some an opportunity to get out and to a safer area then mingle with the crowds.

Gerald said, "And if we have the M79 launcher in the front area, that could be a distraction to maybe allow some to get out the back. Thinking that puppy could be a great diversion and take out some cops and/or SWAT, I am thinking that by the time we get to this point, the area should be cleared of civilians, so we should be okay on that and not harm any of those. Between that and the .50 cal., we might have a chance."

Durham said, "We just need to be sure the van gets in the best possible spot to have a clear shot at the front area and be safe. And have a chance at driving away. Those one-way streets can be a real pain!"

Hawk said, "Is it a consideration that the M79 is used outside the VA? Maybe one of the squares or parks offers a clear shot at the cops. Lafayette Park or McPherson Square maybe, as a sniper spot?"

Tyrell said, "Should we all head into town tomorrow to recon the area in full? Raoul, I know you have a camera, and those of us that have cell phones can all get shots of the entire area as well as the exterior of the building to have a better idea of what will work."

Ben said, "Great idea. Let's all go on and gather all the details we can. Stagger your times, try not to be obvious, and don't see each other. If necessary, grab a bite to eat while out, or remember, leftovers are so easy to nuke if needed or wanted."

Sarge asked, "May I bring up one other thing we do need to consider as we go forward?" And as everyone nodded yes, he went on. "I know we do not want to harm those who are not VA connected, vendors or Veterans themselves, and have been trying to figure out how we handle that. I thought maybe we could carry indelible markers and anyone we are sure is one of the above mentioned, mark them, perhaps with an *X* on the forehead, and then we tell them to go sit by the entrance we are planning to leave out of, and blend in with them when we release them, perhaps putting *X*s on us as well. That may be one way for some of us to escape."

Tom held his hand up to ask a question, and Ben told him that even though they weren't in school, he could speak now, smiling as he said it. Tom said, "Habit, I know, but it just seemed right. What I am also wondering is if we should not consider using some of those people as hostages? One of those things, where if appropriate, it could give leverage. We need to think that through and define if and when that may be appropriate."

Ben said, "Great points. Let's mull over everything we discussed today, head into the city tomorrow, check out things, and meet tomorrow again at eight p.m. to figure out what is what. Good night, men. All sleep well!"

RECON

THE NEXT DAY THEY ALL spent time wandering the VA area yet again. They really needed to be sure they were covering all potential bases, and as Hawk and Raoul headed out to catch transport into the city, Raoul heard Hawk mutter, "Freakin' twenty degrees out. Couldn't do a summer attack?"

Raoul smirked at him and said, "And where or how would you hide any weapons and not be obvious in shorts and flip-flops weather?"

As they were still in the resort area, neither felt threatened having this conversation, Hawk responding with, "I know, the timing makes perfect sense, but brr! Thank God we had the money to get real winter clothes this year. Cannot believe the stuff we did get at the Goodwill store!"

Everyone was back by 6:30 p.m., and somehow, donuts and pastries appeared as well. It seemed multiple people had the same thought, because there were boxes from two different donut shops as well as some from a grocery store. As Tom grabbed a glazed donut, Mike said that coffee and/or hot cocoa was also ready.

It had been discussed previously that maybe the M79 might be a good option for a potential sniper outside, and Raoul, Hawk, and Ron advised they would look for locales that might work if that was the direction things might go in. The M79 was a smaller weapon and would be easy to conceal under a coat, as well as being a quiet shoot!

Gerald commented, "Man, great minds do think alike. These donuts look killer. Thanks to whoever had that great idea. A sugar high sounds good. Ben, as long as we are all here, can we proceed?"

"Don't see why not. Everyone agree?"

DECISION MADE, FIGHT TO THE END

AND SO EVERYONE GRABBED COFFEE or cocoa, with the exception of Hawk—well, he kinda grabbed coffee, then hit it with a shot of JD—then they all took their places at the table. Some had handwritten notes, and some sat their phones in front of them. They had either used the phones to take notes or pictures, and Raoul, he set his camera in front of him. Sarge couldn't resist, first with an exaggerated groan, then he asked, "Please tell me you haven't filled up that thirty-two-bit card in there and want to show all your pictures off, like you did on the fishing trip?"

"Nope, not that many, Sarge. You are safe. However, as cold as it was today, I was able to get shots of pretty much the whole exterior of the building as well as the surrounding area, and I figured that may be something we all can use somehow, and I can move them to a jump drive and have the card for later if we need it."

"Good job, Raoul. Now let's all share our impressions, observations, and potential location details then maybe nail down some final plans, or at least what could be final, if we all agree." That was Ron, and everyone agreed that they would all have their say and then discuss the potentials for each area and locale.

Raoul cleared his throat and asked, "First?"

Everyone nodded, and he began, "We really got a lot of information to hopefully help us decide who and what can go where. After looking at all the variables for using the M79 as a sniper gun, we realized that Lafayette Park near H and Vermont would be a good place for a sniper. Even with it being winter, there is shrubbery there that provides cover. The trees, of course, aren't gonna provide a lot of cover, but those holly bushes are fairly tall and would help. The other corners did not seem to have as unobstructed a view of the front area, so those did not seem as reasonable, because here we could have clear shots at the entry as well as traffic, if necessary. Hawk also noticed a great spot for the van. We have it noted on the pictures, and I have noticed you all reviewing those. I think the parking spot is about frame 10. There is a blue van in it when I took the pic, so you can be sure it is the one we thought would work. Hawk, Ron, did I miss anything?"

"Nope," said Hawk as Ron shook his head, and Hawk added, "But I want to be the sniper."

At that point, Ben interjected, "Let's see what comes down the pike on that, Hawk. Kinda hard though, isn't it, for you to be in two places at once? I am thinking any sniping action may end up being Isaiah and Jon, but let's see who has other info to add before we make any decisions."

Isaiah and Jon at that point shared their thoughts on the entrance-exit coverage. Jon spoke, and as he did so, Isaiah nodded periodically to show his agreement, "Looking around the entire building, the front is the easiest and probably most important to protect. Just remember, guys, when you secure the first floor to also be sure any other doors that allow egress are locked, and locked tight. We found out from some of you and some other sources that all the doors have electronic locks and are accessed from outside with card swipes and internally opened with a keypad and numerical sequence. There is a box in the monitor room that appears to lock down the system, if activated, and from the details we have, activation only requires hitting the red button. In the back, where the deliveries are made, those have bars, so drop 'em. I know for you guys going in, that adds a little extra time, but maybe as some of you head up to the other floors, you can check them to be sure it worked then, if necessary, jam them with something, but I think the lookdown mechanism will work."

"That's a good points, thanks. But do we know for sure doing that will not jeopardize the mission?" asked Sarge.

"Thanks, I try. It was one of those things that hit me as we were walking around and realized none of you or us had said a thing securing doors. However, you have a good point. If we lock down the building, it could make it harder for us to get in and/or out, so maybe we should leave them not on lockdown mode but perhaps jam them as we go so we know we can use them if necessary. Not sure what is actually best for the mission. Guess we need to revisit this as we go. Now back to the streets. If we secure the other doors, that main entrance is it. In or out, we can monitor it. Raoul and company, you three actually hit it on the head. To place the van, that spot you marked is pretty much spot on. Then when time to move it, drive east on H one block, right on Fifteenth, leave that puppy on New York, then head for the area around the White House and get lost in any crowds or at least act like a tourist if it isn't crowded yet. Being the time of year it is, there may not be people out that early, but if you just act normal, people don't usually pay attention. And if you get to Pennsylvania Avenue in front of the White House, there is no car traffic allowed, so that should help with cop coverage. Oh yeah, forgot one little thing. We dump the van, and thirty seconds later there would be a big-assed boom. We would be sure that it was big enough to leave no van behind. Plus it would be one hell of a diversion."

Hawk at that point excitedly spoke up, "And with the sniper in the park, hit a couple of cars on H to stop traffic in the area as well! More diversion!"

Isaiah cleared his throat at that point, and everyone realized he wanted to speak, so Ben gave him the floor. He then solemnly looked over everyone, and once his eyes rested on Hawk, he began, "I know and truly understand why you want the sniper spot. One of the guys shared that you could pretty much hit a specified spot on a leopard, and that is a talent. But," and with a big sigh, he continued, "you need to be with your team. And your team is in the building. Let us concern ourselves with the exterior. Jon and I will cover your backs and protect the main entrance. That is our contribution, and we want you to be able to concentrate on yours… Go kick butt and let us keep things outside. If anyone else thinks they have a better idea, we are open to suggestion, but this is what we see in the mission's best interest."

Hawk started to stand up, and Raoul put his hand on his arm. "Hawk, what they say makes so much sense. We need you on the inside. Please think before you speak. This is one of those times we all need to be sure we are thinking about the mission and what works best for all. Johnson and Wane are better equipped to handle the outside, and if they know that is their main focus, it means they have less concern with the interior layout and steps that occur there. We all are more familiar with the interior and the people and more equipped to complete our mission with them holding down the fort outside. C'mon, buddy, look at the big picture."

Mike added, "Hawk, it is clear these two know their shit. It really does make sense to stick to our original plan and let them take control of the entryway and guard station."

Hawk sat back down and looked at everyone seriously. He then took a very deep breath and then said, "Guys, you don't know how much I appreciate all of you. This whole mission has given me a will to live, only to finish this before the cancer catches up. They checked me a few weeks ago, and it appears that the cancer is moving into other organs from the prostate. The irony is, I could probably get enough money to live on now that the cancer is active, but the odds are, I am not gonna live very long, so my goal is to put the hammer down and make a statement. But I know in my heart you all are right. You guys are the best to secure the entry. Thanks for your support, all. I won't be the sniper but will still kick some major butt, and if I don't get out alive, so be it! Go down for the cause!"

"Hear, hear," said Sarge. "I agree. Having the front door secure if not for us to get out of or into too, but for the Vets and others that may not be part of our mission. And I feel this is a My Lai the more I see and hear. Raoul and I did talk while we were out in the woods, and we know for a fact this is truly a take-no-prisoner mission, and we will not be imprisoned when it is over either. So I guess in our minds this is a suicide mission. But with the outcome, I personally hope we make lives better for a hell of a lot of other Vets."

Rice said, "Sarge, I was with you in Nam. I am here with you too!"

Durham chimed in with, "Man, great minds do think alike! I had it in my mind that regardless of what you guys all do, I was gonna continue to climb those floors until I either had done all the damage I could or they took me down!"

Ben said, "Geez, are you sure you weren't with Tyrell and I when we were in front of the VA? We decided that seeing as how there are eight floors, it was imperative that we hit 'em all. Tyrell asked why they should get lucky, and that made me realize I wasn't gonna allow them any luck from me. I would continue the attack as long as possible. They gave us nothing. I could at least return the favor."

Robert said, "I have thought a lot about what happened when I came back from Nam and put those SOBs in the hospital. Those idiots had no idea what they were talking about. Some had lied about their health, some families had paid someone to keep their precious offspring out of danger, and yet they were trying to make those of us who went feel guilty or bad. It was hard to come back and be treated like second-class citizens and/or attacked. However, those punks ended up in the hospital. They didn't realize who they were messing with, did they? And I consider these people even lower than them on the food chain because they have impacted lives and taken away lives. Hospital? No way. Pine boxes for all! That's my take!"

Mike admitted he wondered how and if this hit-and-run tactic was even feasible, and now it looked like everyone was in for the duration. He was declaring himself in as well but stated he knew there might be some who want an out, and hopefully the plan in place would allow for those if they wanted that option.

Gerald informed them that as a former Green Beret, you don't quit and you fight to the finish—in this case, to allow the other Vets the opportunity to have the right to the benefits they were promised.

Ron said that he and Tom, who at one time were collecting benefits and living the life, having a wife, a house, and a life, had it all yanked out from under them when the VA stopped their compensation. "Playing God can have karmic repercussions, and this will repay some of that debt. They tore down my house and wrecked my life. Call it vengeance or karma, I don't care which phrase you use!"

Tom was looked to next, and he just smiled, nodded, and high-fived the room. "Guess y'all know my feelings."

Ben, not sure how to proceed at this point, looked around the table, and his eyes teared up a bit. "I wish I knew what to say at this point, but I honestly don't. I knew we all thought alike, but this is a whole different game than the original plan we were looking at. One thing I want us all to do in the next few days is write a letter. It can be to a family member, friend, newscaster, newspaper, whoever you feel appropriate to write to. This is your "WHY?" letter. You know as well as I do why will be the first question asked. We all need to know our why. The night before the mission, they go out. So have them addressed and ready. We can keep them safe here 'til then. I think we all need to back off this now unless anyone else has anything that can't wait."

Wane spoke up then, "This may require a bit more thought on our end. Does that mind-set change how we handle our portion of the mission? Is it a better idea for us to attack somewhere else as a diversion before you start yours, or is it still better that we are there with you and also continue to attack 'til we are taken out? I am more than willing to take the hit as well, but if Isaiah wants the opportunity to run, we can work that out. He is one sneaky guy all on his own, trust me!"

Isaiah replied, "No runner here. Guys, this dedication is incredible, and I am with you 'til the bitter end!"

Everyone nodded, and Sarge spoke up. "Maybe we should stop here and really think things over. Is this the route we want to go, or is there something we are missing? If we all contemplate the ramifications and are still sure this is it, move on and run with it. We have to remember, it is not just us we are affecting. Some of us have family, and our decisions could hurt them, financially, in some cases, as well as mentally."

There was complete and utter silence for about three minutes, then Mike spoke up. "Sarge, all that is so true. We do need to be sure this is the way to proceed and think about those we do care about and all other factors that come into play."

"So are we okay to stop here for tonight and reconvene on the eighth to make final decisions and reaffirm our commitments?" Ben asked.

Again, the rather extended pause, and then everyone said they would be okay with this as a stop point. However, it seemed no one wanted to leave immediately. Everyone poured themselves a fresh cup of coffee, all thinking this meeting required a bit more thought, and they sat around for a while drinking that cup before the ones who needed to go home headed out, albeit slowly, and the side conversations that transpired before the evening ended, and all that was quiet would remain unspoken.

CONTEMPLATIONS

BEN WOULD NOT SPEAK OUT loud what was on his mind, but he knew he was not alone in feeling that at this moment, he could blast anyone and everyone to pieces who had anything to do with the VA. *Kinda like those Indians dancing around the fire, ready to attack*, was the thought process running around his brain.

ALL IN

ON THE EIGHTH, DINNER AT six was barely eaten by anyone. They actually had everyone pull leftovers for that night, and once everyone had eaten what they would or could, the table was cleared, and the men settled in to discuss everything.

Hawk finally broke the silence, as he was getting uncomfortable with everybody being so quiet, and said, "I have come to the conclusion that I will go in. I will kill until someone stops me."

Ben replied, "I guess our best bet is to vote and be sure we do all agree. Paper vote, though, so no one feels the need to not vote their true feelings. In simple terms, yes if you are for the suicide mission, no if not. Nothing will be held against any man here, either way, nor will it be a majority-vote win. We will discuss anything that may need to be talked over, or anyone who wishes to leave may do so. Any other comments or questions?"

When he saw all heads shake no, he handed out the papers. They all folded the papers in fourths and threw them into a bowl that Raoul had gotten from the kitchen.

Ben asked if it was okay if he counted them out as their conductor but added, "I will place them in front of me as I count. Fair enough?"

This time all the heads were nodding yes, and he began.

"One yes, two yes, three yes," and on it went, until he had a pile of fifteen yes votes in front of him. "Well, I guess that settles it. Gentlemen, we are a go. This My Lai mission is on, and we are gonna give it our all. I am honored to serve with you all on this, probably our final mission."

Everyone gave a war whoop and then settled in to talk. They knew that now the smallest details needed to be plotted and planned and were dedicated to being sure they covered all the variables that might occur.

Becker advised the others he was wondering how it would play out for the higher floors that had not yet even been discussed. "It seems to me after all the ruckus is heard on the first five floors that the guards on six through eight would be ready to fight back."

Isaiah offered, "When Ron, Tom, and Hawk enter the first floor and wipe out the guard or guards standing there, I see that as the opportunity for us to smash in the entry and move the van to that spot, blocking the door and then stay to guard it. Of course that means the van will not go boom later, or should it be rigged in case? After two of them clear the cafeteria and monitor room, they can secure the other first floor doors and head for the sixth floor."

"Sounds like we have a major strategist amongst us. Maybe you can keep an extra grenade to use if needed."

Ron said, "No questions, but I will volunteer to stay with Jon and Isaiah to help maintain the first floor."

They all approved of both Ron staying and the process to secure the main floor, Ben asking, "Are you comfortable with the amount of firepower and protection this would give you to secure that area?"

Isaiah replied, "I think with the van, which you may or may not realize is bulletproof, body and windows, the .50 cal., grenades, M79, and whatever else we can scare up from that arsenal, I think we will be okay. The local cops are gonna try to wipe us out quickly, but do not see that happening. However, we will take down as many of them as we can, and then they will have to sit tight and wait for SWAT and/or guards or feebies, whoever they decide to try for help. It should work out that our work is done before that all can be put in place."

Hawk asked, "So that leaves Tom and I to head for the sixth floor?"

Ben replied, "Looks that way, if you two are okay with that."

Tom looked at Hawk and nodded, at which point Hawk said, "Oh yeah, absolutely great! Matter of fact, we can finish six and head up to seven. Ready or not, here we come!"

Ron questioned, "How do we know who is where at any given time? Should we not have walkie-talkies to be able to communicate when we change floors or just to know what is going on on the ground floor?"

Durham spoke up, saying, "I think it is too late to get those, because we would need the hands-free, and those aren't at your local electronics store. But wish we had thought of it earlier. They sure helped us in Iraq."

Sarge interjected, "If we all are synchronized on our timing and stick to the plan, we should still be okay with or without direct communication. Plus knowing we can't get the ones that would work the best in time, to me, makes it a nonissue! All agree?"

After some more back and forth as to whether or not regular walkies or cells might be wanted, it was determined that the attempt to get the amount needed to man everyone might create more problems than they needed to address. It was decided no on the walkies or cells to be used during the mission. And back to plotting they went.

Ben said, "So we are good so far. Hawk, Ron, and Tom, as you guys are first in, you for sure get silencers. That should keep the noise at a minimum so hopefully no one on the higher floors gets wind of us right away. Raoul, you and Sarge will also have silencers. I know we are low on ammo for the .38s that have the silencers, but we in great shape with the .45 cal. ammo, so you guys will also have those, as will everyone. Based on the inventory—thank you, Tom, for counting it all out for us—everyone gets a .45 semi with enough clips to hold about 520 rounds, 2 grenades, and a C4 with 2 fuse and caps in case you need them. This way, if necessary, you can gain entry if any doors are locked. Hawk has graciously offered a quick training session and/or uptraining session so we all know or remember how this stuff works."

"Men, as a SEAL, I used this stuff so much I would find fuses in my pockets even when not in the field. What we have in each package is enough to open a door easily, and the fuse gives you 15 seconds to haul ass. The C4 will be baggied, and all together, so if needed, ready to use," explained Hawk. At his final statement, everyone chuckled. "Questions, concerns, comments?"

"Got one question," was from Becker. "What if that puppy doesn't blow? Plan B?"

"If it does not go off, wait 15 seconds. You can than remove and replace the cap and fire it off."

Ben spoke up and thanked Hawk for his training on C4 and then said, "Let's backtrack a bit. We need to get into town first, don't we? I am thinking that I can borrow a buddy's 15-seater van and leave it in a safe place, far enough away for no traces of it being involved, then we all head over. Of course, to keep it from being unnoticeable, thinking it would be best to not park it in 1 spot and have 10 to 13 people haul out of it at once but drop off some of you guys in different locales, then we meet our assigned partners and head over to the target. Agree, all?"

It was determined by all that that would work, and then they needed to figure out the best and simplest way to enter the building. As there was a metal detector at the entrance, the three going in first knew just how important it was to take out the guards ASAP and shut down the monitor room simultaneously so they all knew that they would be in first. And once the cafeteria was cleared, half the guys could enter through the loading dock doors, securing that door behind them as they headed for their respective floors. It was determined that those that had the lower floors would enter through the loading dock area, and the higher, the front, allowing them the elevator access. "So to sum up entry details, you guys all determine where it is best to meet up after leaving the van, and we have Gerald and Mike, floor 4, with Ty and Ben, floor 5, entering the front, and Durham and Becker, floor 3, coming in through the front as soon as they see a wave from Ron, with Tony and Robert, 2nd floor. Raoul, you and Sarge can enter through the loading dock in the cafeteria and wipe it out as you come through before heading to the first floor. The bad thing about this floor is there really isn't time to determine who may not be actual VA, so the entire cafeteria will need to be wiped out," Ben stated. "I am thinking the ground floor attack starts at 8:05

a.m., and by 8:10, you guys have it all secured. At that moment, our other guys should enter, and the van needs to be ready to drive up and block the front entrance. We can all hope not too many Vets are here by then, so that should minimize their danger. Did anyone confirm that Monday is the day they hold staff meetings?"

Jon interjected, "It is for everyone. They actually don't allow appointments 'til nine thirty that day. I tried to make one and was told with total finality that I could not get in as early as I wanted too. Snotty little witch she was too!"

"Good!" stated Tyrell. "Definitely lessens the count of Vets in house."

Rice questioned whether or not they should take out the cops that were always near the front of the building, even though they were not apparently in guard mode, because they were so close, if that made sense.

Mike responded, "My thought is no. We don't want to attract attention earlier than is necessary. Let them figure it out or not. We will have to deal with them soon enough."

"So redundant or not," Tom said, "we three enter the ground floor at eight a.m., clear the guards, Hawk and I sweep the area and be sure all is secure, and Ron is set with Isaiah and Jon moving the van in, while Ron takes care of the monitor/security room and hunkers down to help the guys in the van, right?"

"Got it!" said Ben. "At that point, I really think you all know the drill. Guard first to secure the floor and then clean their clocks. Try for clean head shots to save ammo and mess. We don't want to slip because we made a mess."

"I know we have Kevlar, and we all should be wearing the vest from the get-go. Should anyone have the opportunity to shoot at us, I am guessing it is more natural to go for chest or stomach, so those vests will buy us time too." This was Durham speaking.

Raoul at this point spoke up, "I have the utmost confidence in us all. We are becoming a well-tuned instrument and should do well here. I cannot imagine anyone else with the cojones to do this, and I salute you all!"

At that point, everyone saluted back, and Ben said, "Let's adjourn this meeting and meet on the twelfth at nine a.m. for our prebriefing. We can go over and clarify everyone's responsibility and role in the mission."

RECONVENE AND RECAP

Thursday, February 12, rolled around. Those staying in the resort had had plenty of time to discuss their feelings and fears over the mission but knew this was a definite go. Hawk actually summed it up best one night when they were talking, saying, "I never thought our government would treat people this badly and create a situation that caused people to react this way, but here we are, and I for one am looking forward to this, hoping it helps others, 'cause for me, it won't matter."

That was met with a chorus of amens.

When everyone gathered on Thursday, it had been decided that everyone would bring food for sandwiches and the house would provide condiments and salad. That way, everyone could get their food, and then they could have the meeting and be done at a reasonable time.

"Gentleman, this is it. Fish or cut bait time!" started Ben. "We all are aware of what is at stake here. If I said 'Let's go attack now!' would you all be in?"

"Oh yeah," came back in chorus.

"Even knowing this is probably your last mission?"

"Yes, sir."

"And are we all ready to go Monday, the sixteenth?"

War whoops abounded.

"I only ask one thing. You come here Sunday at twelve noon committed. Because if you aren't committed, please don't show up.

This is it, guys, the final waltz. Either come prepared to dance or don't plan on getting on the floor. Have all your ducks in a row, and let's rock and roll."

Sarge stood up and said, "I think I speak for all of us when I say rock and roll and take no prisoners! Let's show them what we are made of!"

James and Gerald had actually taken the time to draw out a timeline chart:"At 0800 Tom, Ron, and Hawk enter the building, immediately take out the guards' monitor room" was how it began, and they went on to provide an overview of the whole operation.

James explained, "I am a visual person and have to see how things progress. Gerald told me that as long as I needed to see that in writing, we should draft it so anyone who needs that boost has it. I know you guys can't take it home, but they are here for us if needed."

"Great idea. Let's all take a few moments and see if there are any questions or changes required based on this overview," said Ben.

Everyone was in agreement that seeing it all down on paper helped. "Kinda makes it real and ties everything in," said Robert. "One question, though, would it be better to C4 those two elevators?"

Hawk said, "Catch-22 there. It could set off the fire alarm, and that, my friends, would suck."

"Okay, so we leave the elevators alone."

"So we will all be here Sunday at noon to prep for Monday morning. If anyone hasn't finished their letter, please bring them then, with an addressed envelope if possible. We will throw them in a mailbox that night. No, wait, I promise to make sure they all go out overnight delivery. The post office near here has a twenty-four-hour lobby, so all would get to their respective people by Tuesday at the latest. Agree, all, that that makes the most sense?" He saw everyone's heads nod, then he continued, "The easy part is over. Now comes the test. Again, be sure this is what you want to do. And if not, please remember us in your prayers. Final meeting and dinner, Sunday, fifteenth of February, bring your favorite pj's. We are having a sleepover."

Raoul held up his hand to ask a question and looked around the table with a smirk on his face, but in as serious a tone as he could muster, he asked, "Ben, you do not plan on being half a beer late, do you?"

The wadded-up napkin Ben had in his hand sailed but missed, and everyone just looked at Ben then roared.

And again, as serious as possible, Raoul said, "'Cause, partner, we would start without you!"

As the applause died down, Ben responded, "Nope, wouldn't blow this one, guys. Trust me. Sunday, twelve noon, food drinks final prep… all in?"

And on that note, they wound down this gathering. Gerald and James made sure they ordered Valentine's gifts for the wives to be delivered Saturday, with an apology for being gone for that day. The reason they both gave was that they were helping a friend get a place for Vets set up and running smooth. This had been the standard for any trip into DC, and they even had pictures to show the women when they went home each time, not telling them how old those pics were.

GATHERING A DAY EARLY

SATURDAY, EVERYONE GRAVITATED TO THE resort, and by noon, the whole group was there. They spent quite a bit of time going over every detail, thanking one another for their contributions. The time-line was great for recapping steps. Raoul's pics helped, allowing them to be sure things were where and how they remembered. Hawk's training in C4 handling was great.

Some of them went off to one of the campers for a bit of quiet reflective time or to finish their letters, and by 3:00 p.m., they all had flocked together again around the table, some drinking—okay, Hawk was drinking—and some having coffee or sodas.

The conversation got a bit heated, everyone harking back to wars in the past, and Hawk aid, "These people are truly our enemies, and the way they run things now, it will not get better. This is slow death for a lot of Vets rather than just killing them up front. I feel like we are doing a repeat of My Lai, just levelling the whole town."

It became a chant for a brief period and really amped up the guys. Sarge finally took a deep breath and said, "Boy, there is a blast from the past, but you are so right! Now I am gonna suggest we find a game on TV or get the cards out and try to let this go for now."

They did manage to find other outlets to occupy their minds, but side conversations still occurred, and by 6:30 p.m., the only ones left were those that were sleeping there. Ben gave no reason, just said he had business to take care of, and the others grumbled and said, "Valentine's Day, curse it!"

Those that weren't affected raised the drink of choice they had in hand and tipped their heads, laughing.

Gerald and Becker had called home, making sure the background noises sounded like construction noises, and told their wives they should be back by the end of next week. Both promised a nice dinner out. Kathy and Karen had also bonded as neighbors and told the guys that they were gonna treat themselves to a nice dinner as girls' night out as well.

Tyrell had made plans earlier to see a play in the city and then do dinner, so he had to go early to put on a tux. "You own a tux?" and a few snide comments came out over that one, and he shrugged them off as he left.

After all the coupled guys left, Raoul said, "Bet Ben is hotfooting it to Mary for tonight. Almost glad I have no one close to leave behind. Don't know about you guys, but that does make this all somewhat easier."

Sarge replied, "Gonna miss my brother and wife at home, but they will take care of my property and the animals there, and they will understand why we are doing this."

Tom and Ron, both a bit bitter over what had occurred with loss of wives and stability, just sat there and said nothing, but you could see the desire to have someone that they felt would miss them in both of their eyes.

Hawk shrugged his shoulders, tipped his glass of whiskey to the rest of the group, and toasted, "To all those who can, get lucky tonight, and may all our dreams come true on Monday."

To which everyone else tipped their respective glasses or cups back at him and chorused, "Hurrah!"

VALENTINE'S DINNER AT MARY'S

BEN DID OF COURSE GO to Mary's house. They had decided to chill out there. She made dinner, and he brought wine and flowers. Neither wanted to go out and fight the crowds to eat at a high-priced restaurant because it was a holiday. So salad, chicken cordon bleu, and chocolate brownies was the menu.

They decided to have coffee and dessert in the living room, overlooking the backyard and pool area. Ben said, "It looks so peaceful and beautiful out there with the lights on around the pool and the totally unmarked snow. All that is missing is a deer or fox, and we are probably too close into the city for that to happen."

"You are right. Never seen either of those, but maybe a skunk will stroll through," retorted Mary with a chuckle. "A couple of years ago, I had a friend from California here, and she went out for a walk. When she came back to the house, mama skunk and three babies were hanging on the porch. I will give her some credit, she did back off before she called me and asked me if I could make them leave for her."

"You are kidding, right?"

"Nope, not sure why she thought I would even risk opening the front door, but I did open the gate so she could come around to the back."

They sat in companionable silence for a while. Ben thought over his decision to go forward with their mission and knew that the love he had found was too short-lived, but also knew Mary would do all she could to keep the gym going as well as expand the Vet assistance, eventually reaching out to help women Vets as well.

Mary also was thinking about how lucky she was to have reconnected with someone who meant so much to her and had the same moral compass, helping those he could in whatever way he could. When she looked over at Ben, it was obvious his thoughts weren't as pleasant, and she questioned him as to whether or not he was okay.

His response was, "Yeah, sorry. Been busy at work, and for some reason, the last few nights, I have had flashbacks, so been a bit down."

"Hmm, I think I may know how to help erase those bad dreams and let you get so tired, that you'll sleep like a baby!" And with that, she got up, kissed him, and grabbed his hand, and upstairs they went.

Mary made him undress and then take a warm bath, with the jets going in the Jacuzzi tub. She promised him the wait would be worth it but also told him he could not get out until she said it was okay. With the soft jazz in the background, he almost fell asleep in the tub, but his curiosity kept him from nodding off. After what seemed like an eternity, Mary informed him he could join her in the bedroom. He swung over the tub edge, threw his prosthesis on, dried himself in record time, and kept the towel wrapped around his middle. Then he almost fell over. Candles were scattered around the room, and Mary was lying on the bed in a gorgeous red teddy.

"You like, big boy?"

And with that, lights were out, with a long and passionate night enjoyed by both.

They actually were both up and showered by 7:30 a.m., enjoying a breakfast they cooked together, sitting at the bar in the kitchen, and doing more staring at each other than talking, but telling each other what a great Valentine's it was.

At about ten thirty, Ben said he needed to head out, go by the gym, and check on the guys at the resort. He kissed Mary good-bye with such passion, she commented that it felt like a last good-bye kiss.

Ben had to choke back his feelings and the desire to tell her all, but knowing that was not right, he said, "For sure I will see you later in my dreams."

"And in person as well!" she responded.

He winked and departed.

CALLING IN A FAVOR

On his way back to the resort, Ben made a stop at a friend's house. Mark had been a member of the gym since almost day 1 and often told Ben how great it was he did the things he did for Vets and the community. "If you ever need anything I have, let me know," Mark offered.

Today was the day to call in that offer. Mark had a fifteen-passenger van, and Ben had already spoken with him and was there to pick it up and hand over his car. "Tuesday to swap back?" asked Ben.

"Works for me. I will come by the gym to work out and give you yours then."

"Appreciate this. Makes it so much easier. It seems we have guys with appointments at the hospital, VA center, and a couple of job interviews all at once, plus I needed to go into the city for business, so this way we all save time and bus fare," stated Ben. He, of course, did not mention that the van could conceivably be impounded, nor that the title to his car signed over to Mark would be in an envelope without the keys, which he would advise in the note that they were under the mat in the van and where the van would be located.

FINAL SESSION

WHEN BEN FINALLY WALKED INTO the room at twelve fifteen, every-one shot him a look, and Hawk finally said what the others didn't, "Can't break the habit, can ya? We were getting worried, bro!"

"I know, I shoulda called. I am sorry. Had to pick up the van, and there was an accident that delayed me. But we have the van, and I see everyone else is here now, so let's wrap this up. The final round-table meeting is now starting. The van I got will fit all of us and our gear, and I did gas up coming in."

Hawk said, "Would it be better if Tom, Ron, and I rode in with Isaiah and Jon? Three less for you to drop somewhere and as we are the first offense team. What does everyone else think?"

Sarge replied, "That makes sense to me, guys. We do all need to see each other to be sure we got there okay, but I think a way to accomplish that is to be sure each team is visible at least ten minutes before go time. All we need to do is be sure we all show up on one corner or the other and wave or nod to Tom, Ron, or Hawk. If they stagger a little themselves to be seen, think that may do it. That way, should something we don't expect happens, we can abort or regroup."

Hawk responded, "As we are starting with the van parked near Lafayette Park, we can sit on the benches to watch for everyone. I like that idea."

Everyone concurred that that made sense, and Ben went around the room, quizzing everyone on timing and roles in the attack. It was apparent that they had all spent time with diagrams, pictures, and their partners being sure all was in order.

It was decided that they would put on their vests right before they each departed the van. Ben informed them, "That is the one variable, where I drop you each off. Based on opportunity and traffic flow, we can of course be sure everyone is within the range needed to be in place and to allow me time to park the van at the garage on H street and hightail myself over!"

Mike said, "That makes sense, Ben. If we are at a red light, one or two can get out, then and by the time you circle one or two blocks, we should all be on our way. Tyrell, will you wait and get out with Ben or walk over earlier as well?"

"Depends. If I think Ben needs a timekeeper, I will stay with him 'til he parks it. That may not be a bad idea. Ben is not the best at on-time service."

"Hey, I know I have been a bit late in the past, but I promise you, I will be so on the clock you will all think the past latenesses were a figment of your imagination!" Ben said to defend himself.

Gerald questioned the issue about Vets in the building, being sure he understood the protocol. "We X them with the marker and send them down to sit in the lobby, where they will eventually be able to leave, right? But what if an employee tells us they are a Vet?"

Sarge replied, "That is a tough one. If the guy just does filing or something menial, I vote to X them and let 'em go. But if they have any authority, that means they are a turncoat to me. And that leaves only one solution. But these are personal decisions. We can't decide that for you."

They were all good with that and agreed that there could be variables and each man or team would have to decide what worked best for them and the mission.

"We need to be on the road by six a.m., so I think we should be up by five and have the van loaded by five forty-five. Then allowing for traffic and weather, we should be set by seven forty at the absolute latest so we can be on track for eight a.m. All good with that?"

Everyone offered a salute and a "Yes, sir!" Durham stood up and asked everyone's attention for a moment, clearing his throat before continuing. "I know I speak for everyone, Ben, when I say this. We all thank you for stepping up and keeping us all on track. I, no, we, all think you were the perfect candidate for the job, and again, thank you. It's a helluva job you have done here."

And with that, the applause and yesses came out, everyone nodding and agreeing.

Ben hung his head in reflection and blushed, finally responding, "And I thank all of you for your dedication to the cause and commitment to all Vets. Now let's enjoy some food, drinks, and music."

Merle Haggard kicked it off, and they chimed in at the "If you don't love it, leave it. Let this song I'm singing be a warning. You are on the fighting side of me."

The older guys knew all the words to the Green Beret song, but by the time everyone fell asleep, they all knew line and verse of that one too.

Even though the area seemed quiet by about 1:00 a.m., there was an air of restlessness that settled over everyone. Those that were asleep were either dreaming of the mission or past missions, and those that were awake were trying to rest, knowing they needed to be alert when 5:00 a.m. rolled around.

MONDAY MORNING

By 5:00 a.m., everyone was awake, coffee was poured, and some were eating the food that was already cooked. They decided to start gearing up by 5:15 a.m., and the room was quickly emptied, guns with silencers to Hawk, Ron, Tom, Sarge, and Raoul. Everyone else received their guns, and when it was time for flak jackets, Hawk emphatically refused his, starting a chain reaction. Sarge, Raoul, Tom, Ben, and Durham decided they would not bother. "Those darn things add way too much weight," they claimed.

And by 5:30 a.m., they were on the road. Silence reigned in the larger van, while in the armored van they did discuss the exact timing they had laid down earlier. Even though every man had synchronized their watches, they double- and triple-checked them riding on. When they got in the area, it was earlier than anticipated, so they cruised a bit in the armored van, passing Ben and company once as he let one man out of their van about two blocks out. At that point, they again checked the time, realized it was time to be sure their parking space was open on the corner, and headed over. As they drove those last couple of blocks, Isaiah would stop the van two times, once for Tom to get out and again for Ron and Hawk. Luck was with them as they came to the corner at 7:10 a.m., all the other corners that had a space were filled, but facing their target was empty. They knew they needed to have leeway in their timing so all could show up and feel comfortable that they were in place, and the 7:10 a.m. had been the agreed-upon time.

By 7:40 a.m., Isaiah and Jon had seen everyone moving toward their target area. Ron, Tom, and Hawk were sitting on a bench not far from the main entrance. Raoul and Sarge had shown themselves and then moved to a spot right around a corner, where they could enter when the time was right. The others had all breezed by at one point or another, and at one point they just watched employees filter in. And they were carrying donut boxes, so everyone knew they were right about the staff meetings on Mondays. There shouldn't be Vets coming in that early as their appointments would be scheduled for later.

At 7:55 a.m., Hawk, Ron, and Tom started walking slowly to the door, gratefully noticing no police cars presently in sight. Tom was whistling, and when Hawk shot him a look, he just shrugged and smiled.

At precisely 8:00 a.m., they entered the building, Tom and Ron immediately taking out the two guards, signaling Hawk to head for the security room. He did so, ordering the guard to kill the cameras, take out the discs with footage on them, and shut down the fire exit doors. (The last was a calculated risk. Seeing keypads on them, he hoped that they could be secured from the system and was right.) He watched as the guy hit a few keys and was a bit concerned he had sent some coded message for help. But the system responded with Exit Doors Secured, and Hawk breathed a sigh of relief. He then took the discs the guy handed him, waited for the computers to shut down, and finished the job, immediately leaving the room.

He looked toward the cafeteria, noticed Raoul at the entrance, and could also see Sarge near the back, so he knew that area was covered and headed for the stairs, where Tom waited. However, he did yell out to those two that the emergency doors had been secured as he moved on.

Sarge and Raoul had knocked on the door at the loading dock area, and when the door opened, Sarge opened fire, taking out whoever was in his path. Raoul came in and started moving down the left side, also clearing the room on that side, while Sarge moved around the right, being very careful not to cross fire on each other, knowing that Ron would take care of any that got past them. As they finished killing everyone they found in the cafeteria, Sarge looked at Raoul and said, "I see Randy lying there. Sorry, Raoul, was kinda hoping he was off today."

"It happens. Thanks, though. Shall we head up?" asked Raoul as they went toward the stairs, with a quick wave to Ron to let him know they were on their way.

They got on the first floor and immediately saw the guard. Raoul took him down, and they noticed two women walking their way. One screamed "What are you..." and fell to the ground, and the other turned to run and was also put down. They went office to office, and apparently most people were either not in yet or headed for the Monday staff meeting because there were only about forty people total on this floor, including the office marked Payroll and also Admin, so the floor was cleared in record time, and Sarge told Raoul to check the ladies' while he checked the men's.

One stall was locked in the ladies'. Raoul contemplated shooting through the door but decided it was safer and surer to go into the adjacent stall and shoot over the top, which was what he promptly did, ignoring the scream when she saw his head and the gun over the partition. Sarge, in the men's room, saw one washing his hands and two at the urinals and shot the guy at the sink first then the two peeing. There was a yell from one stall, "What the hell was that?" and at that point, Sarge knew where one more was and kicked the door in and shot him too.

He then headed into the hallway to meet up with Raoul, and they nodded to each other as they entered the stairwell to head for the seventh floor. They could hear rounds going off on the higher floors and knew things were moving along.

On the ground floor, a few more employees entered the building, but as soon as one foot hit the doorway, Ron took them down. Those that had no badge, he asked, "Vet?" and they responded "Yes," at which point they got an *X* on the forehead and instructions to sit quietly by the front door. He did explain the reason for his squad being there once Isaiah and Jon had driven up in the van with the .50 cal. and secured the door so no one else could enter.

One guy seemed really fidgety, and Ron asked him very politely to stand up and hand over his wallet. Ron went through the wallet, found a VA employee ID, but no military ID, and asked, "Branch?"

To which the guy replied, "Huh?"

Ron said, "Military, my ass!" and shot him before he could respond. "Not sure which I hate more, cowards or liars!" And he noticed small smiles on the faces of the Vets that still sat there.

Rice and Robert got to the second floor at 8:02 a.m., and the security guard was standing right by the stairwell as they came up. Realizing they needed to wait, they started a conversation, asking of he liked his job, had good benefits, and ever worried about a Vet coming in and going postal on him. The guard said he did like his job and bennies were okay. "Nah, no worries on the postal Vet issue. Our security measures would not allow anyone to get in with a weapon. We got cameras, a metal detector, and guards at the door."

"Really? Well, then, this should really be a surprise!" stated Rice as they pulled their weapons out.

The guard showed his bravado and spoke, so they waited to hear what he had to say. "You may have managed to get those in here somehow, but there would be no way in hell you will get out of here alive, especially if you kill me or anyone else! So I suggest you hand over the weapons."

"You know, that is probably true, so does it matter whether we shoot just you or everyone? I'm thinking no diff either way, so…" Robert said as he locked and loaded and shot the guard.

They then proceeded to hit all the offices on that floor. After they entered the last two offices separately and cleaned those out, they headed back into the hallway and noticed three people entering the stairwell. Rice went to the stairs and managed to hit one of them, but the other two continued down. Rice told Robert as he rejoined him that two had gotten away, and Robert stated they should be handled on the first floor. "Remember, they can't get out the fire exit so should head for the lobby." Restrooms were at that point checked, and Robert did find one guy hiding in a stall in the men's and shot him. Stairs to the seventh floor was their next move.

Durham and Becker hit floor 3 right at 8:00 a.m. Seeing no security guard, they checked both bathrooms and, as both were empty, went back out to walk the halls and see who was where. They heard a door close and saw the guard coming out of an office stirring a cup of coffee. Becker questioned his ability to protect himself and others with that coffee in hand and got the response, "Mind your own damn business and get outta my way!"

Becker smiled, stepped aside, let the guard get about three steps out, and said, "Hey, buddy!" He made sure the guard turned to see him draw on him and hit him dead center in the forehead, turning to Durham and saying, "Oops, looks like that coffee didn't protect him one bit!"

Room to room they moved, killing those that were on the floor. At one point about halfway down the hallway, someone who was running to get to the stairwell realized the guard's gun was still in its holster, reached down to grab it, and had the wherewithal to know how to shoot, focused on Becker, who immediately went down. Durham had returned fire and took out the guy who shot his partner, then knowing there was not time to think things over, he reached down, grabbed Becker's gun and the grenades, as well as the baggies in his pocket containing the C4, and headed for the stairwell going for higher ground. He was well aware that they would all eventually end up on the top two floors but knew it was necessary to move out now.

Mike and Gerald approached the fourth floor carefully. As they exited the elevator, they almost stepped on the security guard. "Sorry, man, didn't expect to see you standing there. Having a good day?" And they bantered back and forth a little, discussing the brutal cold weather and the Redskins, who didn't even come close to a Super Bowl shot that year. After Mike shot the guard, Gerald reached down, took the guard's gun, pulled the slide back, and chuckled when he realized the guard did not keep his gun locked and loaded.

That floor was mostly conference rooms, and empty at that, but one room had coffee cups and donut boxes sitting on a side table and would seat quit a few people, so Mike and Gerald knew they hit it right for the staff meetings and that was why so many offices were empty. This confirmed that this was the reason for so few Vets in the building at this point in time.

Proceeding to check all the other spaces on that floor they had, some realized what was happening and begged for their lives, some asking why, but they stuck to the mission and eliminated everyone they came upon.

Once all was cleared, they also headed up to the sixth floor, waiting in the stairwell for any noises that indicated anyone else was there. It was predetermined that everyone should use the stairs on the west side of the building so they could all meet on the landing before rushing the last two floors. As luck would have it, they were alone waiting at this point for the others. Because it was quiet in the stairwell, they did speak some about what they had done so far, feeling that if everyone else had had things go as smooth, "this mission has been a piece of cake, if that is so," stated Mike. Gerald agreed, and they hunkered down to wait for the others, not having any clue that the actions of two men could change things drastically.

Tyrell and Ben ended up getting off the elevator on 5 with three people who discussed getting down stairs soon for the staff meeting. Ben nodded at Tyrell, and they stood back and let the conversation roll. Sometimes it is better to pretend to be invisible. You quite often are if you keep that persona active. Leaving the elevator, the three employees headed left, and Ben and Tyrell noticed the guard at the other end of the hall.

Tyrell said, "By the time we get down there, it'll be time to drop him, and I want the pleasure!"

"You got it. Let's go. I can take the woman he is chatting with."

After they dispatched the guard and woman at the end of the hall, who did see them and went for his weapon but was gunned down before he could shoot, they continued to process the floor.

This floor housed a call-center-type room. Whether to make appointments or what, it was a large open space with cubicles and could hold probably 250 people. They could lob two grenades in and then follow up with a massacre-style killing of those that survived the grenade. Regrettably, a couple of windows blew out from the grenade attack, and they knew immediately that would trigger activity from the police or someone, so they moved as quickly as they could. About 122 people sat in that area that day, and none survived. Tyrell told Ben, "You know what? We can now blow out the elevator panels and disable them. We have already let it be known something is up here, so does it matter if alarms go off?"

And they did, both heading to an elevator and, using the C4, blew the panels out, each handling one bank of two elevators. Then they went up the stairwell, discussing the fact that they were lucky that it did not take too much time for the elevators to get to their floor so they could disable them all. At that point, they joined Rice and Robert on the stairwell and were comparing notes. Durham came onto the landing with a hangdog look on his face. They all knew immediately and offered condolences, and Durham thanked them, stating, "Let's finish this for Becker and everyone else."

A BAD DECISION IS MADE

Hawk had asked Tom if he agreed that it made more sense for them to go up to the eighth floor and work down, adding, "Maybe we can get the head honcho if he is in today and finish him off, which would give me great pleasure!" Tom thought for about five seconds then grinned and said, "I would love to finish that SOB off. Let's go!" They of course took the elevator up as they were still running and as no one was in it with them, figuring that before they left the floor, they could probably disable the elevators.

As they got off the elevator on the eighth floor, the guard was right there. Hawk was startled to see him right there at the door and pushed him back. This guy was fit and apparently knew how to handle himself, and as he fell, he knocked Hawk's gun from his hand and was able to pull his gun and get a shot off as he landed on his butt. Hawk took the hit full on, and as he fell, Tom realized what had happened, and the two of them exchanged fire. Chuck, the guard, managed to get Tom with two rounds, neck and chest. Chuck was shot in the shoulder, but nothing drastic enough to keep him down, or so he thought. He then took the time to check and see what the two had brought to this party and was shocked to find more ammo, two grenades, two C4 packets per man, and a couple of very nice knives. There were minimal people on the floor. This was where the big dogs had their offices, and no one came in unless they had to.

As Chuck stood there, holding his shoulder that was bleeding fairly freely, he heard a noise and turned to see a door very slowly opening about halfway down the hall. He assumed the position training the gun on the area and yelled, "Show yourself, hands first!"

In a very meek voice, he heard, "Chuck, that you? It's me, Mark from downstairs. Came up here to get some stuff for the staff meeting, and Carl and I are in here. What the hell is going on?"

"Mark? You two okay?" Mark showed himself with a very pale Carl coming up beside him, both nodding. "Guys, not gonna tell you I know what is going on, some kind of attack, for sure, but if these two are not alone, we could still be in trouble. Are you guys up to helping me move the bodies once I check the rest of the floor?"

Mark had gained a bit of his composure back and told Chuck they could help and that he would be able to help more if Chuck could give him a weapon. Chuck offered a .45 or a .38, and they both opted for the .38. Carl also advised him there were probably about twenty people scattered throughout the offices that were unlocked. Those that were secured were the higher-ups, who apparently were on some kind of retreat this week. "In Florida, I heard."

Chuck informed them they should go back into one of the offices that overlooked the elevator area and covered most of the hall, but to only come out if they heard something. He would be sure they knew it was him when he came back down the hall. He then went to check the other areas, finding twenty-four people total in various offices. Those he gathered together in one office, advising them of the need to secure the room and handing one grenade to a woman who stated she had armament training, having been in the Guard for fifteen years. "Thanks," she said, as Sarah, an admin assistant, spoke up and informed them that she had had a call from her hubby, who said the VA was all over the news, and she assured him as best she could that she was okay. She then figured it might be smart to call 911, but when she tried to dial out, their reception had apparently been shut down. Someone then tried the hardline phone, which also had no connection. One guy who had worked in communication said it was not abnormal for all communication to be shut down in this type of situation, so they should do what they could.

Chuck then made sure Marcia knew the drill and when to use that grenade and left them in a room that was big enough to comfortably accommodate all, letting them know he would check in as soon as he could. Sergei said to him, "Before we let you out, let me at least bandage that shoulder. One sec, we have a first aid kit in here, and hopefully staunching the bleeding a little will help. But you need a doc and probably some blood."

"You're probably right, but doubt if one is gonna come flying in right now, so do what you can. Thanks all. Please, please be vigilant, everyone," he implored as he left them.

While one of them locked the door and they made the decision to move the table that was in the room up to the door, others looked out the windows to see cops and other feds all over the place and a chopper overhead, and as they were facing the front of the building, where when you craned your neck, you could see a van blocking the front of the building. They all took some time to speculate what might be going on. They pretty much all agreed that this had to be a terrorist attack, but for the life of them, they could not figure out why the VA and not another locale that might have more impact. And they waited.

CLUELESS

ON THE SEVENTH-FLOOR LANDING AT this point, we had Raoul, Sarge, Rice, Robert, Durham, Mike, Gerald, Ben, and Tyrell. Durham had to explain why Becker wasn't there, and everyone was silent for a moment, before they knew it was time to move on. Assuming that Hawk and Tom were delayed on the sixth, they had no clue that the whole mission had been compromised and jeopardized by their two foolish decisions. Not wearing vests and changing the rules on their own could and had drastic consequences.

While Raoul, Sarge, Rice, and Robert prepared to enter the seventh floor and Durham, Mike, Gerald, Ben, and Tyrell headed up to eighth, things were getting interesting on the ground.

MEANWHILE ON THE GROUND...

THINGS HAD QUIETED DOWN AT this point shooting-wise. With the van in front of the door, no one could enter the building, so now Isaiah and Wane could concentrate on the events outside. The perimeter that was set up to keep out everyone was a three-block radius, and they had evacuated all the buildings in the first block as a precautionary measure as well. As they were literally in the doorway of the building (wide doorways came in handy sometimes), Wane could be out of the van but protected and able to see what Isaiah could not. He had told Isaiah that if at anytime he heard three knocks, he should open the door and open that .50 cal. up out the rear.

As Ron knew the door itself was well protected, he could periodically do a perimeter check and be sure no one was in the stairwells or had figured out how to open an exit door or the loading zone door.

SWAT, of course, had shown up and were trying to secure a spot on H Street, from which they thought they could rush the doorway. That area had enough cars parked to make them feel it would be enough coverage to allow them the time to attack.

Periodically the police negotiator would attempt to get them to agree to give up and hand over their weapons. Wane said, "Not happening, sir. I will recommend that you all stand down and keep your guys alive."

They bantered back and forth, then Jon noticed movement from the area where SWAT was. Three knocks on the van as he yelled, "Right side first!"

Isaiah opened up, and a firefight began. SWAT and the police were giving it a good go, but when Wane joined in with the M79, they had no choice but to back off. It seemed to last forever but was probably a two- to three-minute time frame, when the SWAT team held up a white Tshirt in lieu of a flag. They then took the time to regroup and consider their next move. The Chief of Police requested an official cease-fire and time to remove the bodies that now littered the street.

"Absolutely!" Wane said. "We have no beef with you. Our mission today is to seek justice from the VA. This may seem like a drastic measure, but honestly, desperate times do call for those, to quote an old author."

At that point, the Chief tried again, "Think this through. Violence doesn't solve anything. It just leaves more victims. Think about the families, wives, kids, parents of those that are being killed."

"Like the admin thinks about Vets' families. Chief, do you realize at least twenty-one Vets a day commit suicide? What about their families? Who thought about them and helped them to stop that from happening? Hmmm, let me think. Nope, no one comes to mind. If you call the VA, they say you are okay, if you can even get an appointment. Then the embezzlement that went on. Nice to know money that was to help Vets ends up in staff's pockets. And this is the tip of the disease that riddles the VA. They do not care about the families who lost their people on foreign soil, so maybe if it is felt by them, the reality will click in."

"You could lobby Congress or reach out to legal avenues rather than being this drastic," tried the Chief.

"Do you not think those avenues have been tried? Let me ask a question. No, let me ask two. One, have you heard anything anywhere about the fraud going on in the VA? And two, ever notice the increase in ads on TV for lawyers to help Vets get bennies or appeal them? Doesn't that tell you that every avenue the Vets could try has been? I really don't expect an answer, and I say that respectfully, but we are doing what we must. Maybe they will realize the present format doesn't work. Personally, I would love to see the VA run by Vets because we take care of our own.

"Now, I see you have removed your men, and I do feel bad you lost some of them. I am sure they were good, but is it worth the loss to protect the VA? I wonder. However, please keep in mind, the courtesy we extended once will not happen again! If you try to rush the door or attack in any way, we are *not* honoring white flags a second time."

One of the Vets who was in the building had managed to power up his laptop and found a local news station showing the events at the VA. He yelled out, "Hey, guys, snipers taking place on the roof next door!"

Ron asked, "Huh, how do you know?"

The Vet replied, "Internet TV. There is a chopper circling, showing it all."

Ron called Wane over, who looked at the screen and yelled "Oh, shit!" and ran to the door to tell Isaiah to blast the copter, and if needed, he and Ron would join in with the M79s. They did. All three worked to take out the chopper, and as luck would have it, it went down on the very roof the snipers were on, causing a fire big enough to keep everyone's eyes there for a while.

"Hey, Chief," Wane yelled through his bullhorn, "we have eighteen Vets sitting here in the lobby who probably have better things to do today. Would you like us to let them go?"

And it was agreed. They left the building calmly, saluting the guys before raising their hands in perfect timing and heading for safety. As they were heading out, Ron thanked the guy with the laptop, and the guy responded, "It was the least I could do to help. You guys are laying it on the line today, and even if killed, you are not quitting, are you?"

"No, we are not."

THE ENEMY FIGHTS BACK

ON THE SEVENTH FLOOR, THE four were cautiously approaching one of the offices. The security guard on the floor knew something was going on, and when he heard the stairwell door creak open, he backed into the nearest office and held the door cracked, watching and waiting. Raoul was the closest, and as he opened the door to the office two doors down, the guard, Sam, had a view and took the shot. He actually took two, got Raoul in the leg and hip, and Raoul went down. The other three knew they couldn't help, so they moved into another office to rethink their next move. Sarge noticed as he slid into the room that Raoul had his gun under his chin and winced as he knew the outcome of that move. "Bye, pal, was a great ride!" he said, hoping Raoul heard.

Rice told Robert and Sarge he would watch the hall, leaving them free to handle the other offices they could get into. This floor looked like filing and storage was handled here and had less office spaces to attack, so they felt they could do what needed doing if Rice could hold the guard at bay for them.

Robert and Sarge managed to get into the next room with no incident and continued their mission one by one. The last woman standing had an awed look on her face, and for some reason, Sarge felt the need to question her, so he held up his hand in a stop gesture to Robert. With a very puzzled look, Robert held his gun down at his side and waited.

"Ma'am, you are aware of what is going down here, right?" he questioned.

"Oh yeah, I get the picture." As she started to speak, she held out her right leg so he could see the prosthetic limb sticking out from her pant leg. "Afghanistan, middle of the night attack by al-Qaeda, and I was the lucky one! I work here but am also chair on a committee that tries to help Vets voice concerns and find solutions to some issues."

He continued to look at her, and she took a deep breath and continued. "One of the men in the group is a counselor here and a Veteran of Iraq. He is one who always has things to bring to the table but always has at least part of a potential solution in mind." Michelle had no idea why she was allowed to continue speaking but figured the more time she could buy, the more people might be saved.

"So out of, oh, let's say, the last ten issues presented, how many were you able to resolve?" Sarge questioned.

"Three resolved, two being looked at further."

"Without you guys trying to help, nothing would change, am I right?"

"Yes, I believe we have helped some."

"And family?" he then asked.

"Hubby, current active duty, Navy. One son, eighteen months, and due in six with second."

"You remind me of someone from my past, young lady. I am assuming this is a happy marriage and he treats you right. Sounds like you and I want the same things, a better life for all Vets, even if our methods are drastically different to try to attain that. I can but hope we do both accomplish something for the good of them, and I need to finish my part. You stay in this room and stay safe." And he signaled Robert to go out as well.

Quietly from the room as they softly shut the door, she said, "Thank you. Good luck."

They got back safely to the room Rice was waiting for them in and determined that the next room attacked would be Sarge leading and Rice and Robert covering, then following to be closer to the end of that floor's attack. "Hopefully we can also get that damn person shooting at us too" was also a comment made while planning.

Sarge carefully left the room, and as he started down the hall to get in the next office, the guard shot twice, and Sarge returned fire and ran out of ammo. Before he could put in a clip, the guard fired one more and head shot Sarge, who felt nothing. The other two had gotten into the room and made short work of the five in there. They knew Sarge was down and right outside the door, and because the guard had taken him down, getting the guard became almost more important than finishing the mission. Human nature sometimes is not a good thing; it can cause errors in judgment.

Rice stated, "Good idea or not, I want us to get this SOB, just on general principle. I will go out first, head left to draw his attention, and then you follow and/or get him as soon as you see a chance. Then we can finish this floor in relative peace."

And try they did. However, Sam had won awards for skeet shoots and prided himself on his overall ability in general, often telling friends that had he lived in the Old West and that towns would have fought for him to be their sheriff. So as Rice skittered down the hall, Sam took him down with one very well-placed shot and then turned to Robert, with whom he did have to exchange a few shots before he also fell. At that point, Sam was out of ammo, and in checking the bodies, he realized they had guns and clips, and he took all he could from the bodies. There were also grenades and C4. The grenades, he knew what to do with, but the C4, he left, knowing not what it required to be effective.

He knew there were people in the last office on this floor and was hoping they were all okay as there had been no noise from that end of the hallway. Not sure if maybe another terrorist, which was all he could presently assume had happened, was in there and holding the ten or so people hostage. He cautiously headed into that area. The ones in that room had been set up to revamp some files and computer files as well, so they were working in tandem to coordinate all possible info. As he entered the room, everyone started to hold up their hands, praying for mercy, and Sam said, "Relax, I am not the enemy. Hopefully we can help erase the enemy."

The questions started, and Sam held up his hand. "Guys, gals, I really know nothing. I can speculate, but that may not be the smartest thing to do right now, so let's deal with what I do know. Three guys came onto this floor to try to eradicate everyone. Near as I can tell, they did so with the exception of us. If there is anyone else here alive, I didn't take the time to check the other offices. Felt it was more important to do what we can to protect you first and then see what else is going on. I know there is still something happening, can hear noises upstairs and outside, so let's see what we can do!"

Sam asked if anyone was comfortable with a gun, and seven or eight hands went up. They determined that four should have weapons and the grenades were also an option if things got out of hand, but those were only given to the two that had military background, Sam feeling safer knowing they at least knew the basics. And they waited, listening for any sounds that indicated someone was on the floor. Meanwhile, poor Michelle sat alone in her office, fretting and fidgeting because she knew moving could be a big mistake. She tried to call someone, anyone, but the phone service was apparently disconnected, and her cell was dead.

EIGHTH-FLOOR NIGHTMARES

When the last five hit floor 8, they had no idea what was in store for them—one very pissed, but wounded, security guard, and people who now have custody of Hawk's and Tom's supplies.

Chuck had gone back to the room where everyone was at one point, and one of the guys proposed the idea that it might be better to divide and potentially conquer anyone who tried to breach the floor. The stairwell was blocked on the west side by some of the guys in the room once the decision was made to do this, and then they decided that the best plan of attack was to be in offices that let them get to everyone, be it one or more attackers at once. "So if we are down the hall away, and there are multiple attackers, if we have a grenade coming from either side, that should do it, right?" asked Marcia.

Another voice piped up, "Yeah, sounds right, but I think you guys with guns should be down the hall further or on the other side in case."

"And maybe two more grenades to follow if the first two don't."

Someone else added, "Just be sure it is the enemy, and not our police!"

Chuck said, "Think if they come in, the bullhorn will be first, but you are right. That is why I think the delayed attack is best. All in?"

And with a chorus of yesses, those that had places to go very carefully moved to their rooms, while those that waited said silent prayers and held tight to one another.

They were able to get completely set up before the five entered the floor. Mike actually peaked out into the hall first and looked around. He closed the door and told the others that there was absolutely no activity on the floor, no guard in sight. They decided Durham, Mike, and Gerald would hit the first office to the right of the stairs, and Ben and Tyrell the one across the hall, then move on. As this floor was where the director and other higher powers had offices, they knew there may be inner offices and psyched themselves up to maybe get a major player before this was over.

Chuck was standing in a shadowed area at the end of the hall, where he was hidden completely. They all knew it was a risk to handle it this way, but he would whistle when he felt they should start their attack. Waiting until they cleared the stairwell area and had moved about ten paces down the hall was hard, but at that point he whistled, and out of the two doors at the other end, grenades were lobbed, and the door was immediately slammed shut. Durham, Mike, and Tyrell had not worn flak jackets and went down immediately. Ben and Gerald had theirs on but took in enough shrapnel to be immobile. Two more doors opened while Ben and Gerald lay there, and out came two more grenades to finish them off.

All was quiet for a few moments, and then Carl and Mark stuck their heads out of the room and noticed six bodies.

The five were by the elevators and another at the end of the hall. They very cautiously headed down that way and realized body number 6 was Chuck. He had done all he could to keep everyone safe and then bled out. They somberly headed back down the hall to where the others waited and advised them of the carnage in the hall. No one wanted to head out until they knew it was safe, as much as they all really wanted to run for it and get out of there. So they waited. A couple of people did try the phones and/or cell phones, but still no service either way.

BACK ON THE GROUND

Things had become noticeably quiet on the first floor. Wane was at the side door of the van that was against the entry door of the building, and they were trying to decide next step.

Isaiah said to the others, "Guys, I am not going out alive or alone. We all know our squad is gone," and before they could join him or make any comment, he pulled out his .45, took off his flak jacket, and headed out the driver door, gun blazing. He was dropped within about thirty seconds, and the bullhorn was reactivated by the Chief for another try at getting them to give up.

Ron looked at Wane. "I have heard enough of that loudmouth. Let's give him a shot at taking out the guys who killed some of his men, or I can do that alone!"

"No, you can't go alone. I wanna help scare him a bit myself and not ever hear a freakin' bullhorn again."

And with that, they stripped off the bulletproof, high-fived each other, and stepped out, guns in hand. They fell almost simultaneously, then all became ominously quiet. Things were quiet for at least ten minutes while everyone awaited the chief's orders. He had asked for anyone inside to come out with hands up a few times and, with no response, finally knew it was time to enter the building and start assessing the damage. Chief Conroy had already had his office put all the nearby morgues and hospitals on standby, figuring the dead would number at least one hundred, but not knowing for sure the total fatality count nor the number of attackers involved.

THE WORLD AWAITS DETAILS

THE CITY MORGUE HAD SENT over staff members with as many body bags as possible and toe tags. The chief medical examiner, Kim Liu, had requested that they keep any ID found with the bodies, knowing this whole process would make for a long couple of days and hoping that would help speed up their jobs.

At that point, after thanking Kim for coming out to help, Chief Conroy started setting up his guys to enter. "First, you four," pointing to seasoned officers standing nearby. "You and I will sweep the first floor, make sure all is secure and, if needed, also get the elevators running. I am in hopes that they just found the override in the security room, and we can flip a switch and have them on, or maybe even they are totally functional already. Once we are sure that floor is secure, I want four guys per floor, hitting them from the stairwells, two per stairs, radios on at all times, and if you don't have a fully charged phone with camera, take one of the cameras Carol brought over to document everything. Guys, and ladies too, guard each other, I don't want to lose any more people today!" And with that, he assigned the thirty-two officers to take floors, keeping the ones together that worked together on the street, knowing they knew how the other worked and would not have to question one another's tactics or moves.

As they entered the ground floor, all thirty-two heard a loud gasp, and as they turned to look, the reporter who had managed to sneak by the secured area was trying to get a camera shot with his phone. "Grogan, get that SOB outta here, and make sure the perimeter is secured. If I find out who let that one slip by… oh yeah, and be sure any picture he may have gotten is erased. Ask politely though, got it?"

The reporter started to back away, and Grogan stopped him, realizing this was a guy he knew from a local paper, and politely discussed the situation, explaining the sensitivity of this, but telling him they would meet at the local hangout one day soon to catch up, at which point the reporter left the area.

While the four officers checked the ground floor and started a count, the others stood together and made sure everyone knew where everyone would be. There was apprehension for all. Even those that were seasoned officers knew that this could be their last call or they could make it home safely again, but for so many, this was where it might end.

Outside, the mayor had shown up and was also trying to wrap his mind around this whole situation. He refused to make any statement yet, just saying, "I know this is a tragic situation and am asking for everyone's patience. Until we know more, I can't comment, except to say that my heart goes out to any and all that have been affected by this. Please, please be patient and let our city police and others do their job."

It had been decided that the officers downed outside, which was a total of five, would go to the nearest hospital morgues to make things easier for their families. As they determined who was involved in the attack, those would go to the city morgue to try to keep everything centralized for investigations sake.

Kim, the medical examiner, had offered to stay and, with five of his staff members available also, offered to help by handling the bodies outside the building. Those that had been on the rooftop and in the helicopter earlier had already been transported to a hospital morgue nearby, and they knew their identities, so knew they could wait. The more immediate issue was to get answers to questions that everyone was asking—who and why. Kim hoped they could at least get a leg up on the who question.

The five officers were easily identified, and that made the total count of officers to thirteen, with the two snipers on the roof and six others shot earlier.

They knew that the other three on the sidewalk were definitely shooters, and two of the ME people offered to check out the van looking for IDs but knowing nothing else should be disturbed so the police could also check it out fully later. Luckily all three had left IDs in the van glovebox.

1. Ronald Woods, DC ID with a local address and a VA card
2. Isaiah Johnson, driver's license from White Bird, Idaho
3. Jon Wane, driver's license from Grangeville, Idaho

They were tagged and bagged and sent off to the morgue while the ME's people awaited more detail. By this time, the first floor had been secured, and the officers had started up to their respective floors. Most of the people on the first floor had VA ID badges, so the Chief asked the ME to start there with those they had firm IDs on, processing and clearing the floor. Ground-floor count, forty-three dead, no survivors. As the officers entered each floor, some gasped with surprise at the sight of bodies scattered around, but from the fifth floor, the first words heard through the chief's headset was, "Holy shit! Sorry, sir, this is a large room we are in with quite a few bodies and some injuries. It does look like a lot of people weren't here today or away from their desks, but I am guessing total on floor deceased and/or not at 140–150. Can we get paramedics up here?"

"Elevator's inoperative, but we know stairs are cleared, so yes, will do. Any idea how many injured?"

"Looks like three with major injuries, ten to twelve with minor, and over one hundred dead," responded Kelly.

"Will get you some help. Hang in."

"Thanks. Those with minor injuries are staying with those that aren't unconscious. Will let them know."

As Officer Kelly and the other three officers checked the area and tried to help those injured, one asked, "Do you guys know what happened here? We were getting ready to start our day, and bam, apparently grenades were thrown in, then some guys started shooting."

Officer Smythe asked, "May I have your name, sir? And if you are up to it, can you tell me what you all do on this floor?"

"Cornelius Maplewood, and we were an information area. If anyone calls needing to know how to file a claim or to reach a certain area, we provide help. Definitely not a threat to anyone!"

"Appreciate that info. Please let those know we are trying our damnedest to figure this out and medical help is on its way. Is that cut over your eye your only injury?"

"Luckily, yes, I was over in the far corner and had accidentally kicked my plug loose so had crawled under my desk to fix that. When I heard the noise when the grenade went off, figured I should stay put. Believe it or not, I hit my head coming out from under when all was quiet, so I did this to myself."

"Sounds like me, never get hurt in the normal way. Thank you so much, Cornelius, for helping keep everyone calm and giving me what info you could."

"Took a couple of those Red Cross courses ages ago. Glad I could do something, even if not much," he said sincerely.

While they were discussing this, the other three officers were checking in with those injured and letting those that were alert enough know what they could, i.e., that medics were on the way and to please try to remain calm.

The Chief had received the details on the three shooters from out front and had to admit to himself from what he knew so far this was an impressive attempt at something. He just wished he knew what. Based on what info was provided on the three out front and the firepower involved, his thought was now geared to a potential military tie. They all appeared to be of a similar age, and two were from the same state. Ties might be VA, stationed together. All this needed attention and created more questions.

While he was mulling over this information, he kept getting updates.

"Floor 5, I have the body count, sir. It's 122."

"Floor 2, 27."

"Chief? This is Morgan on 6. You are not gonna believe this, but no fatalities here."

He then requested details from the other floors that had not yet checked in.

"On three, 17 bodies."

"Four, 44, sir."

"Seven, 30 bodies, 11 survivors."

"Eight, 6 dead, 12 survivors."

"So with the 43 on ground, 38 on first, and the ones outside, that totals 335 people dead. Can anyone tell yet how many are the bad guys? I know there are three accounted for here."

From the third floor, the officer noticed one man in the hallway with a .45 in hand and said, "Think this one can be confirmed, sir. Gun in hand and ammo and grenades, plus I think an explosive in pocket. He actually has ID, and it states James Becker with an address in Charlotte, NC. Surprised to see ID on an attacker, though."

On the eighth floor, Carl and Mark had updated the officer on what had transpired there, showing tremendous composure in light of the situation, but being emphatic in the fact that Chuck needed an award, Carl saying, "I can't believe he didn't make it. He actually saved us! What the hell caused this?" as the sniffles were held back as much as possible. Detective Close shook his head and said, "First, let me thank all of you who helped Chuck. I am so sorry he did not make it and wish I could tell you more, but at this point, we really know nothing. You all can ID the bodies there as shooters though, right? I know that is a lot to ask, but it will help tremendously as we try to figure this all out."

Marcia interjected at that point. "Detective, those five were definitely out to do us all harm. I was the grenade launcher, and never happier to see bodies scattered in a hallway, because I know there would have been no survivors if not for us. If that sounds cruel, so sorry."

As he took names and information on those that had survived, Officer Michaels was checking the ID of those that were attackers and reported to the chief, "Sir, names and IDs on seven perps on eighth floor. Ready?"

1. Murdit Durham, MD
2. Mike Jackson, VA
3. Gerald Washington, NC
4. Ben Goodman, DC
5. Tyrell Dyer, MD
6. Jason Hawk, DC
7. Ron Woods, DC

"Am taking pics of IDs so they can stay with bodies for ME work, and we have people here who are needing to sign statements and more than willing to do so ASAP."

Chief Conroy responded with, "I want everyone to know how much I appreciate the cooperation we are getting from you, my men, as well as every person we have spoken with. Guys, please don't let the opportunity to thank those involved at every chance you get. Have a hunch this is far from over and is a puzzle that may continue on for a while, but I hope not. There were some things said earlier that may help, but as we all well know, we need all the details to be sure."

"Chief? This is Officer Gerard on seven. The security guard has introduced me to Michelle, who apparently spoke with one of the shooters and was left alone."

"Interesting. Get the details, and I will also speak with her later to follow up."

Michelle told Officer Gerard all she could remember about the discussion with the "slightly older gentleman" who acted as if this was just a normal conversation, and told her to "go back to work" once he found out about her history, both on working at the VA and personal life. She knew that both men in the office at that time had been military, mostly because of stature and the fact that the older man told the younger one to "stand down." "That is not something you hear every day, officer," she stated. "Military or police, yes. Normal citizens, not so much."

Gerard took notes, thanked her, and advised her everyone was working as fast as they could to get things to the point where people could go home. Michelle thanked him and said she understood, and as long as she could speak with her husband as soon as the phones came up, she would be okay.

Meanwhile, Officer Tompkins had gotten the details from Sam on the events that had transpired there and was looking at the four bodies there that had attacked that floor.

"Chief, got four here that were shooters. One sec, will give names if they have ID. Oh yeah, got 'em."

1. Raoul Martinez, DC
2. William Lewis, CO
3. Anthony Rice, ID
4. Robert Ellis, ID

"And I will take pics and keep for records and info, Chief. I know Gerard has spoken with the lady here and will share his info ASAP."

"Thanks, Tompkins."

A LONG DAY WINDS DOWN

WITH A CONCERTED EFFORT FROM all, police, the ME office, local morgues, and the fire department, the building was cleared of bodies, alive and dead, by about 7:00 p.m. Crime scene investigators spent another five hours that night going back through the building to be sure they had not missed any evidence or potential clues for later. Between all the pictures taken by officers and the subsequent investigators, there ended up being not one square inch of the building not on file. Everyone knew that more was not less in this case. More was needed to figure out why, how, and who.

The six-o'clock news was pretty much this story only, with each station speculating the whys as well. Some thought mad employee, some thought mad Vet, some thought terrorism, and some thought pissed at the government as a whole. But what threw them all was the fact that even though the mayor and Police Chief was not giving a lot of detail, everyone was baffled, because with all they did not know, they did know there were multiple shooters, and that muddied the waters even more.

By 8:00 p.m., the president was ready to speak. He was in town and knew that it was in his best interest to be involved. He had the mayor with him and started at promptly 8:00 p.m. "I am not addressing only the citizens of DC but the entire country at this time. I wish I had more information to provide at this time, but regrettably I do not, so let me tell you what I can. No questions will be allowed at present for a few reasons: one, we either can't answer or won't so as not to jeopardize the investigation, and no names will be released pending notification of all of next of kin. This is a tragedy of a magnitude we all feel deeply, I know, so I do request sensitivity and awareness of others' shock to let you in the news industry move with caution. At eight a.m. this morning, sixteenth of February, approximately 15 people entered our local VA office and proceeded to execute anyone and everyone in their path. We have 335 persons who have died at this time and are not sure if any of the perpetrators did get away. Everyone who can assist is helping in processing names and details, so those who are wondering where and if their family members are safe are working as fast and hard as they can. Again, would that I had more details I would provide them, Mayor? Anything you care to add?"

"No, we will keep you up by briefing every opportunity we can. Please accept my prayers and sympathy to those of you who are waiting word. I do know how rough this must be on everyone. And I also ask for patience from the media and the public. Please, please be patient, and thank you all."

Even though there were people around the building all night, police officers guarding, a few crime scene people checking and rechecking details, it was eerily quiet. When people bumped into one another, they bowed their heads, and no one really spoke all night.

When the director of operations did arrive, rushed back from their retreat in Florida, he knew things were not going to be status quo for quite a while. The police had given him numbers of companies that could clean a building, and they advised him this would take at least a week, so he had to suspend operations for that time, as well as try to figure out why and what they could do to protect others. After he gave his speech on the 8:00 a.m. briefing on television, he started lining up those to clean the building, repair windows, etc., as needed. Little did he know what the day held for him once information started coming in.

TUESDAY MORNING, MARY RECEIVES MAIL

As LUCK WOULD HAVE IT, today was Mary's day off, and she was worried. She had tried repeatedly to call Ben since the news came on last night and gotten no answer at either his apartment or cell, and this morning she had tried both again then called the gym. David informed her that today was his day to open but had not heard from Ben or Tyrell, and it looked like no one was out back either. When she questioned him if he had seen the news, he got really quiet, and they both were mulling this all over. Finally, he told her that he would call when he heard from Ben because he knew it was just a flat tire or something and Tyrell was probably with the girlfriend. Neither mentioned the guys out back, and they finally disconnected, somewhat unnerved on both ends.

When the mail arrived at her house at about 9:30 a.m., she was surprised to see a large manila envelope with Ben's name and address on it, not realizing it was an overnight delivery, not normal mail. Pouring a cup of coffee, she wondered what Ben had done as perhaps a belated Valentine's surprise. Curling up in her favorite spot overlooking the backyard, which she loved even in the winter, she smiled and settled in to see what Ben was up too.

As she started to read, a big smile came over her face. Ben declaring his love in writing was something she would treasure always, and share with her daughter, if they were blessed with one later. However, as she read further, incredulity and shock came over her. "Oh no... no, no, no!" she screamed as her coffee cup hit the floor.

"Darling Mary," the letter began.

First, let me thank you. I never thought I would love someone as much as I love you, nor have it happen so quickly. When you helped me after I lost my leg, I did feel a bond, but when I left the hospital and you didn't ask for an update, I thought, who in their right mind would want to be saddled with a one-legged gimp, and went on. When we reconnected and things went so quickly and smooth, I thanked God for the second chance.

Now for the apology! I am sorry we are ending up like this. If you are reading this letter, the mission we went on failed, and we are no longer of this earth. While I know that sounds corny, I hate the other phrases people use as a description, so now you know.

What happened yesterday was a compilation of events, and perhaps I helped too much in getting the ball rolling. Were it just me who had complaints about the VA, I may have just sucked it up and gone on. As you know, I had to fight to get benefits when I came home and fight to get any training to help me find work. Then I found out how much help I could give with the gym and made it work. Of course, the VA then reduced my benefits, claiming I no longer needed them. I could have lived with that, but then I started hearing other stories. You know, most of the guys that hung at the compound, their stories were worse. Vets shouldn't be homeless. The military promises to take care of their own, but I guess only while active duty! Before we realized exactly what we had put in place, fifteen men with issues, be they medical or psychological, had decided it was time to let the world know what was happening. And maybe, just maybe, make a difference. You and I have talked about this. Twenty-one vets a day are committing suicide. How many more are that don't show on the rolls?

So should anyone ask you why, feel free to explain. Show them this letter. I could cry "Poor me" and tell more of my story about trying to adjust, etc., but in the large scheme of things, others have had it harder. Much harder.

Love you 'til eternity, Mary,
Ben

Once she finished, she headed for the bathroom, lost her breakfast, and sat in a trance for about half an hour. Then the anger kicked in. Realizing she had the answer to everyone's why question, she decided the best person to call was the chief that was leading the investigation. Finding out what precinct house he was at was not hard, and she called him, advising him she had very pertinent info about the shooting. He asked if she wanted a car to pick her up, which she quickly declined, and she made copies of Ben's letter to take to him, knowing the original would never leave her.

Neither one of them realized at this time how many other letters were circulating, but from the Chief's perspective when he read this, it tied together the events of that day.

Later that afternoon, Mary, Chief Conroy, and Mayor Richards gave a press conference, with Mary reading Ben's letter and closing with this statement, "I know some of you are still awaiting word on your loved ones' status. I am sorry for everyone impacted by this. I feel especially bad for those who felt this was the answer. They lost their lives to hopefully help others down the road, not suffer as they did. Please help make sure this does not ever happen again, help those who need it, make our government do as they promised, and support our Vets."

Not everyone involved saw this newscast originally, although it ended up being replayed on every news station, local and national, as days went on.

People were being informed of the family members lost in the attack, and letters were arriving at locations as the day progressed. Why was still being asked in houses around the country. For those who had family employed, it was, "Why my husband, wife, son, daughter?" For those related to the attackers, it was, "Why the need to act now and in this manner?"

Perhaps the entire logic, or lack thereof, would never be completely understood, and perhaps synchronicity is not always for the good, but the following letters that the others wrote might help explain their frustration and mind-set that caused this to happen.

MAIL CALL FOR FRIENDS AND FAMILY

SERGEANT BILL LEWIS'S LETTER TO his brother and sister-in-law, John and Carol, arrived at Sarge's farm on Tuesday morning. (Ben had sent them all overnight, thanking the USPS for the capability to do so after hours due to technology.)

Carol got the letter first as John was out in the barn, and as she was reading through, she could barely move to go to the door and scream for John. He could hear the tremor in her voice and came running. "Hon, what? Are you okay?"

She realized this was going to be a major shock for John and, hiccupping and trying to get herself under control, said, "I am fine, really, but..." and the tears started again. "John, I am so sorry. Sarge was family to me too. That newscast we saw last night? The VA attack."

"No, not Sarge! Oh my god, please tell me no."

"John, I am so sorry. His letter tells what he could. We need to do what we can as well to help each other through this."

"Pour me a drink, please. I know I am gonna need at least one to get through this."

And he sat down to try to get through his brother's final letter.

Carol and John,

I know this may be hard for you guys to believe, but it was time to end this. I tried for all the years

248

since Nam to hide the pictures and bad memories at bay and hidden from the world, but the replay was continual. I never had a break from seeing those who I fought with every day drop around me or disappear, never to be seen again. I felt so responsible for so many of them. Then I came home and got the job at the penitentiary. It became a harsh reality that some of the people who had committed crimes, especially murderers, had been in war, and suffered from PTSD. These men were trained to know it was okay to kill, and I firmly believe this is what caused some to turn to that life. Saddens me to realize they can get no help from the government who trained them and then never helped—for lack for a better phrase, untrain them. Or at least address the mental issues caused by the situation.

Please, you two, understand my need to do this. We are going in there to let the world know that this is a situation that needs help. Vets are dying daily, some actually taking their own lives, and others because they are denied care and the medical issues take their lives much earlier than they should. The government needs to stand up to the plate and help our guys and women who went into these situations, really believing they were backed if necessary.

Guys, a copy of this is going to our senator and the local news station in the Springs, but your copy has all the info on a separate sheet with lawyer and will details.

You two take care of yourselves and the land. It will love you back, always, and I love you too.

Sarge

At that point, Carol and John hugged close, and both had the cry of their lives. When the phone rang, Carol answered, realized it was the news station that had received their copy, and stated, "No comment!" She hung up and took the phone off the hook.

Raoul's letter went to a buddy in Mesa, Arizona. He had no family and figured that the pal might want to know what had happened to him. Turned out the guy read the letter and threw it away.

Nate,

Remember when we were kids and played cowboy and Indians? The cowboys always won 'cause they were the good guys! Had I known that that isn't always the truth, I would have headed for Canada when Vietnam came along, never to return, even after Clinton granted amnesty. I am embarrassed and ashamed at the way we are treating our Vets, and it makes it sadder that the damage done to them was not even on our soil but rather to help and protect others.

So with this offensive, I stand on US soil fighting for the Vets who deserve so much more, like a real life rather than living on the streets or hoping they can see a doctor before something bad happens. If I have to give my life, let it be for my fellow Vets, who hopefully benefit from this. Perhaps they will get the things promised that so many of us have not!

As Nate was wadding the letter up to toss it, under his breath, he muttered, "That guy was always weird. Why me?"

Tyrell wrote to Sue and his family to explain.

I guess what is making me be a part of this mission is what I saw in Afghanistan and Iraq. In Afghanistan, you continued the attack until no one was left standing. There was no retreat. It was all or nothing. Because dying beat getting caught and tortured before dying. And it continues, not always the Military doing atrocious things. Look at the beheadings attacks in non–war zones, people. We didn't accomplish a thing! But we did honor the Geneva Convention, unlike the others, for what good it did us.

Then we leave all the weapons behind to help. Help who? They sure as hell are helping al-Qaeda and probably ISIS now. This is not over, nor is it going to end well. But our Vets need a voice here at home to help them get the things they need, and I think we are it.

Durham Murdit sent his letter to his wife, Shawna. He was truly not sure if she would share with anyone as they had always kept things close, not telling outsiders or family a lot of things, either good or bad.

> I was proud and excited to become part of the group known as the Rangers, and not just Army. We had to do the impossible, and even though we were well trained, sometimes it felt we fail, but we never gave up. But it cost men and equipment, and even some of us who survived came away broken. Matter of fact, most of us are broken one way or another. I still see those that were lost in the field and, Shawna, you lived the nightmares with me all too often.
>
> When I was shot, the leg and shoulder was hard enough to take, but the groin shot kinda put a damper on us, and I know how hard that has been on you. Never mind that I really thought I wouldn't make it home, and was halfheartedly hoping it would end before you heard the news. When I got home, I knew our sex life as we knew it was done, and that hurt. I want you to go find someone who deserves you, cares for you, and can give you everything you need and deserve.
>
> And I want the VA to realize we did this because... because we want better for our Veterans, and their families, not those employed by the VA, who apparently are doing well, until now that is. Perhaps this mission we embarked on will make them care about us and not themselves and nothing like this will ever happen again!
>
> Love ya... Will miss ya... Be strong and move on.

James Becker to his wife, Karen, and the local Charlotte newspaper.

As a POW for five years in Nam, I saw a different side of the war. Others heard about the conditions and tortures inflicted on our guys. I saw and lived them. I ate things that I still don't know if they were animal vegetable or mineral and, truthfully, don't think I want to know. I saw people broken, both physically and mentally, and truthfully, can say have no idea how I managed to survive, or did I?

Some starved to death, others broke down completely from the mental games, and some did escape. Well, kinda escaped. They either never returned, and quite often you heard noises outside the camp that clearly indicated they would never return, or worse, they brought them back, with new cuts and bruises, and one time brought the three guys back, made us watch while they shot them, then we had to bury the bodies. As hard as you try to forget these things, I think any rational human would know it is pretty impossible to do.

Then I get to come home, home to a country I really don't recognize. People are treating us like we are the enemy, and the VA? They are supposed to help us, and I am so disappointed in their version of help, that I am taking part in this offense. Yes, they gave me dentures when I needed them, and oh yeah, compensation, for a while, anyway. I did get 100 percent comp for a while, but at one point they determined I was doing better and lowered it to a 20 percent amount, which then was removed from my retirement, so in effect I was paying myself...

Sometimes I wonder why I stuck it out after Vietnam, but I really felt that the twenty-year retirement would be worth it, and boy, was I wrong. It is a good thing we invested wisely, Karen. I do feel guilty leaving you like this, but I have to do this. You see, I was no help to the guys who did survive while in the camp, but maybe I can make up for some of that now.

Stars in your eyes, sun at your back,
Me

It was the closing he used in every letter he had ever written her.

Tony and Robert, who coauthored their letters, sent them to Tony's sister and Robert's cousin.

> When we met in grade school, the phrase "brothers from another mother" was not known, but we were that. Robert was the tough guy, and even though we always had each other's backs, he was the one who usually threw the first punch and got the last one in as well. So no surprise, that when I, Tony, joined the Army, Robert had to one-up me by going Marine! He told me point-blank, "You can be the wuss. I will be the one to kick ass and take names!"

Tony had been chosen to actually write the letter and, as much as he grumbled, knew that was the best idea, as Robert's spelling and penmanship was a bit, shall we say, bad. His writing was chicken scratch, and for spelling, well, better people could understand.

> Robert saw his fair share of brutal battles, and I saw my share too, being Infantry. The death tolls were high, and many of those pictures stayed with us, even after coming home. I guess we both were lucky, or stupid, going in police work and the fire department, but we both think that being able to help people, rather than shooting them, helped us keep the bad memories at bay, allowing us both to feel we were negating some of the bad.
>
> But once we retired and had nothing to occupy our minds, those bad dreams and memories returned. The VA had a solution, drugs! Of course, most of those either made the memories worse or put us to sleep, neither of which helped the situation. We both kept trying to come to grips with this and had many discussions on the

porch at the cabin as to why we were not getting real help, then this opportunity came along, and here we are!

Isaiah sent to his family this letter:

I remember the horrific nightmares my dad had that not only woke him up but the screams making the whole family get up as well. Vietnam caused these, it was apparent, and we all knew the neighbors were awakened as well. I know they were waiting for the cops or an ambulance, 'cause they had to think someone was being killed in our house. Come to think of it, this would explain why old man Jones was always on the porch when we left for school and work in the morning. Bet he was making sure we all came out alive and whole!

If any of us tried to ask any questions about the nightmare, or even an innocent question about Vietnam, it was made very clear the subject was taboo, with you, Mom, trying your darndest to get us to hush before we could even finish our sentence. Dad made us promise though to never join the Military, any branch at any time, and we all but had to sign that promise in blood to keep him happy!

Things were actually calming down after he had been home about a year and working in an office, but then orders came out, and when Dad knew he had to go back to "that hell hole," and he decided to blow his brains out, rather than do that, you, Mom, had to bust your ass to keep us kids alive and in food. You should have gotten the help you deserved, and I know at this point I can't help you, but with these guys' help, maybe we can make things better for others in these situations.

WHY?

Hawk addressed his to the *Washington* newspaper and *NY Times*.

I want it clearly understood that in my mind, this mission is for ALL Veterans. I know that there have been inequalities in the treatment of Veterans throughout history and feel the need to try to help the ones I can. And if this achieves that, we are not in vain.

I remember my uncle who served in WWII. He had stories to tell, and even though some were sad, and people died, there was a degree of pride in those stories, knowing that these things were done for the good of mankind. Because of him, I knew at a young age that I wanted to join the Navy and follow in his footsteps.

So as soon as I was legal, I did so. As gung ho as I was, I actually became a SEAL, one of the elite, so I thought. I still cannot or will not discuss some of the missions I went on but will say this. I never thought I would wear black pajamas, sandals made of old tires, and what was called a coolie hat to infiltrate places I should not have been in. And do things that cannot be spoken of!

But I did survive this and came back to the good ole US of A, where people made me feel like the bad guy, no idea why, but hey, I moved on. Got a job in construction, loved it, had no one looking over my shoulder constantly 'cause I was good at what I did. Kept that up for about ten years, then felt bad, and someone told me to go to the VA. So I did. They found prostate cancer because of the Agent Orange. I decided on the seed implant and radiation treatment option. Removing the prostate scared the crap outta me, and all was good for a while. I got VA comp and was fine 'cause couldn't find work then.

Everything had also made me depressed, and the building slump was on. And who wants to hire a clinically depressed Veteran? Then boom, the VA decided that I was doing better, PSA was 0 (of course it was, for a while), so they dropped my compensation. And now? Last month I had a CT and bone scan, and it appears the cancer is moving into other organs and bone. Do I want to fight them to get money back? Hell no, my quality of life will never be good again. Do I want to die and have it mean nothing? Again, hell no. Dying means I get no money, but I get the satisfaction of taking some of those worthless SOBs with me!

Mike to his wife, Jean.

> I wish I could say that our government learned something from Vietnam, but I am afraid that didn't happen. When I landed in country on the USS *Paul Revere*, I felt proud to be a part of Operation Double Eagle. And doubly proud to be a Marine.
>
> I didn't realize at first just what was going on. As we moved in to take over other hills and towns, Charlie just kinda hung back and let us go out and fight their war. Also didn't catch on to the fact that our government was aware we were the ones fighting the Chinese and Russians while the natives stayed alive. So now I wonder if the over forty thousand lives lost in that little conflict could have been lessened or not have happened at all. And of course the residual deaths since. Looking at some records online, the death toll of Americans as of 2008 based on Vietnam causes was over fifty-eight thousand.
>
> Then we leave, finally. And do it again later, sending our men into Afghanistan and Iraq, to die yet again for other countries. I understand someone has to be there to help those less fortunate, but then we leave behind our weapons and equipment, hoping it will help those fighting for real freedom, but in essence handing it all over to the oppressors, like alQaeda and/or anyone else who wants it.
>
> So of course this causes more injured Vets, who also cannot get help from their overworked VA, which I have to assume is the reason it takes over a year to settle a claim, and it just continues to snowball. Perhaps if the government had

to go fight these wars themselves and then work through the aftereffects, things may be different.

Jean, we have had our ups and downs, and you are appreciated for putting up with me all these years. I know that we never got the VA to give back what they took away, and I know we are not alone in this. The number of Vets who are fighting for benefits that were promised and negated is astounding, believe me. A couple of guys in this with me are in our boat as well. However, I know you, Ms. Stubborn, if there is a way, you will at least get back what they took away when they reduced our benefits a couple of years ago. Perhaps you can band together with others that are in the same boat and give 'em some more grief. I hope you understand the reason for this. Actually I know you do. You have always seen the big picture better than a lot of people do and get the fact that sometimes the loss of a few makes for the better of many!

Always

WHY?

Gerald to Kathy and Charlotte news station.

> Let me start by thanking you. While I know all too well running may have entered your mind now and again, or shooting me and burying me in a swamp somewhere, you stayed and tolerated me. I hope you can understand how this all came to pass. It was hard to fight those that had no beliefs or intentions of following the Geneva Convention, nor having a government who wanted to protect you from those atrocities. And also a government who in certain cases pulled your men, Green Berets, and others out if they went outside the rules. It made it hard to know who was really on whose side. Or what we could and could not do to help win this war.
>
> And we also know this was never actually called a war, referred to as a conflict, which I think was part of the problem. Our politicians didn't want to treat victims of said conflict the same as those that were in a war, so they hoped if it all was swept under the rug, it would go away.
>
> Regrettably a few things happened that made that impossible. Agent Orange came to light, and it was realized that there were far-reaching effects of that little goodie. However, I feel that the government (read VA there) hoped Vets would die of those effects before they could file for benefits, and then of course, the Afghanistan, Iraq, situation has brought the issue of Vets to light, making things harder to continue to sweep away.
>
> But now of course the VA has more Vets requiring help, Vietnam-era Vets still alive hoping for help as well as newer Vets requiring help. The problem, however, is they have forgotten what

they are here for. Look at all the things going on with them. There was even a request not long ago for more funds to go in the VA admin. If they had been better stewards when people needed less, they would not be scrambling now to figure out who they can ignore and how many may pass on before they resolve their issues. Hopefully this helps others by bringing awareness to the world.

SUMMATION

As the letters were received, and in some cases forwarded to news media or other family members, it became more and more obvious that sometimes synchronicity makes for strange bedfellows. On the national news five nights after the attack, one newscaster summed things up rather succinctly, "In a world where attacks on people and places has regrettably become commonplace, we need to take a few moments and reflect. What message are these fifteen men trying to give? For me, it is fairly simple: we as a country and people have forgotten the basics, that everyone deserves the best life they can have, and that we have gotten away from being sure we protect and help our own. Those who fight for our freedom, protect our freedom, deserve better! And it is truly sad that these men felt the need to remind us of this in this manner."

ABOUT THE AUTHOR

PJ CURRENTLY LIVES IN JACKSONVILLE, Florida, with her husband of forty-plus years.

She grew up with a father, who was a disabled Veteran, always fighting for his benefits and appropriate compensation. The fight began again when her husband (also a Veteran) was diagnosed with cancer and PTSD. To this day, the fight continues to receive his benefits, with the government continually denying all blame and requests.

Realizing these were not isolated instances but experiences many of our Veterans continually faced was the reason for this story. To bring to light the plight of so many that will not speak out but are fighting for medical, psychological, and monetary help.

CPSIA information can be obtained
at www.ICGtesting.com
Printed in the USA
LVOW03s0537230817
546015LV00001BA/2/P